reverberation

reverberation

A.M. CAPLAN

copyright

Cover design by Natasha MacKenzie
Typeset in Palatino by Chapter One Book Production, Knebworth, UK
Printed in the United States

dedication

This is for you, Mom

1

Hannah carefully pulled the frame from the hive. A single wakeful bee wobbled drunkenly around its edge, and she picked it up gently with her thumb and finger and set it back in the hive. Placing the frame in the tub beside her, she reached for another, repeating the process until the tub was full, then lugged it up the hill to the house. She let it slide, heavy with honey, to the floor of the porch with a thud.

Flopping down into the lone chair next to its tiny table, she took a sip from her lukewarm tea and looked past the hives, across a field of clover to where it rolled down and out of sight into Seneca Lake. In the sun, the blue-black water sparkled with diamond flashes, and sailboats tiny as toys skated across the surface like water bugs.

Another bee, a sneaky worker who had hitched a ride up the hill, buzzed out of the tub and landed on her arm. She let this one sit, watching it fidget its minuscule front legs.

"You're allergic to bees, you know."

"Don't tell the bees that." Hannah had drawn the gun before she finished speaking, aiming in the direction of the voice. There was a figure standing at the far end of the porch, blurred by the reflection from the tall bank of windows.

"You stay right there." She leveled the gun and scanned the tree line around her, making sure she wasn't being hemmed in on all sides. Her phone had only signaled this one intruder, with nothing else showing up on the perimeter sensor. She didn't see anything to make her question its accuracy.

"Han," the man's voice said, "there's no way you're going to shoot me. Put the gun down." That voice.

She stood slowly, knees bent, weight shifting forward, hands steady on the gun's grip. The figure took a step forward from the shade into daylight.

It just wasn't possible.

Hannah didn't twitch, bead locked on the slowly moving target.

"Now, Han, that's no way to be."

No one else ever called her Han, because she hated it. Except for him. But it couldn't be him—because he was dead.

The gun started to wobble and she lowered it slowly as he came out of the blinding reflection. "Uncle Joel," she said, her voice choked off to a whisper.

It wasn't possible.

"You need to come with me," he said. "I'll explain everything, but we need to go. She's headed this way."

He was dead. How was he here?

Alive.

Perfect.

Too perfect.

He was one of *them*.

Her gun dropped to the porch with a thud. Boneless with shock, Hannah started to wilt into her chair, but Joel caught her in a bear hug, hauling her back to her feet. Being crushed by arms that were absolutely real was enough to convince her she wasn't hallucinating. The feeling was so familiar, all flannel and wiry muscles and the smell of coffee and beat-up leather.

There was a time when Hannah would have questioned her sanity, being squeezed breathless by someone who was supposed to be dead. Not anymore. She snaked her arms around him and stood there for a moment. The man who'd raised her, the man she loved and missed and had mourned and accepted as gone forever was here. Alive.

Hannah hugged him back so tightly her shoulders creaked, basking in the strange, unnatural warmth. But only for a moment.

"Joel, you'd better let go," she said. "This is one of those occasions that turns into someone getting a black eye real quick."

When he laughed and she felt the up and down jiggle it made, Hannah smiled against his chest.

"Fine," he said, "but only because I taught you how to throw a punch." He grew serious, pushing her out to arm's length and studying her face. "Really, kid, I'm not sure how much time we have. We need to head out."

Twisting away from him, she sat down. "Not until I get an explanation." Hannah pulled out her phone and turned the screen toward him. "There's no one else here. I knew someone was coming the second you crossed the first line of sensors. There hasn't been anything else since."

Hannah was damn proud of the defenses she had set up. "I've got the entire perimeter on motion detectors from ground to tree tops," she said, "and there are enough guns and ammo in the house to take down a small army. Even if it isn't the normal kind."

Not so normal was what Hannah was expecting. The intruder she'd gone to such great lengths to detect had a lot in common with the man she was staring at. The too-perfect skin had given him away the instant she'd seen him clearly. Knowing what she knew now, Hannah had instantly recognized Joel for what he was.

There were two types of people walking Earth: the kind that died and stayed that way, and the kind that didn't. Hannah had learned that the hard way. What she hadn't known until now was that Joel was part of the second group.

Someone like Joel died, just like anyone else. But when they took their last breath and their life ended, they just vanished, disappearing without a trace. They didn't stay gone long. They quickly found themself somewhere far away, alive again and perfect—even slightly better than before. The cycle kept repeating and repeating. Forever.

At least it had been forever, Hannah thought, correcting herself. For the first time, there was a way to break the cycle. Her.

"I have a dart gun loaded with my own blood, if the standard arsenal inside doesn't make you feel better," she said. "There are enough loads to turn you into a regular person a couple times."

Joel didn't look bothered by that; not that he needed to be. The darts weren't meant for him. Hannah had a specific target in mind, and she had a pretty good idea that person was why Joel was here and so insistent on leaving.

"Good girl," Joel said. "I don't have time to explain the details, but Amara is on her way."

Just hearing the name out loud yanked Hannah's stomach up into her throat.

Amara. Last time the two of them had met, she intended to use Hannah as a weapon to kill every other immortal person like herself and Joel. She needed Hannah's blood in order to wipe out the others and make Amara one of a kind. If she'd succeeded, Hannah would probably be strapped to a table somewhere with a tube in her arm, being drained dry one drop at a time. Or dead.

Before that could happen, Hannah had bitten her own tongue bloody and then taken a bite out of Amara's hand. She hoped it had been enough to make Amara a regular human, the kind you could put bullets into that stayed there. She'd also been holding out hope Amara had been hit by a bus, or maybe pushed down an elevator shaft. The fact Joel was looking ready to shove her out the door made Hannah think that wasn't the case.

Amara's heart stopping for good had clearly been too much to ask. Now she was coming back, and whatever her plan for Hannah was, revenge would be a big part of it.

"Is she human?" Hannah asked.

"I don't know," Joel said. "No one knows. Maybe not even her."

She looked up at him, eyes narrowed. "But you do know she's coming here, and you think we should go to a safer location? Where exactly would that be?"

Wasn't Hannah safest where she was? It was secluded, protected, and she was armed to the teeth. Living like a hermit inside her little fortress had been working out so far.

Joel looked at her and smiled and her irritation melted away. She had missed him so much and seeing him again was like a miracle. She threw her arms around him, snugging her head against his shoulder like she'd done when she was a child. So much had gone to hell when he died.

Except *died* wasn't the right word anymore. For a moment, it didn't matter. "I missed you so much," she whispered.

He kissed the top of her head. "I missed you too. You can't even imagine."

"I'm still not going anywhere, at least not until you sit down and give me an explanation."

"We don't have time. This location won't be safe for much longer. I may have gotten here ahead of Amara, but she won't be far behind."

"Inside then." Hannah jerked her head toward the door. "The sooner you start talking, the sooner you might be able to convince me to go," she said. "Might."

Ballistic glass was expensive. And really freaking heavy. The sliding glass door stuck in its track, and Hannah had to rock it back and forth, putting her weight behind it until it closed. Reaching behind the long blackout curtains, she pulled the retractable security gate across the glass, securing it to the steel plate bolted through the wall.

Metal grids were already pulled down over the room's two small windows; Hannah checked they were locked and yanked the blinds down over them. The front door was dead bolted—as always—and she dropped a steel bar as wide as her arm across it and pushed it into its slot, where it fell into place with a comforting, solid clunk.

Tapping the screen of the tablet on the kitchen counter, Hannah brought up a visual rendering of the security system with rings of green, yellow, and red arranged in a concentric cylinder like a 3D bull's eye. The black target at the center was the shape of a tiny house.

Joel leaned over her shoulder. "How far out do the sensors go?"

"Motion detectors start four hundred yards out in all directions.

There's a ring every hundred yards until you get to the house." Hannah pointed to the two places where the outermost green ring was overlaid with a large dot. "There are overlapping sensors at the obvious points of entry—the lakefront and driveway. They're programmed to disregard anything that's obviously not human. A black bear tripped them a couple times, but otherwise it works."

Satisfied everything was quiet, Hannah pulled up a four-way video feed. Each quarter of the screen showed an image from one of the cameras mounted on a corner of the roof. "These are high resolution and you can see out to the hundred-yard mark, at least where there aren't trees in the way." She changed the view again, pointing to a screen split in two. "There are extra cameras at the same places as the redundant motion detectors."

The top half of the screen showed a gravel driveway with a chain stretched across it, the rusty no trespassing sign hanging from its center swaying dejectedly back and forth. On the bottom half of the screen, inky water lapped against the rocks on the shoreline. The picture was so clear she could make out individual maple leaves, white bellies showing like flags of surrender to the storm hovering somewhere over the lake.

The security hadn't come easy. It had taken her weeks of tree climbing and beating her head against the computer to get everything up and running. It wasn't until then, when she was sure nobody was getting to her doorstop unannounced, that Hannah had finally stopped sleeping in a chair with a gun across her lap. She still spent plenty of nights with her hand under her pillow wrapped around the grip of a handgun, but it was an improvement.

"Good girl," Joel said, nodding in approval at the security camera images.

"Stop good girling me, Joel." Hannah pulled out a barstool. "Sit down and start talking."

He paused, eyebrow raised. She stared pointedly until he sat.

Propping the tablet up against the coffee pot where she could see it, Hannah stood across from him, leaning back against the counter.

Joel stared at her for a moment, head tilted to the side, but didn't speak. Fine. If that's how he wanted to do it, she'd ask the questions.

"So who was in the can, Joel? It clearly wasn't you."

That was where it all started, with the little metal urn she'd believed held his ashes. Seeing him alive now, her tight-lipped expression slipped a little. Hannah reined it in, but it wasn't easy. Her happiness at seeing him sitting in front of her was at serious odds with the gravity of the situation and how pissed she was about his neglecting to mention not being dead.

"No clue," Joel said. "Did you know you can buy human cremains online? I feel especially bad now, since whoever they were got cremated twice." The can that had held the remains had been lost—along with everything else she owned—when Amara burned down her last house.

"It's not funny, Joel," Hannah said. "You faked your death, and you left me."

"I had to."

Hannah slammed a hand on the counter. The tablet slid flat with a clunk. "You *had to*? That never would have flown as an explanation when I was a kid, and it certainly isn't flying now. Try again."

"I really did have to," Joel said. "You've obviously recognized what I am. You know we don't age. Someone was going to notice." He *was* different than she remembered, and not just because she'd learned to recognize the slight differences that gave his kind away. She studied his face.

"I know. I don't look quite the same, do I?" Joel ruffled the front of his hair. "It was a relief to stop dyeing it. Do you know how hard it is to get a convincing fake sprinkle of salt and pepper?"

She remembered the silver that threaded through the hair at his temples. The thick curls were all dark brown now, and his sharp, thin face didn't look a day older than hers. His eyes at least were the same—crystalline green, the corners crinkled in amusement.

He stroked his chin and laughed. "And you thought *you* hated the beard? It was so scratchy, but I was stuck with it, since it made me look

7

a little older. Which still wasn't enough. I'm glad I was able to find that tattoo artist. She was an absolute wizard."

Joel saw her confusion. "Wrinkles. Inked-on crow's feet. They were so good, I swore I was going to be able to feel them. Impressive, since I can't imagine she'd had much practice. How many people walk into a tattoo parlor looking for wrinkles?" His grin fell away. "Even that wouldn't have worked forever. You would have figured it out eventually, that I hadn't really changed in twenty years." Joel reached over and took her hand. "It was time. You were grown up and perfectly capable of taking care of yourself. You didn't need me anymore."

Hannah jerked her hand away. "Easy for you to say. You have no idea what it was like after you left. You could have just told me." Did he think she wouldn't have believed him? It turned out his secret was well within her ability to handle.

She hadn't found out about Joel's world from him, though in a small way it was because of him. So much had changed since the night she glanced away from the road to pick up the container of his ashes from where it rolled under the seat. Hannah had looked up just in time to see the man in the road before she'd ended his life. Or so she'd thought. The man had returned.

And brought a whole lot of trouble with him.

Joel opened his mouth, but she didn't give him a chance to speak.

"You should have told me the truth," she said. "I knew nothing about who I am. My entire life was a lie." A lie, and a dangerous one. Keeping the details secret about what he was—and who *she* was—hadn't protected her. It made her more vulnerable, ignorant of the danger that was going to come for her. Joel hadn't warned her about her father.

Referring to the man as her father was distasteful, even in her mind. *Michael.* Hannah hadn't known Michael existed until a year ago. She certainly hadn't known he'd been like Joel, living over and over again.

Unlike Joel, Michael hadn't been interested in seeing Hannah alive; quite the opposite, in fact. She didn't feel any remorse that Michael was dead now—permanently dead—because of her.

"You have no idea how miraculous you are," Joel said. "It's hard to believe you survived at all. Whatever intuition your mother had about him saved your life. If Michael had been in the picture when you were born, you wouldn't have made it to your first birthday."

Pity the intuition hadn't saved my mother's life as well, Hannah thought. And miraculous? There wasn't anything miraculous about Hannah. It was sheer luck Michael hadn't managed to kill her.

"Did you know?" she asked.

"Know what?"

"What I am. Did you know? Is that why you rescued me and raised me?" Hannah picked up the tablet and flicked back and forth between the images on the screen. She didn't want to look at his face while he answered. He'd kept enough else from her; would it be so hard to believe he'd kept the knowledge of what her blood could do to immortals from her as well?

He reached over and put a finger under her chin, forcing her to look him in the face. "I had no idea. None whatsoever, not until I found out Michael was dead for good. No one could've known."

Maybe that was true; Hannah wanted to believe him. And Michael had been fathering children and killing them to see if they came back like he did for hundreds of years. As far as anyone knew, she was the first of his children to survive. Could anyone have known what she was?

Joel shook his head and smiled. "I picked you up and took you because I didn't want to see another child die at his hands. I hid you, because I knew he'd be back to finish you off some day. I intended to erase your identity and place you with a family somewhere so he could never find you."

"So why didn't you?"

"Because after a couple days, I couldn't bring myself to give you away." Joel smiled at her. "You were a very cute baby."

A ping made them both freeze, the tone reverberating around the bulletproof box of a room. Hannah picked up the tablet.

"We have company."

2

The ring of green dots on the screen was bouncing up and down excitedly. Hannah silenced the pinging. "There's movement coming toward the front of the house, just off the main road." As soon as she spoke, the ring of yellow dots began to jiggle. "She's still on the same course," she said, "heading straight this way and fast, staying just a couple yards left of the driveway."

Hannah pulled down the backpack hanging by the front door and unzipped it, quickly checking the contents. Satisfied, she slung it over her shoulder and reached into the coat closet, pulling out the shotgun and making sure it was loaded. When she chambered the shell, Joel sidestepped away from the barrel.

"Traded in the old side by side for the pump action, did you? That's different," he said.

"A lot of things are different."

"I think we should—"

"We should what? She's coming. You wanted to go, let's go."

Before today, Hannah had every intention of hunkering down and waiting for Amara to come so she could face her head on, but now that it was really happening, Hannah was scared, and a little less assured of her chances. If Joel had found her, she wasn't as well hidden as she'd thought. Now it looked like Amara had found her too. Amara, who'd been killing people since before the guns in Hannah's bag had been invented. Were the defenses here likely to do anything more than delay the inevitable?

Hannah had trusted Joel her entire life, and knowing what he was, it was likely he'd been around for a while. He might know a couple of things. If he thought they should go, maybe they should go.

Punching a code into the keypad by the side door, she paused impatiently until the alarm turned off. In the garage, Hannah clicked open the locks on her SUV and tossed Joel the keys. "You drive. I'll cover us," she said. When she pulled up the rendering of the motion sensors on her phone, the innermost row of red dots was going crazy. "Still coming on the same track. She's just hugging the edge of the driveway."

It wasn't the stealthiest approach, but who knew what Amara was thinking. "She could pop out on the road right in front of us," Hannah said. "If we have to, I guess we'll just go through her." It wouldn't be the first time she'd run Amara over with a car.

Pulling the secondhand Beretta out of her bag and carefully racking the slide, Hannah hit the button on the garage door opener with the muzzle.

Joel tore out, roof scraping the bottom of the door. Hannah's driveway immediately cut left under the cover of trees, the tight turn forcing them to move more slowly than she would have liked. After the bend the gravel track straightened he floored it.

The approaching figure, hidden in the shadow of the tree line, stepped out into the road in front of them.

"Stop!" Hannah screamed. Joel slammed the pedal to the floor, the heavy back end of the SUV kicking out. He deftly corrected out of the slide as the car began to turn sideways. It slowed, skidding to a halt in front of the person standing stock still in the center of the road.

Asher.

Asher blocked out the sun, casting a shadow over Hannah where she sat. His knees touched the grill where it had come to a stop against them, and when he put his hands down on the hood of the SUV, the front end dipped.

11

He was staring a hole through the window tint.

Though Hannah had thought about Asher every day in the months since she'd seen him, being face to face still came as a shock. He was not the same as she remembered. This Asher was a darker, sharpened version, close cropped and narrowed. He was still abnormally large, but pared down to more severe angles.

"Get out of the car, Hannah," Asher said. His voice was so low and gravely she could barely hear him, but the shapes of his slowly formed words were clear enough through the glass. His odd, pale eyes, more deeply buried in their sockets than before, were narrowed into slits.

Joel grabbed her sleeve as she opened the door but she shook him off. The woman she was running from might be Asher's sister, but Hannah had nothing to fear from this man. Outside of the car, her face broke into a smile.

It wasn't returned. Hers faded.

"Nice to see you too, Ash," she said. She heard a car door open behind her, and Asher's posture somehow managed to grow even more menacing.

"Stay where you are," Asher said to Joel.

"It's fine." Hannah waved off his concern. "He's my uncle." Asher's hand slipped into his jacket. "This man is not your uncle." Not at all fazed, Joel took a step forward to stand beside her.

"Not technically," Hannah said, "but anyway, this is Joel."

Joel crossed his arms, eyeing the hand Asher had tucked inside his coat, where the bulge of a holster showed.

"Go ahead. Shoot me," Joel said. "I think you and I both know it won't do any good, at least not for long." He turned around to get back into the SUV, pausing by the open door. "Besides, I'd hazard a guess you're here for the same reason I am." Joel slid into his seat and shut the door. Hannah gave Asher an appraising look, and followed.

"You coming?" she asked. There was more she wanted to say before she ducked inside, but she closed the door and fastened her seat belt. Hannah watched Asher stand there for a moment, deciding. He finally shook his head and squeezed into the back seat.

———•◆◆•———

They flew, threading their way down the narrow road that clung to the border of the lake. No one spoke, but Hannah could feel Asher's presence behind her. She'd forgotten how completely he tended to fill up a space. It was a welcome break in the silence when Joel's phone vibrated. He answered it and listened briefly, then cursed under his breath. Murmuring a response she couldn't make out, he tucked the phone into his pocket and pressed his foot down more firmly on the gas pedal.

"I *had* a plan in place," Joel said. "I intended to slip in here and get you and slip out before Amara arrived. I knew where she was, that she was headed this way, and that I was ahead of her. But something spooked her. She's disappeared." He whipped around a slow-moving car in their lane. "I can only guess what tipped her off." He shot an accusatory glare over his shoulder. "Now we don't know which way she'll come at Hannah. Only that she'll come. And now we're out in the open and a whole hell of a lot easier to spot."

They skidded into the opposing lane, dodging a minivan. Joel whipped back into their lane just in front of oncoming traffic. "Time for plan B. We have to get clear and ditch this car," he said. "Once we know for sure she isn't following you, I'll get you to a safe location."

"I have a vehicle, tied to no one," Asher said over Hannah's shoulder. "Take us to it and I will get her to safety, before my sister can follow."

Joel scowled at him. "Blue sedan, parked behind a barn two miles from Hannah's? Registered to the alias of an immortal the size of a bus? You were picked up the same time we lost track of Amara." They swerved around a Sunday driver, everyone lurching sideways with the motion, then back into the right lane through a salvo of angry honks. "If you followed your sister here, you did an unimpressive job of hiding."

Turning toward Hannah and apparently not paying attention to the road, Joel said, "No need to worry, I've got it all in hand. I'll get you out of here."

"And make her an easy target, sitting still?" Asher scowled. "It would be best to put as much distance between Hannah and my sister as possible. We need to find another mode of transportation and flee." His voice was booming like the bass was turned up too far on the speakers.

Joel was louder. "Flee to where? To what end? So Hannah can just run forever, hoping to stay ahead of your sister? Were you thinking maybe you could pop Amara off before she gets a piece of Hannah?" Joel shook his head. "I've seen the narrow misses you've gotten her into."

The tires screamed when they shot into the oncoming lane and back again. "She'll catch up with you, like she always does," Joel said. "You won't even see her coming. I know more about you than you think, Asher. I know all about you two. I never believed in the twin crap, but she finds you like you two are sharing a brain."

They blew around a pickup truck, narrowly avoiding clipping a party bus.

Hannah made a grab for the panic bar above her head.

Suddenly Asher's voice was in Hannah's ear, low and insistent, not intended for Joel to hear. "Hannah, I do not think you should blindly trust this man. We should consider an option other than his."

"There isn't another option," Joel said. These immortals, they heard absolutely everything. "I don't know what gave you the ridiculous impression she's going anywhere with you."

Hannah could feel her seat pushing forward when Asher leaned against it in response to Joel's words. It was vibrating with anger.

"You've never done anything but bring her danger," Joel said. "My plan doesn't include you. I had everything in hand. And I will again as soon as we get Hannah clear of your damned twin."

"Who are you to be trusted?" Asher was shouting past Hannah's ear. "You could well be part of Amara's plan. You abandon Hannah to her fate and conveniently reemerge just when my sister makes a move. For all we know, *you* led her to Hannah."

"This isn't up for debate. Hannah is safest with me," Joel said. "The resources at my disposal are far beyond what you can even imagine."

They screeched to a halt behind a line of cars at the red light on the edge of town. Before anyone could react, Hannah unhooked her seatbelt and jumped out, slamming the door behind her.

Maybe it took them some time to find her. She doubted it. More likely they were surveying the area, on the lookout for Amara. Either way, they were smart enough to give Hannah some space for a few minutes. She had a beer in front of her and was watching the water slap against the boats in their slots when she heard the scrape of a chair next to her.

"Parking in this town is a nightmare. It'll be a miracle if we aren't towed," Joel said. He leaned back in his chair and examined the faces of the few people sitting outside. There weren't many braving the gray skies and the wind that was throwing white spurts of water up over the jetty.

"Put away that piece," he said. "Someone's going to see it. I think we're clear of Amara, for the moment at least."

"I have it out because of you two," Hannah said. Still, she slid the handgun out from under her menu and laid it in her lap. She looked out across the lake, to the point on the horizon where the roiling clouds tumbled into the black lake.

Another scrape, and Asher sat down on the other side of her. "I did not see any evidence that my sister is near," he said.

"Good," said Hannah. "If you're finished yelling at each other over my head and making decisions for me like I'm not here, maybe we can figure out what to do next."

Joel leaned toward her. "Sweetheart, I really don't think this is the time." She picked up her bottle and shook her head.

"Don't patronize me, Joel. I'm not a child."

"You're acting like one. I will pick you up and bodily throw you in a car rather than sit here until we're attacked. We're pinned down at this location."

"I have a gun. Asher has a gun. I don't know where you're hiding it, but I *know* you have a gun," Hannah said. "I'm not looking forward to seeing Amara again either, but it's happening. Like I knew it would eventually. So what now?" She took a long drink from her beer and set it down carefully on the coaster before she continued. "I'm actually glad you two showed up to hassle me. Probably makes my odds of survival a lot better. I'm just an okay shot, but the two of you should be able to handle her. Besides, what's the worst she can do, kill you?" She gave a sidelong glance at Asher. His sister had killed him plenty of times. He was the expert.

"That may be, for him and me," Asher said. "We can take a bullet and be no worse for it. But you …"

"Exactly," Joel said, nodding. "Whether Amara is human or not, she's not going to barge in here, guns blazing, and give us a clear shot at her. She's smarter than that, no matter what shape she's in. She wasn't ever going to come at you in a way that posed any risk to her. The sensors, the layers of armor, she would have found a way around them. You wouldn't have seen her coming."

"He is right," Asher said. "She will not come rushing in here, especially if there is any chance she is human. Now that you are not alone, Amara will find another way. Likely she will isolate you by injuring or killing Joel and me to get us temporarily out of the way." His voice dropped to nearly a whisper. "If that happens," he said, "I may not be able to find you again in time."

Hannah slid her bottle out in front of her and rested her head on her arms. "So I have to leave. Fine." Not fine really. She was starting to shake now that she wasn't jacked up on adrenaline any longer. Here she was, faced with death, *again*, stripped of the false safety provided by all her stupid little preventative measures.

She sighed. "Okay then. Where to? What's the most reasonable course of action?"

"I have a location—" Joel said.

"It is best that we keep—" Asher spoke at the same time.

They could work that part out later. "Whatever. Just stop arguing like I'm not here and let's get going," Hannah said. At least they didn't argue about that. "So Asher's car is out. Joel, you had to get here somehow. Where's your ride stashed? On the lake?" she said.

"No, I was dropped in. I was—"

Joel didn't get to finish. There was a long screech of brakes, followed by a crunch of metal and glass that carried over the top of the restaurant behind them. They froze, ears tuned in the direction of the noise.

Asher and Joel were on their feet.

"Didn't you just say she wouldn't come in here guns blazing? Could just be a car accident, right? There's a lot of traffic today," Hannah said, still sitting.

They heard a scream. "Or not. Shit, I knew I shouldn't have opened a tab." She stood up fast.

Joel had drawn a gun and was eyeing their exits. There were only two, and they were both bad choices. They were hemmed in along the narrow strip of waterfront. "Where are you going?" he asked, as Hannah started running.

"Hopefully taking my boat the hell out of here, unless you want to go back the way we came?" Hannah said. "Up to you."

When Hannah hit the dock Asher was at her heels. Joel gave one last look behind them and followed. She whipped the cover off the boat and climbed in while Asher undid the dock lines and pushed them away from the slip. Joel made a graceful leap over the gap in the water as the motor sputtered to life.

"A boat?" Joel said. "I never would have guessed."

Hannah ignored him, too busy trying to back out and unable to resist looking the way they'd just come. She heard raised voices and then a series of faint pops. She looked at Asher whose grim expression confirmed it was gunfire.

The second they were clear of the surrounding boats, Hannah opened up the throttle, the bow lifting as she gunned the boat over the choppy water. She sped around a pair of kayakers, tossing them sideways with her wake. She could hear their angry shouts as she cut in front of a sailboat tour coming in early, trying to get ahead of the wall of rain moving over the surface of the lake.

Behind them, Hannah saw a dark figure standing at the farthest point of the ragged stone jetty. They were too far away for her to identify, and it didn't look like a woman, but at that distance, Hannah couldn't be sure.

"Is it her?" Hannah looked at Asher who was staring, wide-eyed. He had a horrified look on his face.

Joel turned to him for clarification. "Is that Roman?" Asher nodded.

"What? Mass-murdering, screwed-up-childhood Roman?" Hannah shouted over the noise of the engine. Great. She'd hoped that particular figure was just a cautionary tale.

Like Asher and Joel, when Roman died, he didn't stay that way. The difference was, when he'd died the very first time, he'd only been a few years old. It was as long as he'd ever live again. Immortals never did—never lived longer than that first span of years.

Roman only ever had a short time before he was ripped away again, thrown across the world. At best, he might have been found and taken in, cared for well enough to live out that short period of life. But how many times, instead, had he found himself alive again only to perish almost immediately? He'd died countless times—alone, helpless, and scared.

It had broken him, twisted him into a detached, warped being. By the time he finally reached adulthood, he was so devoid of human emotion that life or death made no difference to him. He snuffed out human life without conscience. For enjoyment. He'd never had a reason to stop.

Joel looked at the figure shrinking in the distance, then back at Asher with cold eyes. "What has your sister done?" he said.

Asher had no answer.

3

Hannah pushed the throttle forward as far as it would go and didn't back it down until they were clear of the lakefront. She eased the stick back slightly when she didn't see any boats in pursuit, and because they'd crossed into the storm hovering over the lake. The rain was coming down in heavy gray sheets.

"Where are you going?" Joel said. He grabbed for the wheel when Hannah began to turn toward the western shore. "Keep going up the lake." She smacked his hand away.

"I'm heading for my car. I have it parked at a hotel near here, just in case," she said. Hannah had stashed her old, beat-up compact there, a car both men were familiar with. One of them had bought it for her eighteenth birthday; the other she'd killed with it. It was parked there for the same reason she owned the boat they were in—to give herself an escape option if a day like today ever came.

"If this keeps up, we aren't going to be able to see where we're going and we're going to be swamped," she said.

Already there was a pool of water collecting at their feet, accumulating faster than the bilge could cope with. Hannah pulled hard to the left, aiming toward where she thought the hotel's dock was, already struggling to make out the details of the shoreline.

"I think the bar is still open for the season," she said. "Maybe we can stop for a margarita. But then you'll have to drive."

"That is not humorous," Asher said.

He was wrong about that. She was totally funny, and besides, he should know by now that her mouth kicked into gear when she was scared.

Currently she was terrified.

"I don't know what part Roman plays in this," Joel said, "but it isn't a coincidence they're both after you." He considered their path for a moment and didn't stop Hannah pulling the boat toward shore. "If they're working together, they'll be trying to figure out the best way to get us coming off the lake. Maybe we can be off the water and on the road before they catch up."

Finally close enough to see the floating docks tossing up and down, Hannah slowed the boat slightly, ready to bump against the dock and use the forward momentum to give her a running start. She'd just taken her hand off the throttle when Asher smashed it back down. He pointed.

"What is that?" Hannah said.

In front of them, on the shoreline below the hotel, was a thatch-roofed tiki bar with a row of neon plastic palm trees. In the parking lot that overlooked it, she could see something blurry and bright. It looked like someone was having a bonfire, though what would be burning in this downpour she couldn't imagine.

"Oh my god, is that my...?"

It was. It was her car. In flames. And it was moving. It picked up speed, jumped the guardrail, and fell like a comet into the bar below. There was a mute second where Hannah watched, shocked, before everything blew toward them in a ball of fire.

"Get down!" Asher ripped the throttle backward and threw the boat into reverse. It struggled and churned, not moving fast enough to escape the rolling wall of flames. Hannah felt her face blistering, until she was pushed to the floor. She stayed there until they were clear of the docks and the boat turned. Risking a look backward as they tore away, she thought she saw the slender figure of a woman through the scrim of smoke.

<hr>

"What now?" Asher yelled over the noise of the engine and the rain beating against the fiberglass. They were fighting their way farther up the long lake, slogging across it diagonally in an attempt to get as far away as possible from where they'd just narrowly missed Amara. It was—of course—the path that led directly into the storm.

"We have to get off the water," Joel said, calling to them from where he was standing on the stern. "Once the storm passes we'll be too visible." He was looking backward into the thick gray wall that was wrapped around them. The drops hitting the water were kicking up a bank of mist, making it even more difficult to see. The combination brought visibility for Hannah down to exactly crap.

"How many miles is it around this lake?" Asher asked from beside her, where she'd taken back the helm. At least he was blocking a decent amount of the rain, not that it made a difference at this point. Hannah scraped a hank of sopping hair away from her eyes.

"Almost eighty miles." She wasn't sure how far they'd come up the length of the lake and, unable to see the shore on either side, she looked down at the compass mounted in the dash. Hannah readjusted again, pushing back against the wind that had pulled them off course.

"Even my sister cannot cover that distance without time," Asher said.

"And we left Roman on the southern tip," Joel said. "If we ditch the boat on the opposite shore, maybe we can be gone before they catch up with us. Of course that's assuming there are only two of them."

That was a frightening thought, that there might be more people after her.

Wherever it was they landed, they were going to have to do it soon. Under the deluge, fighting the uneven chop, they had collected an ankle-deep pool of water. Add to that three people in a tiny ski boat, one of them the size of Asher, and you got a gas gauge that was sinking at an alarming rate.

"Why did she do that?" Hannah asked. "She could have just waited until we landed and, I don't know, blown up the car with someone in it." She turned toward Asher. "And why does she keep burning up my stuff?"

He shrugged. "My sister has always had a strange affinity for setting things on fire," Asher said. "What is that sound?"

"Probably my boat dying a premature death," Hannah said. "We've been beating it like a rented mule for the last half hour."

Even if they didn't run out of gas, there was a good chance that if she kept the engine pegged much longer it was going to go up in smoke. She could smell it burning. At least the rain would put out the fire.

"No," Asher said. "It is not our engine."

Whatever he heard, Joel must have heard it too, his head swiveling the same direction as Asher's.

"Damn it," Joel said. "She wasn't trying to catch us coming off the lake, she was trying to keep us on it. We have incoming."

At first she couldn't make it out, but a moment later Hannah heard what they did—the high-pitched drone of a jet boat motor. Soon the craft broke through the wall of rain, close enough for even Hannah to see.

The sleek boat was painted a bright, solid black that stood out—the only distinct thing in all the gray. It was clearly a much newer, faster boat than hers, and it was making a beeline for them.

"Get out of the way." Joel shouldered her aside and took the helm, pulling her clenched hand off the throttle.

"What are you doing?" she yelled.

He whipped the wheel around, sending them into a tight turn that threw her sideways against the gunwale. She scrabbled on the slick side for purchase, a hand yanking her back just before she went over.

"It's Roman. We can't outrun him," Joel said. "We're too heavy and too slow." He looked accusingly at Asher, who had just pushed Hannah down into the seat and was reaching into his sodden jacket for his gun.

"Get down!" Joel and Asher both yelled at her.

Hannah hit the deck, sliding down into the accumulated pond just as the black boat blew by. There was a whizzing sound and a thud, and a spidery hole opened up in the middle of her windscreen.

"He is coming around again," Asher said. He jumped up on the bow, gun drawn. She couldn't hear anything over the struggling engine and the approaching jet motor, but she saw his hands kick back once, then twice.

The other boat blew by a second time.

When it passed, from her angle on the floor Hannah could see the shape of the black-clad figure at the helm. She threw herself down face forward into the water on the bottom of the boat at the sight of the ugly, long-barreled handgun he was holding. It jerked away when a trio of holes appeared on the side of the black boat, Joel squeezing off one-handed shots as it passed.

Hannah came up armed, yanking her weapon out of her backpack in time to watch the more agile craft wheel around again. This time it was Asher who laid down a line of fire. She thought she saw the driver of the other boat jerk backward, though he quickly recovered. If they'd been shot, that small twitch was the sum total of their reaction.

"He's armored. And coming around again. Port side!" Joel yelled.

Asher was already shifting, going down on one knee, following the new track of the black boat. It blew by again, the figure at the wheel calmly leveling their weapon at Hannah where she was crouched, helplessly exposed. Her own weapon was drawn, but the boat was rocking so violently she couldn't hope to hit anything, even if she got the chance.

Hannah braced for the thud. She'd been shot once before; it hurt like hell. At the last minute the gun swung sideways, away from her. There was a grunt of pain that hadn't come from her.

"How bad?" Joel yelled. Asher struggled up from his knees, one of his shoulders drooping in a sickeningly boneless way. There was already blood pouring out the bottom of his sleeve, running in rivers from his fingers. "Fine," Asher said. "Nothing. Hannah, stay down."

What was the point? They were at a hopeless disadvantage, and now Asher had just taken a bullet. They were right, Joel and Asher. The driver of the boat could have easily killed her, but he was picking the others off one by one until she was alone. Then she'd be an impossibly easy target.

There was no way they could outmaneuver the other boat. It was already coming around again. It would keep coming; maybe finish Asher off this time, maybe Joel. Then Roman would come for her.

Joel had turned them around and slowed the engine to an idle. They were standing nearly still, white belly wide open.

"Joel, what are you doing!" Hannah yelled.

He wasn't paying attention to her, and he wasn't trying to get out of the way of the oncoming craft. He was looking at Asher. Asher nodded.

"Get down!" Joel and Asher both shouted at her again.

She obeyed, mostly, ducking down onto the floor in front of the seats. Just over the shattered plastic windshield she could see it clearly, the small dark boat. Asher stood beside her, gun in his good hand, but he held it down at his side. Then he suddenly sprang in front of her line of vision, stepping up onto the stern.

"Ash, get down!" Hannah screamed. They were on a collision course, the small, fast rocket of a boat bearing down on them at full speed.

At the last possible second, Joel slammed the throttle forward and jerked the wheel, sending Hannah surfing across the floor. She saw Asher sailing through the air.

The momentum of their turn carried him over the side of the boat and into the driver of the other craft. Asher locked his arms around Roman when they impacted. His weight drove them both out of the boat and into the dark, churning water.

⚫⚫⚫⚫⚫

Hannah hauled herself to her feet, recovering her gun from the murky pool in the bottom of the boat. "Joel, circle back. When they come back up, maybe I can get a shot."

"Hold on," Joel said. He didn't pull around or even pause to look where Hannah was combing the water with her eyes. Asher hadn't reemerged and she scanned the water, waiting for him to resurface. Instead Joel throttled it, steering them in the direction of the shore.

"Stop," she said, "what are you doing?"

He shook his head. "He's fine. Asher bought us some time, just like he intended. He'll keep Roman away from us one way or another. Hopefully far away. We can't wait around and give Amara time to catch up."

He said it so casually, like they hadn't just watched Asher get shot and throw himself off a boat into a waiting madman. Hannah slid back down into the seat, stunned, struggling to catch her breath.

Joel looked back at her. "You know how it works. Asher's probably in a beach chair somewhere with an umbrella drink."

That might be true if Asher was any other immortal, but Joel didn't know what she knew.

When the others died, they popped up in some far-off, random location. It didn't work quite the same for Asher. He had an inexplicable habit of turning up a little closer to home—or at least closer to her. He had every time since they'd met. Since before they met. More like since she'd been born, though neither of them had known that until recently. If he wasn't back here where she was, then he was still alive, somewhere under the water.

"Joel, we need to go back. What if he's still out there?"

"What's that over there?" Joel said, ignoring her question. He was pointing at a large building perched on the hill above the opposite shoreline. The rain had finally slowed and she could see well enough to identify the familiar building.

"Nothing. A winery."

"Perfect. Hold on." Joel goosed the failing engine, pointing them toward shore. Hannah couldn't help but turn again and scan the water behind them. The water was growing flat as the wind died, the white caps replaced with a surface that was only interrupted by dimples of rain, nothing else. Hannah kept searching as they moved toward shore, until a choking sound from the engine made her turn.

"That's not good." She pushed Joel aside and took the controls just as the motor wheezed itself out. Hannah didn't bother trying to restart it when she saw the gas gauge. They quickly started to slow; their remaining momentum wasn't going to be enough to get them to shore.

Joel jumped into the water, disappearing long enough to make her worry. His dark head bobbed back up. "It's deeper than I thought. Come on. It's not that far," he said, already starting to move away from the boat. With one last look behind her, Hannah pulled the straps on her backpack tight and jumped in after him.

If it had been any later in the year it would have been a dangerously different swim, but at least the water near the surface retained a little bit of the late summer's warmth. As she dog-paddled ahead, wishing she'd taken the time to shed some layers, she shuddered to think of what it was like closer to the bottom, where the center of the lake was a black abyss and the water never warmed.

"Almost there," Joel urged her on. Hannah still wasn't close enough to shore to feel bottom under her feet when she stopped to rest for a moment. The minute she wasn't moving she started to sink, pulled down by her wet shoes. She struggled, weighed down and tiring quickly. Everything was so heavy. She fought to drag herself forward through the water.

Her head dipped under for a second. Joel grabbed her by the front of her jacket and pulled her up. A few strokes later he was hauling her onto the slick, slimy rocks at the shoreline. She lay there on her back, spitting up lake water, looking straight up into the ash-colored sky.

"Almost there, kid. We can't stop now."

———

"Isn't this going to be a little noticeable?" Hannah said, squeezing a stream of water from the hem of her shirt, grateful for a moment to rest. They had dragged their way up the hill, through the rows and rows of grapevines and around the side of the winery to where they stood, ducked behind a corner of the building.

"I don't see any better option right now."

Joel was right; there were only a few cars in the parking lot on such a dreary day. And the one in front of them was conveniently running. "No time like the present," he said.

She hesitated, but he yanked her along with him. Joel bulldozed their way through the wobbly high-heeled assembly waiting to climb into the limo and threw Hannah in, slamming the door. He pulled the driver out of his seat and they were moving before anyone had a chance to react.

Hannah popped her head up just in time to see a woman in a short white dress with a satin sash across her chest standing slack jawed, before they swerved out of the parking lot, sending Hannah sliding the length of the vinyl seat.

She bounced around the inside of the limo like a pinball when they careened onto the highway, coming to a stop in a jumble of coolers, wine bottles, and white tulle decorations in the rear. By the time she clawed her way back to the front and squeezed through the divider, they were tearing downhill at breakneck speed.

"Well, darling," Joel said, "you never did make it to the prom. Now you know what all the fuss is about."

———◆◆◆———

Joel put the keys in the visor and pushed the door of the limo shut. After a quick look around, confident they hadn't drawn any attention, he led the way toward the building they had parked behind.

"Come on," he said. "Someone will find this quickly enough."

Probably very quickly. Even if the limo company didn't have some sort of tracking on it, hiding thirty bright white feet of tacky wasn't easy. She didn't think anyone had seen them squeeze it in behind the convenience store, but based on the carpet of cigarette butts, someone would be out there before long.

Joel crouched low at a sound she didn't hear and pulled Hannah with him behind an overflowing dumpster. A moment later he shooed away the cat that had wound its way out of the shadows to investigate him. Once it was clear that the stray was their only observer, they scraped through the narrow gap between the building and a chain-link fence. In front of them were gas pumps, and beyond them, a long stretch of parking lot.

"Far side. Next to the trucks," Joel said.

She looked toward the opposite side of the parking lot where a row of old cars was crammed in next to a line of semis. When they stepped out into the open, Hannah pulled her damp hood up over her head. Joel reached over and pulled it back down.

"It's sunny now. It's warm out. And you look like you just robbed the gas station. Try to act casual." Joel started walking at a leisurely pace, hands in his pockets, head up. She matched him as well as she could as they strolled across the cracked lot. At least she attempted to stroll. Hannah couldn't stop her head jerking toward every sound, convinced she heard sirens in the distance.

"You're terrible at acting casual," Joel said as they passed the gas pumps.

He smiled and nodded to a woman in a stained cobbler apron with the gas station's jaunty cow logo on it.

"It's hard to act relaxed when we're about to steal a car. *Another* car. I feel like I have a grand theft auto sign on my back," Hannah said.

"I think you need to steal at least three to get the official shirt. This looks promising." Joel eyed the beat-up hatchback in the middle of the line of cars.

At least it was subtler than the limo. "Yes," he said, "this one will do nicely."

Hannah squished to a halt beside him and he tapped the hood of the wired-together car. She didn't necessarily approve of stealing a second car in less than half an hour, but at least Joel made it look easy. It only took him a few seconds to snake a wiry arm through the partially open window and pop open the lock.

"Do you think this is employee parking?" she asked, pushing aside a pile of fast food wrappers and climbing into the passenger seat.

"Exactly. If that was the owner and their shift just started, maybe they won't notice we've borrowed it right away. But the limo will no doubt be found before then, and this place will be crawling with cops, so we shouldn't linger."

Joel pulled the plastic cover off the steering column and yanked out a handful of wires. "In this decrepit wreck's case, we've probably done the owner a favor stealing it. It's worth far more in insurance."

He separated out and stripped a few of the wires and touched them together. The engine sputtered, then choked to life.

"I didn't think hot wiring cars was really a thing," Hannah said as they backed out of the parking space.

"It's a miracle we found a car this old. Otherwise it's nearly impossible. Only vehicles manufactured before—"

She cut him off. "Maybe later with the lesson." She was looking behind them, craning her neck back the way they'd come.

"We're fine," he said. "I doubt the local authorities will pose a problem once we're out of the parking lot. As for our more pressing pursuers, I think we're clear of Amara for the moment."

He didn't seem as concerned about anyone else. When Roman and Asher hadn't come back up, Hannah was certain Joel had been relieved at the thought of them far away—both of them. Amara was the threat Joel was looking out for.

Hannah scanned the parking lot in the rearview mirror as they left. She wasn't looking for threats; well, not *only* for threats. She was looking for Asher.

"Looks like somebody found the limo," Joel said.

Hannah dropped face first into the dash when two police cars blew by them, lights flashing. She snuck a peek after they'd passed, then looked at Joel. He only glanced briefly in the rearview mirror before slipping out of the parking lot.

"What now?" she asked, when they didn't get back on the highway heading away from town. It was the fastest way to anywhere populated, where they could hope to blend in and disappear. Instead, Joel was headed east. The only things immediately east were a smattering of small villages and a whole lot of heavily forested nothing.

"Miraculously enough, we've managed to veer pretty closely back to my original plan. This route is just going to take us a little more footwork. I hope your shoes have dried out."

4

The two-lane road turned into a rutted single lane, then finally petered out into a narrow dirt track, a thick thatch of grass growing down the middle. They left the path with a thump of the tires and a scrape of the axle across the ground. Joel coaxed the little car into the trees, and they spent a few minutes scavenging fallen branches, making the car all but invisible from the road.

"Remember when we used to go camping?" Joel asked as Hannah followed him into the woods. She remembered. It seemed like something she'd done in another lifetime, with another person, but she remembered. "Sometimes we'd stay in those little cabins the park service rents out," he said. "There's a couple of them near here—relatively near. We're headed for the closest one—"

Joel froze, like he'd heard a distant sound, but apparently decided it was nothing. Starting again, he led the way deeper into the trees. Hannah hitched up her soggy backpack and followed. "It's a perfect place to reconnoiter." He paused to pull aside a branch for her to duck under. "We'll just hang out while I contact my people to pick us up. Amara won't be any the wiser."

"Wouldn't it have been better to just get farther away?" Hannah said. She saw him shake his head from where she was trailing behind now, getting snagged by the grabby underbrush.

"Amara managed to find your house, your car, and figure out Asher and I were coming in time to change her plans. There's not a lot of roads in and out of this area, and you can bet she has every one of them covered. I considered that might happen and looked at the alternatives. This is the best way we can keep from being found long enough to get picked up without her tracking us."

It sounded reasonable enough, Hannah guessed. That didn't mean it was going to work out even remotely the way it was planned. Hardly anything ever did.

She had plenty of time to figure out what could possibly go wrong while they hiked. When Joel had said a little more footwork, he'd meant a lot more. The blisters that formed on her feet during the first half hour of walking in damp shoes burst, the open skin rubbing painfully. She could feel the added wetness of the open sores—or maybe blood—as they continued to weave through the woods.

Joel looked back over his shoulder. "Have you kept hiking, since I—"

"Pretended to die?" she said, frowning.

He laughed but didn't apologize. "We used to hike all the time. Remember that three-day trip in the Pennsylvania Grand Canyon, to the Western Rim Trail?" he said. "You couldn't have been more than fifteen but you kept up, thirty miles out and back, camping rough every night."

That was a hard trip to forget, for a couple of reasons.

It had been the perfect combination of weather that year, and the turning leaves had been so nearly neon bright it seemed impossible they were made by nature. Every time they topped the edge of the trail and got a peek down into the gorge, they were hit with a breathtaking shot of oranges and reds and yellows. The colors were almost as memorable as the other highlight.

"Oh, I kept up all right. But you were moving a little more slowly than usual if I recall," Hannah said, letting out a snort of laughter. "You went to the bathroom in the wrong patch of woods and ended up with a case of poison oak where the sun doesn't shine."

She heard him laughing softly ahead of her. By the time they'd made it to the end of that trip, Joel was walking like they'd spent the time on horseback instead of on foot. It had been a continuous source of amusement for her and discomfort for him, even after they'd returned home. It wasn't until he came back from a last-minute business trip that it cleared up.

Or had it? It struck Hannah then that he had come back completely healed, and strangely without the tan they had both picked up over the three sunny days. She'd wondered if he was ill—she had been worried about him because he'd gone so pale.

"You died after, didn't you?" Hannah said. She saw him nod, but he didn't say anything. How many times had that happened, when she was growing up, that he'd died and she hadn't known? A great deal of her life must have been very different than she'd realized.

"We aren't that far now," Joel said, pulling her back to reality, slowing to let her catch up. "If we keep going at this pace we'll be there before we lose all the light."

They had to be close then, because there was next to no light left. The sky had become so dim Hannah was struggling to see where she was going. The trees blocked out most of what little light remained, and beneath them there was no color, only a hundred different shades of gray. It was that period before night fully fell when everything took on a surreal quality. It gave her false frames of reference about depth and distance, and made objects look like they were moving and shifting in the corners of her vision.

Stumbling, Hannah reached for a tree that turned out to be closer than it appeared, dragging her hand across the bark painfully, cursing under her breath. Joel wasn't hampered by the lack of light, only stopping to reach back from time to time to steady her before she face-planted. She was grateful for the break in the trees ahead, a clearing where it was marginally lighter.

"Is that it?" Hannah asked. She hoped so and picked up her pace, following so closely behind Joel she could feel the heat coming off his body. She collided with his back when he stopped without warning. He whipped around and clamped his hand over her mouth.

"Be still," he whispered. "There's someone behind us."

His chin brushed across her hair as his head swiveled back and forth above hers, his hand still firm across her mouth. His voice was so low and quiet she barely heard his words when he spoke, though they were said directly against her ear.

"Don't move. Not a muscle," Joel said, his breath stirring her hair. "Stay right here. I'm going to cut them off." He slipped away and Hannah swayed, suddenly unsupported. She cringed at the sound of her own foot shifting against the ground to keep her from toppling over. Joel had left her here.

She attempted to do what he said, and tried to only listen, but she couldn't filter out the sounds that didn't belong from the creak of branches and the noise of the wind bothering the leaves. The only other thing she could hear was her own heartbeat, and that was threatening to drown everything else out.

It was too dark; Hannah felt helpless, like she was floating in night. Keeping still became harder because she was so afraid. The fear was starting a little quake in her middle. She focused on the reassuring heft of the bag on her back. If she had something in her hand to defend herself with, it would be better than standing there like a target tacked to a board.

Hannah lowered her shoulder, letting the weight of the weapons carry the strap of her backpack down to her elbow. The slip of the nylon against her shirt seemed absurdly loud, and she froze again, holding her breath. She let it slide a little farther, and paused again, listening.

Better to approach it like ripping off a Band-Aid. Hannah quickly pulled the bag in front of her in one movement, getting her hand on the zipper. She froze again. She didn't hear anything; there hadn't been a sound. But something was moving. Somewhere, not far from her, something was coming. She could feel it.

Even if she could get into her bag, anything inside it was useless, here where she couldn't see her hand in front of her face. Something was headed her way, and the only thing Hannah could see was the brief break in the darkness of the clearing ahead. It was the only light, a patch of flat gray in the black. It couldn't be more than twenty yards away. If she could make it there, maybe she had a chance.

She took a step forward. Face first into a tree. Hannah threw her arms around it to keep from falling. *Where the hell are you, Joel?* She cursed him mentally. Had Amara found them already and taken him out? It was possible there was nothing left of him now but a dent in the ground, leaving Hannah the easiest prey imaginable, blind and alone.

Hannah charged forward, one hand struck straight out in front of her, the other trying to find her gun in the bag. The strap was yanked from behind, a hand jerking her backward. Hannah slid out of the straps, leaving the bag. Now it was even more futile. If she even made it the last few yards to the clearing, she was defenseless.

Suddenly she hit the ground, falling hard onto her side. Whatever Hannah landed on rammed into her ribs with so much force she heard a crack. A yelp of pain forced its way out before she could stop it, and Hannah slapped her hand across her mouth, pushing herself along on her knees, anything to be moving forward.

There was the swish of fabric against leaves to her left. She wheeled away from it, finally pulling herself the rest of the way to her feet. Unarmed and in pain, she could see the light only steps away. It wasn't going to save her, but at least she would go down able to see what she was facing. Hannah rushed the last few feet through blackness. Her shins crashed into something and she went headfirst over a log, the forward momentum rolling her over in a somersault and back up onto her feet. Hannah launched out of the tree line and into the faint gray light.

Skidding to a halt, she turned back. She was shaking, taking slow steps backward, one foot shuffling against the ground after another. Nothing materialized out of the blackness. Nothing moved toward her.

Because it was behind her.

She heard the faintest whoosh before an arm slammed her hands down and wrapped across her chest, pinioning her arms to her sides. Another hand clamped against her face. Hannah thrashed, struggling against the iron grip that made her sore ribs creak and squeezed the air from her lungs. The person holding her gave her a small shake, picking her up off the ground.

"Hannah, stop," Asher said.

"Yes, stop. Really, barreling around like that in the dark," Joel said from where he had materialized beside them. "You could have broken your neck. I wouldn't have left you there if I thought you were in danger. I found Asher, and we were coming to get you when you bolted."

"There is no one else in this wood now. We should go while it is still thus," Asher said, loosening his grip on Hannah, holding her up as she swayed for a moment, then stepping away.

"Amara wasn't out there?" Hannah said.

"No," Asher said. "There was only me."

Hannah let out a whoosh of breath.

"Let's get going. We're almost there," Joel said, leading the way. Hannah stumbled almost immediately, and he stopped and crouched in front of her. "Hop on," he said. She didn't protest. All the fight had wilted out of her, and anyway, they were quieter without her clumsy footsteps.

The two men carried on a low conversation as they wound their way upward. She was able to catch most of what was being said, because she was quite literally in the middle of it. Asher had slightly more information than she and Joel did.

"I lost Roman in the water and could not relocate him. We struggled for a long time, but he slipped away from me. It may be that he expired. It may also mean he simply managed to evade me," Asher admitted. "It is possible he made his way to shore to resume his pursuit."

Joel slowed. The incline had lessened and they dropped onto the beginnings of a trail. He let Hannah slide to the ground.

"How did you find us?" Joel asked, whispering over his shoulder.

Asher didn't answer immediately. Hannah had an inkling why. If it was the way he had always found her in the past, that meant the story he'd just told them might not be entirely factual. If she was right, there wasn't a bullet hole in his shoulder anymore.

"It probably had something to do with us having every flashing light in the county pointing our direction," Hannah said. "It happens when you plow through town in a stolen limo and dump it at a gas station." Her voice sounded so much harsher and louder than theirs, echoing back at her from the trees.

"I trailed you from there to the odd little car you buried in the underbrush," Asher said, picking up her story. "I was delayed in rejoining you because I stayed and made a circuit of the area, to ensure I was the only person that had come as far in your pursuit."

"Are you sure we were clear?" Joel asked. His voice had an incredulous tone. "You managed to follow us, and your sister hasn't ever had a hard time following you."

"I am certain," Asher said in a manner that didn't invite further doubt.

They stopped abruptly. "We're here," Joel said. "Let me do a quick lap to check things out." He melted away into the dark.

Hannah walked a step back, close to where she knew Asher must be. "Did Roman kill you?" she asked. Her words barely made a noise, and she couldn't see where he was, but she knew he heard.

"We both went into the water. I did not come out. He struck a blow I did not anticipate and cut me somewhere so I could not move. I have died in countless ways, but never have I felt anything like sliding helplessly into the blackness of that lake. I sank in blindness for what felt like an eternity."

Hannah shuddered at the thought. The lake's depth was astonishing, hundreds of feet of water that never grew warm, home to boats long forgotten, bodies that would never again reach the surface. Hannah imagined him falling and falling, settling onto the bottom, stirring up a bloom of rot and silt.

"He is still alive, for now," he said. "Roman will still be trying to find you. As will my sister."

"But he couldn't have followed you, could he?" Hannah said.

"No. I found myself at your car. *On* your car. I would have come after you more quickly, but there was the necessity of reequipping myself."

The corners of Hannah's mouth tugged up in the dark. One of the few perils of immortal life was waking up stark naked every single time.

"You did not tell Joel about this?" Asher said.

She felt him shift his attention. Joel must be returning. Then she heard it too, someone coming toward them.

"We're clear," Joel called out from a short distance ahead of them. "Follow me up."

"I didn't tell him," Hannah said.

Asher stepped past her, following the sound. "You should not," he said.

———⟡———

She kept watch over the black hole that swallowed the dirt trail leading from the porch, the only break in the band of trees wrapped close around the tiny cabin. It was eerily still; not a breath of air stirred the limply hanging leaves.

The only sound was the far-off call of a lonely, late-to-retire owl.

Hannah had been sitting like a sentry for hours, though Joel had assured her that—for the present at least—they were alone and not in danger. Still, she'd sat, and watched the light peel back the layers of dark one by one, until the forest that had felt crowded with shadow figures finally felt like just a forest.

"Still bewitching the wildlife, I see," Asher said. The pair of tiny sparrows that had been picking at the dust in front of her, unbothered by her presence as animals always were, skittered away at his voice.

The porch swing groaned painfully when he started to sit, and he stood back up before it collapsed. Asher leaned gingerly against the railing in front of her instead.

"Let me see it, where you fell," he said. She shrugged him off. "Hannah, do not be a stubborn ass."

She smiled before she could help herself. Asher almost never swore. He never even used a contraction, his English was so old fashioned and stiff. Hannah relented and pulled up the side of her shirt.

It really wasn't anything more than a purply-green bruise on the outside, maybe a couple of cracked ribs underneath. She'd had worse. In the dark, it had felt like her whole side had caved in. Everything seemed so much worse in the dark.

"See." She dropped her shirt. "Nothing."

Asher scowled and ran his thumb over his chin but didn't disagree. "Now let me see your hands."

Hannah stuck them out. They'd been in better shape. She hadn't felt it happen, with all the running in fear and flailing around like a fool, but she'd managed to ram a sliver of wood the size of a paperclip under the skin of her palm. The other hand wasn't as bad, just a scraped-up, oozy mess. A couple of the swipes and creases were deep enough to have bled and had crusted over with dirt that didn't want to brush off. She wondered if it was just her weirdo blood, or if everyone else's turned into contact cement the minute it left their body.

"Look what I found." Joel's voice came through the screen door. He pushed through it with her backpack in hand.

"You found it?"

Joel nodded. "One strap over a tree branch like you'd hung it there." Hannah reddened. So much for the hand that had reached out and grabbed it from her. Joel looked at her outstretched palms and grimaced.

"Give it here," Hannah said, reaching for her bag. "I've got a first aid kit." He unzipped the backpack and rifled around, pulling out the little bag. "With your history of accident proneness I would have thought you'd spring for the bigger kit."

The sarcasm wasn't appreciated, but it was true. She reached for the kit but he pulled it away.

"I've got it," he said. Joel grabbed her hand, and before she could react he whipped the sliver out of her palm. Ripping open an alcohol pad, he dabbed at the blood welling up, brushing off the bits of debris as he went. She didn't even react to the stinging, just gaped at him.

"Geez, be careful," she said, trying to pull her hand away. "I didn't know you were so interested in the normal human thing."

Joel rolled his eyes, continuing to clean up her palm. "I wasn't planning on licking the blood off. Other than that, it doesn't really work that way." Satisfied with the job, he tore open a Band-Aid and slapped it over the biggest gouge. "There," he said, "good as new. Now the other one." She held it out and he went to work.

"How do you know it doesn't work that way?" Hannah said. "Things didn't end so well for Michael or Gabe." Both were men who had expected to live forever. Both were now very permanently dead after a run-in with her blood.

"Think about it," Joel said. "I raised you. I've been spit up on, sneezed on … hell, I've even been peed on. I've fixed every cut, scrape, and bloody nose you ever had, all without any idea I might need to be careful. If it were that easy, don't you think I'd be dead, or at least old by now?"

He stood up, crumpling up the wrappers and putting them in his pocket. "I'm still my usual unusual self. Believe me, I died last week and here I am, good as new. I'm pretty certain it's a little harder than you think, or I'd be an average Joel by now."

It was Hannah's turn to roll her eyes.

"Then how does it work?" Asher's voice surprised her when it sounded from where he'd gone to sit on the steps.

"Hannah's blood can undo what we are, but not anything else about her, at least that I've encountered. It's clearly not airborne or passed through casual contact," Joel said. "It's blood, introduced internally. At least that's my educated guess. Gabe got it by injection. Michael got a face full of it when you were a baby. I put a dart in him when he was about to kill you and he fell down with you bleeding all over his face. It was purely poor timing on his part. Bad luck for him. Good luck for you."

Joel squeezed past Asher and down the steps. "I don't know how much it takes, but I hope you got enough into Amara to do the job. I'm going to take a look around." He jumped off the last step and disappeared through the slash in the trees.

Asher's head slowly turned, probably tracking Joel as he moved noiselessly through the woods. She watched Asher from the swing. He was different again.

Even though it had only been a few hours, he'd changed from when she'd seen him disappear into the water. Whatever life did to him, his death always knit him back together perfectly. This time was no exception.

The changes weren't drastic; they might not even be apparent to someone who didn't really know him, but they'd brought him around again to the person she remembered. His skin was fairer, his hair just a shade darker, his face softer. He'd returned to his usual gold-colored sort of perfection. Only the strange blue-gray eyes staring off into the distance were exactly the same.

"Did you think your sister would tell anyone?" Hannah said. She couldn't know what he was thinking about, but she knew what was at the top of her mind. It was one more reason she felt like a fool, a child playing amongst the adults. She had built herself a little sandcastle, hidden herself behind the walls. Why had she even imagined she could stand against the tide?

"Tell anyone what?" he said.

"About me. I didn't even consider it." It seemed like such an obvious idea to Hannah now. "I was prepared for your sister to come. Part of me even wanted her to. I thought I could end all this. I never even thought that she might tell anyone else what my blood does." It didn't make sense to Hannah. "Why would Amara want anyone to know she might be vulnerable? But once again, what the hell do I know?"

Hannah watched the slow movement of his shoulders up and down, waiting for him to chime in and reassure her that she couldn't have known.

He didn't.

"I guess I'm the only one who was surprised then," she went on. "I was expecting Amara to waltz up the driveway all by herself. I was going to have plenty of warning with my stupid sensors and cameras. I was going to open the front door and put a bullet in her if she was human, and a dart in her if she wasn't. And maybe then a bullet."

Asher finally turned toward her. "I wish we could know for certain if my sister is truly human. But even if she is, and she knows it, I do not believe she will have shared *that* information. I did consider that she might let the knowledge of your ability get out though. It would ensure her revenge against you, even if she cannot exact it herself."

"How would that help her?" Hannah said. "Why would it matter to anyone else but her?"

"Because your very existence is a threat to our kind," Asher said. "We cannot know to whom she has spread the information, or what she has told them, but it appears there are some—like Roman—who might not like the thought of someone who could undo their continued existence."

Her fear of Amara had been bad enough. Now that the word was out, how many more would there be? It was a new fear, a cold kind that raised gooseflesh on her arms.

"You never did tell me why you came," Hannah said.

"You left me." His words were flat. "When you walked away from me in Savannah, you did not tell me where you were going. It seemed clear you did not wish me to know." Asher got up from his step and came to stand in front of her. "You did not wish me near. If I was not with you, I could not ensure your safety. In that case, I thought my best option would be to find my sister. If I could locate her and follow her closely enough, I would know when she was coming after you. I might be able to warn you before she put you in danger."

He was still trying to protect her from Amara. He'd been doing it since they met. Unlike his sister, who didn't appear to possess a conscience, Asher was trying not to pile the weight of any more deaths on his. Hannah found it hard to believe his soul had too many dark stains on it, even after nearly a thousand years. Regardless, his wish not to add to it was the only reason she was still alive.

For now. There was a good chance her death would come relatively soon. Hannah's chance of survival was looking more and more grim, especially with other immortals joining the mix. She hoped Asher wouldn't feel responsible when one of them eventually did catch up with her. Hannah understood guilt, and she couldn't imagine the thought of carrying it forever.

And he would go on forever. Hannah could have changed that, but he'd made it clear he wasn't interested. When he knew what she was, he'd put up a wall between them, so she couldn't accidentally end his immortality. It was the reason she'd left.

Hannah had opted not to spend her possibly short remaining

time pining for someone who—if they remembered her at all after enough time had passed—would only recall her as a guilty blot on his conscience. Or worse, someone who would forget her altogether a few lifetimes after she was gone.

Grabbing the chain on the swing to pull herself up, Hannah yelped in pain.

"That will leave a scar," Asher said. He took her hand and peeked carefully under the poorly stuck bandage.

"What's one more?" Hannah said, pulling her hand away. She had plenty. The hairline split across her cheek from when she went off a bridge. The faint diamond pattern up and down the side of her legs from being blown up in a bar. The deep divot across her upper arm where Amara had shot her. A dozen others, large and small. At least it didn't hurt where the scar tissue was. Better to be all scars.

"If they scar, at least that means I was alive long enough for them to heal," she said. "Hopefully these get a chance to turn to scars too. I don't get a clean slate, like you. I have to carry mine around."

"I carry mine too," Asher said. "Not all scars are where you can see them."

5

A clap of thunder shook Hannah awake. Fat bullets of rain were beating against the tin porch roof, and she uncurled from where she'd dozed off on the swing. Over the rain she could hear strained voices and smell the bitterness of burned coffee.

The murmuring stopped abruptly when she put her foot on the floor—damn their unfairly good hearing. Inside the door, Asher had a tin mug waiting for her.

"Is everything okay?" she asked, accepting the scalding cup.

"No." He ran a hand across his head, standing his hair up the way he did when he was agitated. "Your *uncle* and I have spent the last hours trying to agree on our next course of action. Our opinions on what would be wisest differ a great deal."

Asher's words were clipped, his face tight around the mouth. Joel popped around the plywood partition that divided the single room. He had a cast iron skillet in one hand and plates in the other. He was wearing a mischievous smile that she knew well.

"There's nothing to agree on," Joel said. "I have it all worked out, but I don't believe your friend here trusts that ensuring your safety is my first concern."

"Oh, I'm *so* sorry," Hannah said, making no attempt to hide the sarcasm. "Are you running into problems deciding my future without consulting me again? Were you planning on letting me know what you decided, or were you just going to let whoever wins your little pissing match throw me in a sack and drag me away?"

"Language, young lady." Joel filled a plate with fried potatoes and plunked it down on the table with a grin.

"She is capable of far worse, I assure you," Asher said. He pulled over his plate and dug in hungrily.

Joel just poked at his with an exaggerated sigh. "As you can see, we're sorely limited in the comestibles department. That nasty black tar is all the coffee"—he waved his fork at the enameled pot— "and we have exactly half a bag of ancient potatoes that I found in the cupboard. Thankfully we won't be here long enough for it to matter."

"And where exactly are we going?"

"That, my dear," Joel said, "is where we're struggling to find common ground."

Hannah looked at Asher. From his expression, he looked ready to *struggle* Joel right through the window.

Joel took a halfhearted bite, not at all bothered. "I have a supremely safe place I'm going to take you to. My plan was to get you away from your house, make sure no one was aware of our location, and then have us picked up from here and transported there. The team that's waiting to extract us just needed our whereabouts and an all clear." He gave up playing with the rock-hard potatoes and pushed the plate aside. "Nothing has changed really, except for my ability to get a message out. Sadly, due to our time on the lake, we are short exactly one satellite phone."

From his expression, it was clear he'd overcome that problem. He looked unworried, maybe even a bit smug.

"But you have that all figured out, I gather," Hannah said. "Are you going to find some hiker and knock them over the head for their phone? Maybe sneak back to town and steal one?"

"Of course not. Neither would be particularly secure, and all the to and fro would only increase our risk of being discovered. No need for all that anyway. There's a place near here where I can send the message. They'll pick us up and you'll be off to safety. No one that means you harm will have any idea where you are."

She stabbed at a chunk of potato; it shot away from the tines of her fork. "Seems like you're pretty confident you have it all figured out. But then again, you always did." It was a quality she'd admired, Hannah had to admit to herself. He'd tried to pass it on, but he was always far more adept at planning. "Considering every contingency ..." Hannah said.

"... is the best way to ensure a favorable outcome," Joel finished. "Exactly. The problem is that Asher on the other hand—"

"Asher can speak for himself." He glared over his empty plate at Joel. Hannah pushed her uneaten potatoes toward him while they weren't looking. "Does this not sound a little unbelievable to you?" he asked Hannah. "Would it not be best to simply flee now while we all agree our whereabouts are unknown? It would give us a considerable head start, enough to allow us to disappear completely. You would be safer this way. I would ensure it."

"How? By doing what?" Joel said. "On the slim chance we could manage to get out of the area without being seen, which with you in the picture would be next to impossible, then what? Run? Run forever? Run from people you won't even know are after you until they show up?"

Asher ignored him, turning to Hannah. "This man is not your uncle," he said. "You cannot simply trust him. He has been lying to you for more than twenty years. He faked his own death and abandoned you. He walked away and left you to be killed."

Hannah raised an eyebrow. It was true. She'd automatically fallen back into her relationship with Joel, relying on him automatically the way she had for most of her life. It was second nature to trust his decisions. But the number of unknowns Joel was throwing out hadn't been lost on her. Granted, there hadn't been a whole lot of time for explanations, what with all the running from Amara and Roman.

"Left her to be killed?" Joel said. "Whose fault was it that was even a possibility? I left everything perfectly arranged. She was completely safe. Then I hear my house is on fire and people are dying left and right. If I'd come back a minute later your sister would have killed Hannah. Where were you when I had to take Amara's head off? Was that you ensuring Hannah's safety?"

"That was you?" Hannah said. It had been a mystery, who had saved her from Amara at the last moment, allowing her to escape. "Wait, why were you—"

"She was safe enough," Asher interrupted, leaning forward toward Joel. "You underestimate her ability to take care of herself. And what place could you possibly provide that would be better than being on the move?"

"Why would I tell you anything? Your inability to hide from your own sister is the stuff of legends. I wouldn't want you anywhere near—"

"Both of you, shut up," Hannah said. Joel opened his mouth to speak again. "I said shut up. Did you hear something?" She thought there had been a rumble somewhere in the distance, from a motor maybe, though she thought it was unlikely she'd picked up on a noise before they had. Then again, her mouth had been closed.

"She is right. Someone is coming," Asher said. "Some sort of small vehicle. More than one. The place you would go to—to send the message—it is near here?"

Joel nodded. "Take her then," Asher said. "Go."

They were moving before she even registered what was happening. Joel pulled Hannah's gun from her backpack and handed it to Asher, shoving the bag over her arms. "Come on." Joel grabbed her by the hand and pulled her toward the back door.

Asher stopped her for a moment, catching her by the wrist. "I will find you," he said. Joel nodded, but she knew he'd meant it for her. *Without fail*, she added silently to the end for him. He disappeared out the front door.

"Let's go," Joel said. "Now. There's no time." He pulled her through the cabin and out the back door, and they crossed into the trees. "Faster. If it's Amara, we can't hide. He'll give us some time." Joel pushed her in front of him. "Hannah, you have to run."

————————

"It's just up there." Joel leaned down, reaching a hand back for her. She couldn't take it without losing her hold and sliding backward, so

Hannah gritted her teeth and heaved herself up over the ledge, the jagged shale scraping the skin off her stomach. Joel was already moving forward again so she didn't stop to rest, even though her arms felt like jelly and her legs were burning like she was knee-deep in hell.

"We just need to get over the top of this ridge to where the ground levels out," he said. *Level.* What a beautiful thought. They'd been making their way uphill since racing out the back of the cabin, moving as fast as she could manage over the rough terrain. Parts of their route—like the stretch they were facing right now—were nearly vertical, and the footing was unpredictable, with loose rock hiding under a skin of leaves. It was daylight, so at least she could see where she was going, and there was no one behind them—for now.

Joel was pulling himself quickly up the steep slope, zig-zagging forward tree by tree. Ignoring her protesting ribs, Hannah started again, picking out a path after him. He looked back, and seeing how far she'd fallen behind, slowed for a moment to let her catch up. She was almost even with his shoe when the roots of the sapling she grabbed slithered out of the ground.

Scrabbling her feet didn't do anything but send a shower of rocks and dirt behind her. Joel's hand shot out and snagged one backpack strap before she was out of reach, but it wasn't enough to stop her completely. It slowed her descent, though, until Hannah managed to get her arm around a branch that held.

"Up you come." Joel hauled her back up. He took the bag from her back and slung it over his shoulder, and she followed him more carefully the rest of the way up, over the edge of the cliff to where the ground finally flattened. He paused to look back below them, and she tried to stop breathing so loudly so he could hear if someone was following them.

"It's nothing," Joel said. "There's no one. Keep going." The ground was more even now as they wove their way around humpbacked tumbles of rock and pushed through thickets of thorn bushes like barbed wire strung between the trees. Soon her hands were criss-crossed with scratches, and she was leaving dots and droplets of blood everywhere. Maybe if she was lucky Amara and Roman would stumble through this particular patch of heaven in their pursuit.

Joel paused at the edge where the trees finally gave way to a clearing. "There it is," he said. Hannah couldn't see anything through the hair and sweat in her eyes. She wiped her face with her sleeve and looked up. Way up.

"Conservation Department fire tower. We'll hole up in there," he said, and dashed across the flat space, Hannah close behind.

The switchback flights of narrow steps to the top were a brand new form of torture, but at least it was a short sentence. Her panic on the way up was worse than the climb. Hannah felt like a tin duck target, nothing between her and anyone looking for them but slim wooden struts. At the top, Joel twisted off the padlock with his hand and pushed open the trapdoor. Hannah pulled herself through the opening and collapsed into a puddle on the floor.

"Anything?" she said from where she was lying flat on her back, panting. He circled the space in a crouch, then sat down beside her, below the level of the windows.

"I didn't hear a thing the whole time we were coming, and I don't see anything now. I think we're clear here."

Here was a square wooden box. Perched on long, spindly legs, it sat squarely on top of the highest part of the land, at the best possible vantage point over the forest. Windows in shrunken wood frames ran all the way around the single room, from waist high up to the low ceiling. A narrow cot was built into one wall, a bench into another. A squat storage cupboard painted dark green set into the corner between them was the only furnishing. There was a calendar for the current year tacked to the front of the cupboard, but it was several months behind, showing a wilted picture of fireworks.

Hannah rolled over and started to get up. "Stay low. Just in case," Joel said. On her knees she took a careful look out the bottom of the closest window. She couldn't stick her head up high enough to see what was directly below them without being visible, so from her angle all she could see was a strip of blue sky, clear except for a few clouds like smeary fingerprints, and below it, the top edge of the forest. It was a stretch of solid green, uninterrupted except for a spattering of dead pines, like white splotches of mold on the forest surface. It was a deceptive scene. There could be anyone beneath the layer of trees. It could be Asher catching up with them, or an army slinking in their direction, all tucked up under the branches.

Joel fiddled with the lock on the cabinet, then gave up and twisted it off like he had the last one, easily pulling the screws that held the hardware in place out of the cheap plywood. He rifled through the contents, taking something out. He set it on the cabinet and bent over the familiar object.

"What are you doing?" Hannah scooted her way over.

"I'm sending the instructions for our pickup."

"Is that a good idea?" Hannah knew enough about the radio he was playing with to guess that it wasn't the most private form of communication in the world.

"It's ideal really," he said. "It's the reason we came here. It's so low tech it's genius." Joel pulled open a plastic cover on the side and flipped something down. "It's not technically secure, but it's highly unlikely anyone would pick up a short message, unless they just happened to be listening in on the frequency. Unlike cellular, you can't trace a transmission back to it. I doubt even someone as wily as Amara would consider something so archaic."

He began to spin a crank at a dizzying speed. There was a snap and crackle as he coaxed the battery back to life.

"And you just happen to know someone will be listening on the correct frequency?" Hannah said.

Joel nodded, smiling. "Always plan for every eventuality."

"We used to have one of these," Hannah said.

"That was a long time ago, when you were really small. How do you even remember that?"

"I remember perfectly. We used to talk to people from all over the world. You always claimed you knew what they were saying, but I thought you were making it up. Nobody could speak that many languages."

That was what she'd thought then. Now she knew he'd had more than the usual amount of time to learn any number of them.

The radio whistled. Joel stopped cranking and adjusted the dials, then picked up the handset tethered to the box by a coiled cord. He hit transmit. "Skarbeck. Skarbeck this is Déricourt. Are you QVR? Click twice for QSL."

He switched to receive and waited. There wasn't a response, just a crackle.

Clicking back to transmit, he repeated the original call. This time when he hit receive, there were two short but definitely purposeful clicks.

"QSP zero, eleven, dash, eighty-eight, sixteen, dash, thirty-one, oh-four, ninety-nine, sixty-nine. QSL?" Two clicks again. "We are forty-two, dash, thirty-eight, seventy-two, by seventy-seven, dash, double zero, twenty-six." A short wait, and a final two clicks. "Step two accomplished," Joel said.

"What was that all about? Aside from giving them our location?" Hannah cocked her head toward the gridded latitude and longitude map on the inside of the cabinet door. That was about all she'd caught, besides the bits of shortwave lingo, but not enough for it to make any sense. "Are you sure that was smart?"

"The person on the other end and I, we go way back, to when wireless was the height of communications. We both retained a soft spot for it. They'll call the sat phone number I gave them and let the team know everything is a go," he said. "Hannah, really"—he waved her down— "stay below the windows, at least until it's dark."

She turned to face Joel where he was leaning casually against the wall, looking unconcerned.

"We're clear. There's nothing to see anyway," he said. "Unless you're looking for Asher, in which case, I don't know what you're worried about. You forget he isn't exactly human. It's not like he's in any real danger."

Hannah slid back down to the floor.

"We'll be out of here before you know it. Then you won't have to worry about anything," Joel said. "Won't it be nice to feel absolutely safe for a change?"

It would. But she wasn't convinced there was a single place in the world where that was possible.

"You don't look convinced, but I promise you, it's a better plan of action than moving around aimlessly, trying to stay ahead of your enemies."

Joel made it sound like such a stupid move, but when Asher proposed running, she'd considered it. At least she knew what it entailed; they'd done it before. But it was too late anyway; it wasn't an option now. She was going to have to trust that whatever plan Joel had in mind was really as safe as he said.

The sun had dipped low enough that Joel must have been convinced they were invisible, because he stood up and looked out the window. He didn't wave her down again when she joined him.

"There, in the tree line," he said, pointing. She didn't see anything clearly, but there might have been a smudge of dark moving near the border of the forest. Whatever it was, Joel raised his hand in a small unemphatic wave. "Asher," he said, though he didn't look especially thrilled. Now she could make out a shape moving from under the cover of trees and across the ground toward them.

"You're sure you weren't followed?" Joel asked Asher a moment later, shutting the trapdoor behind him after he squeezed his way through. The room felt like it had shrunk by half.

"At the cabin, it was not them," Asher said. He pulled the gun from his waistband and handed it back to Hannah. "But it will be, next time."

The people they'd heard coming, before Hannah and Joel took off, had been the state police. It was good she hadn't been there, because she was the one they were looking for.

"They were searching for a missing woman. One who was kidnapped by two dangerous armed men," Asher said. "A concerned family member supposedly found the car the victim was abducted in hidden near one of the park entrances." Hannah had a pretty good idea who had reported her "missing."

"I had few options," he said. "They clearly had our descriptions, since they drew their weapons the moment I opened the door. I left them tied up in the cabin. They will be found soon enough, but it gives us a little more time than if I had let them go. As soon as they are free, however, everyone will know we were there."

Joel stared out the window for a moment. "It's genius really," he said eventually. "Once she found the car, Amara knew we were out here somewhere. Soon this whole mountain is going to be crawling with people searching for us, doing her job for her." He went to the radio and snapped it on with a pop. "QSP to same as before. Stand by to record." Then Joel began to click the receiver rapidly. Hannah thought at first it was Morse code, but she knew Morse well enough to tell that this was something else. "QSL? Two clicks." There was another series of clicks on the other end. He snapped the set off again.

"What was all that?" she asked.

"Just a small adjustment. It's all in hand. Everything will go exactly as planned."

6

Joel pulled something out of the cabinet and threw it. A block of beige sailed through the air at Hannah's head—she bobbled it, of course—and it landed on her shoe, making Joel shake his head in amusement.

"Dinner is served," he said, tossing another block to Asher, who of course easily caught it one-handed.

"Do we really have time to be sitting here eating?" Hannah said.

Joel ripped off the top of his meal and sat on the narrow bunk. "We'll be moving out as soon as we get a signal. Might as well eat while we have a chance."

Hannah turned over the MRE, reading the label. It took her a minute, but she figured out how to use the chemical heater to warm up the mushy-looking chicken and rice. She whipped her oatmeal cookie at Asher like a foil-wrapped flying saucer. He snagged it without looking up and opened it. "If we have that kind of time, you can tell us who's coming to pick us up. And where we're going," she said. "There's been an awful lot of running and not a lot of details."

"I started to, but we keep getting interrupted." Joel poked at the contents of his pouch with a look of distaste and set it aside. "We're being extracted by my best people, a team at the top of my organization. It's been around in some way, shape, or form for a very, very long time. It wasn't always the efficient outfit it is now, of course, but from the start, its purpose has been to keep people safe from dangerous immortals."

"And this organization, which you never once mentioned over the course of my life, is made up of people like you two?" Hannah said, waving her spork at them.

"Of course I couldn't tell you about it," Joel said. "And not anymore, as far as being made up of people like me. At this point the majority of the people involved are entirely human. That's strictly a matter of staffing; it's grown to be a rather large organization and there aren't that many immortals. But it's still driven by people like me who are concerned about the threat some of our kind pose to the human race."

"I was under the impression that people with your *condition* weren't really joiners," she said.

"That isn't true at all. The only one of us you've really known up until now is Asher, and he just happens to be particularly antisocial."

Asher snorted. "I am not antisocial. And this is nonsense. I have never heard of any sort of organization amongst our kind. If it existed, why in all my years have I never encountered it?"

"Why would you know anything about it?" Joel said, shaking his head at Asher. "You've never appeared particularly interested in the world at large. Have you spent a single lifetime as an actual part of the population, or even considered doing something to be an asset to humanity?" Joel got up and walked back and forth in front of the windows, looking out into the darkness. He reminded Hannah of a big cat pacing a cage. He stopped and turned back to Asher.

"And you're certainly of very little interest to us, except when it comes to your sister. Every time she decides it's time to come find you, her body count goes down, and we don't have to worry about her killing a hundred people just because she's bored." Joel's expression now was thin—sneering, almost—a look Hannah wasn't used to seeing on him. "That's your service to humanity, I guess. Amara's less of a threat to the population when she's trying to kill you. Just think how many more lives could've been saved if you two hung out more often."

Asher was staring at him with a blank expression, the kind that was a thin cover over a simmering anger, a lid chittering on a pot about to boil over. Hannah had only seen Asher really fired up once, and if this was going to be anything like that, there was no way this cracker box was going to survive. "None of that matters now," Joel said. The accusatory tone, the superiority, disappeared and he turned to Hannah, coming over and grabbing her hand. "All these years of protecting people were leading up to this. Everything's about to change. It's time to protect the most important person."

Hannah shook her head and pulled her hand away. "That's the dumbest thing I've ever heard. Now where are we going?"

"To my headquarters," Joel said. "It's secure as a fortress. You won't ever have to worry about your safety again." He got up and snapped the radio back on, then walked over to the trapdoor. "Listen for the double click. It's the signal to move out. I'm going to scout around the area one last time."

Asher stood up, still looking livid. He put a foot down on the trapdoor, holding it shut.

"Is it wise to be waving yourself around like a red flag, going up and down?" he said. "They know we are on this mountain now. If you are seen, Hannah might be trapped up here."

Joel looked up at Asher and shook his head. "So protective. Even if there was someone out there, which there isn't, I won't be seen going up and down. I'm too fast for that." He winked at Hannah.

"If you insist on leaving, I will send you down in the swiftest way possible." Asher kept his foot on the door. At his full height, his head pushed up against the ceiling. There was a vein in his neck that looked like it was going to explode.

"Let him go," Hannah said. No one moved; the tiny space was vibrating with the tension. "Ash. Just let him go."

He stared a moment at Joel, who just raised an eyebrow, then he pulled his foot away.

Hannah stood beside him as he watched Joel go, though all she could see through the window was darkness. She laid a hand on his arm and he bristled. Then he looked at her and let out a deep breath.

"Thank you," she said.

"Thank you for what?" He was calmer now, marginally. His eyes weren't as dark, and there was no more feeling of electricity crackling around the room.

"For not throwing him out the window," she said. "For once again putting yourself in harm's way so I could escape. That's twice now since you showed up. You didn't need to come here at all, but I'm glad you did."

He grabbed her by the shoulders and turned her toward him, leaning over and staring at her. "Hannah—all of this—there is more going on. I feel like we have delayed here too long. Why would he have you wait, giving danger time to come to you?"

Letting go of her shoulders, he took her hands instead, swallowing them up in his. The gesture struck her. Since the moment he'd found out what her blood could do to him, Asher hadn't come near her, hadn't been close to her a second longer than was absolutely necessary. His hands were as feverishly warm as she remembered, and his stare was still a little too intense, the oddly colored eyes locked onto her.

"Joel wouldn't do anything to put me in danger," she said.

"Would not put you in danger?" Asher's words came out in an incredulous rumble. "Look at the danger you are in right now," he said. "Look at the danger he has put you in for the past twenty years. Joel let you walk around ignorant of the murderous father who would certainly come looking for you." Asher rocked back on his heels. "He endangers you the same way I did. You might have avoided a great deal of pain and danger if I'd been honest with you about what I was from the beginning."

Ifs and regrets. They meant nothing now. There wasn't a single thing about the past they could change. A person who'd been alive as long as Asher should know that better than anyone.

"Maybe that's true," she said. "And you're right, Joel should have told me. I don't know as much as I thought about him. But I've always been able to trust him and I know one thing for sure; he's incredibly smart. If he has a plan, it'll be a good one. He'll have thought of everything, and he wouldn't have come back to get me without having covered all his bases."

"I do not share your trust," Asher said. "If there were any way to take you from here right now, I would. I would have you far away from my sister and that monster, rather than allowing them to draw near. This plan—it waits for danger. We should have run."

"Maybe," she said, "but it doesn't matter. It's too late now."

Asher let go of her hands abruptly, and she felt suddenly cold and shivered. She heard the ping of feet against the steps at almost the same time a double click came from the radio. Hannah looked at Asher as the trapdoor squeaked its way open.

"It is too late now," Asher said.

"All clear." Joel's head appeared through the hole. "As an added bonus I broke into the outbuilding down there." He pulled up a bag and set it down with a clunk. "Six pack of warm beer and an expired box of Twinkies." He pulled himself inside and shut the door. "But what did I always tell you?" he said to Hannah. "Expiration dates are just a suggestion."

"What is it?" Joel asked, when he saw the expression on their faces.

"There were two clicks."

"Then it's time."

———

Asher gave Hannah one last look and turned away. Sliding her backpack over her arms she walked toward the trapdoor, peering out the windows as she passed. The moon had finally risen, but it was tucked away behind the clouds, only an anemic glow making its way through. It wasn't going to be much to see by.

"Where are you going?" Joel asked. He was standing on top of the trapdoor.

"You said that was the signal? It's time to go, right?"

"That was the signal. But we aren't going anywhere just yet."

"What is going on? Where is your promised pickup?" Asher's voice was angry. Hannah was angry, too, but it was outweighed by how worried she was growing, knowing somewhere outside—mixed in with all the people looking for them—were Roman and Amara.

She'd hoped to be down from the fire tower and headed somewhere far away by now.

Joel paused, holding up a finger, his head turned toward the window like he was listening. "Wait for it …" There was a muffled thump against the roof that made Hannah jump.

"What was that?" she said.

Joel walked over to one of the windows and pushed against the top, tilting it outward. "You can come in now," he said. A pair of feet dropped in through the space. The rest of a slender black-clad figure slithered in after.

"Did someone order room service?" a woman's voice called out. Joel laughed and helped her to the ground. She reached back out and pulled a bag in behind her, then pushed the window shut. When she turned toward Hannah, the woman was tucking her hair back up under her cap and pulling the brim down over her unfairly lovely face.

"The second package is right behind?" Joel said.

The woman nodded, looking at her watch. "We pushed it back half a minute. Didn't want him getting here first, in case the wind threw my chute off or something. Should be here in thirty seconds." She unzipped her bag and pulled out a bundle. "Drop this onto the first landing there, would you?" She handed it to Joel. He opened the trapdoor and tossed it down to where it landed with a thump.

"What's going on?" Hannah said, eying the new addition warily.

"This is Paige," Joel said. "She's—" He was interrupted by a quiet beep from Paige's watch. A second later something else landed on the tower, just below them, making the whole thing shake.

"And there he is. Right on schedule," Paige said. Joel reached over to open the trapdoor, but Paige grabbed his arm. "Better give him a minute." It was less than that when the door pushed open on its own.

"We can roll now. The good-looking decoy has arrived," the man said, smiling broadly under the stocking cap pulled down low over his head. He looked around the crowded space. "There's no way I'm gonna fit up there. I'll be waiting at the bottom." He disappeared again as quickly as he'd appeared, letting the door fall silently closed over the top of him.

"Joel?" Asher said, eyes narrowed. He didn't need to say more.

"Hannah, Asher," Joel said, "I already introduced Paige, and that guy was Noble. They're part of my organization, the one Asher doesn't believe exists. They're our ticket out of here. Plus a little."

"Plus a little what?" Hannah said.

"Explain," said Asher. Again, the single word was enough.

"Calm down," Joel said. "Hannah will be out of here soon enough; we all will. But by now the men you tied up have been discovered, and the whole world knows we're up here. That's what Amara was going for. I just did her one better." He smiled, looking assured. "I had my people feed the authorities a little extra information. Any minute now they'll report we've been seen leaving this tower, heading toward a particular exit point. I promise you, that information will make its way straight to Amara, and she'll head right for us. It's ideal."

"Ideal, Joel?" Hannah said. "How is this ideal?"

"Because the new arrivals and I are going to walk out of here, and Roman and Amara are going to come after us. We're going to capture them. After that you can just walk out."

"What!" Hannah said.

"What!" Asher said. "Capture them?"

Joel calmly raised a finger for them to keep their voices down. "They'll know we're here any minute, so stay quiet after we leave, just in case. Amara probably thought it was genius when she cooked up the story about you being kidnapped. It got the authorities to do the work for her, and it almost guaranteed we wouldn't get off this mountain without being seen," he said. "But she made a mistake, relying on the authorities for information about where we were. It allowed me to shape what she heard and get her and Roman to head exactly where I want them. This really is the ideal outcome."

"You said that. I really don't think that sounds ideal, sitting here, just hoping they fall for it," Hannah said.

"I'll get you to safety, I promised I would," Joel said. "And those two crazies will be put away forever. It was far too good an opportunity to pass up. Really, you two, this is why I didn't tell you. You're missing the big picture."

"Big picture?" said Hannah. "I should've stayed in my own damn house. It has guns. And at least if I fell off the porch there I would mother—"

"Really, dear, your language has gone downhill." Joel cut her off. "Must be the company you're keeping."

It was already stiflingly warm inside the little room full of people with overly high body temperatures. Now that things were growing heated, it was approaching combustion level. If Joel wasn't careful, Asher was going to take his head off and Hannah thought she might help.

"We need to head out soon. Paige, unpack and hand out the supplies."

"Wait, what are Asher and I supposed to do?" Hannah said.

"While Paige, Noble, and I head to where some search vehicles have been conveniently left waiting for us to pretend to steal, you and Asher are going to wait here until Roman and Amara are in custody."

"You couldn't have clued us in on any of this plan before now?"

If Joel noticed the snark in Hannah's voice, he didn't respond. He reached down for the weapon Paige handed him and deftly dropped the clip, reinserted it, and checked the chamber before sticking the gun into his waistband.

"You might not have agreed. You aren't in a position to see the value of this little side operation. Getting you out of here is still the first priority, of course, but capturing Amara and Roman is a bonus that adds a great deal of benefit and no danger to you. It was a simple choice."

"This is crazy, Joel," Hannah said, exasperated. "And I've only heard half of it. You still haven't said how I'm supposed to get out of here." Hannah appreciated the idea of Amara and Roman under lock and key, as much as she wasn't happy about being left out of the loop again. But until they were actually captured, Hannah was still stranded seventy feet in the air with people trying to kill her running around.

Maybe she should go find some of the nice police officers who were looking for her and tell them she *had* been kidnapped by crazy people.

"Anything I need to know, heading out?" Paige broke in, oblivious to the argument going on over her head. "They were thin on details on the decoy act."

"Nothing difficult. Just try to pass for Hannah on the way down in case they zero in on us earlier than expected, to be sure they take the bait and don't get spooked and run. Miss a step or two on the way down," Joel said. "Don't move too confidently. It needs to be convincing. Stop to catch your breath. Look clumsy."

Hannah bristled. She was struggling just to survive in the midst of all this immortal bullshit—sorry she couldn't manage to be as fit and stealthy as they were. Easy for them to waft through the woods like a fart.

"Sorry, I haven't had a hundred and fifty lifetimes to improve my balance and vision," she said, not trying to hide the attitude anymore.

"Paige hasn't either," Joel said, looking down at the phone Paige had just handed him. Hannah looked at Paige more closely. Great. Finally there was another regular old human in the room, and they could pass for an immortal in the low light. It might have been exhaustion—or the long period of abject fear—but whatever it was, Hannah was irritable to the point where her ability to hold her tongue had been severely compromised.

"Jesus, Joel, even better. You're sending someone out there who's going to be just as permanently dead if Amara or Roman get their hands on her?" she said. "I know it's a long time ago for you to remember, but were you dropped on your head as a child?"

Asher snorted out a laugh behind her. Joel shook his head in an infuriatingly parental manner. "Paige is a highly trained professional. She's familiar with the challenges posed by working with people like myself, and all the possibilities have been considered. She also has enough tranquilizers on her to drop a bull elephant if things go south."

Hannah scowled. "And what other direction were you planning for things to go? I know I'm not G.I. Jane over here, but can you at least tell me what's next? I mean, unless you think the details are beyond me."

"Han, dial it back a notch with the attitude," Joel said. Hannah thought she saw Paige's mouth twitch into a smirk before she recovered and returned to organizing the objects from her bag.

"Gee dad, sorry dad," Hannah said.

Joel closed his eyes in a put-upon manner for a second before he answered. "This will all be over soon. Your part is still the same. When we know they've taken the bait you'll be whisked away to safety. You don't even have to move."

Asher said, "So this woman is going to disguise herself as Hannah and hope to capture my sister without being harmed, all while Hannah waits when she could have been far away by now? You endanger far too many people in your plans, Joel."

"No one will be in danger." Paige laughed. "Oh, before I forget, Hannah, trade me your clothes. I need to look like I'm you."

Hannah sighed. Fat chance there. She awkwardly shuffled out of her jacket and pants—she was past caring who saw her unattractively sensible underwear at this point—and squeezed into Paige's cargo pants and shirt.

Paige pulled Hannah's jacket on and zipped it up.

"There. We need to get going. Oh wait." Joel tugged on Paige's sleeve—Hannah's sleeve—before she stepped through the trapdoor. "Also, make sure to breathe really hard. Like the effort is killing you. Make it realistic."

Fortunately they didn't linger much longer, because Hannah was a second away from giving them both a quick trip down. Wouldn't falling the whole way be the most convincingly Hannah thing they could do?

7

Hannah heard Paige's foot slip off the rung with a ping when she pretended to miss a step. She listened to the exaggerated noisiness until the sounds faded away. At least the irritation had been a good distraction from the concern—and not just for herself. Now someone else was out there heading purposefully into Amara's sights.

The wind had picked up and blown the moon clear of its curtain of clouds. Able to see better, Hannah reached into the bottom of her backpack and pulled a small, zippered pouch away from its velcro fasteners. Taking out a length of elastic, she wrapped it around her upper arm and tied it off. A hand encircled her wrist and pulled her arm out straight.

"What is this, Hannah?"

She tried to jerk her arm out of Asher's grasp and failed. He stared at the mess of bruises and needle tracks.

"I need to reload while I have time, just in case. I gave them everything I had."

This time when Hannah twisted her arm away, he let it go. Hannah had given Joel and Paige each one of the darts loaded with her blood from the dart pistol. If they were going after Roman and Amara, she couldn't begrudge them any defense she could give. She didn't like the idea of her blood floating around out there, but it was the only thing she could really contribute. Plus, she could easily get more.

"I was going to put a permanent port in, to cut down on the damage, but I was afraid it would get infected." Also because she wasn't sure she could have managed to put one in on her own—you couldn't just walk into a hospital and get someone to install a permanent blood draw channel without a good reason. There would have been at least a couple questions.

She rifled through the bag, then set it aside, irritated. Grabbing her backpack, she searched it as well, running her hands around the bottom, not finding what she was looking for. Hannah returned to the small blood draw kit, setting aside a couple of sterilely wrapped butterfly needles and alcohol wipes.

"How often are you doing this?" Asher said.

Hannah shrugged, looking for the parts for the aero syringes in the bag.

"A couple times a week. Everything I've read online says human blood doesn't have a long shelf life. I don't know how fresh it needs to be." She shook the little bag upside down. The only thing that appeared was a small yellow tail, the piece that was supposed to clip to the end of a vial—a vial she didn't appear to have.

When they were assembled—with the tail snapped onto one end and the needle tip screwed onto the other—they looked like regular darts, the kind you threw at a beat-up board in the rear of a bar. Loaded into the dart gun, they became the best weapon she had against people like his sister. Unfortunately, now she only had one dart left in the chamber, and its age was a little dubious. Hopefully it wasn't chunky blood by now.

"Not a couple of times this week," she said, letting the strap around her arm go with a snap. "I'm out of the parts I need." She crammed the kit back in the bag and changed the subject.

"You think everything will go okay? Are they going to let us know as soon as they have them?" It was a happy thought, that if everything went as planned, she could walk out of here without having to look over her shoulder for them, maybe ever again.

Hannah started to stick her head up, to peek over the edge of the window, but resisted the urge and ducked back down out of sight. "Will you be upset?" she asked.

"About?"

"About your sister."

There was a possibility that soon his sister would be completely and permanently dead.

Amara had been dead a hundred times, maybe hundreds of times. Asher was responsible for some of them himself—Hannah was too—but always with the knowledge she would come back. This time when it happened, it might be for good. Would that hurt him? Amara might be tied for the worst person on the planet, but even after nearly a thousand years of crazy, she was still Asher's family.

Asher looked over at Hannah. His eyes gave off a silver sheen, like the eyes of an animal in the dark, picking up every last bit of light.

"Did I ever tell you about my friend who was a king?" he said. *You must have forgotten to mention that,* Hannah thought. She would have remembered. She was certain she remembered everything he'd ever said to her.

"It was a very long time ago, when the movement of funds was not as easy as it is today. When I was not near a cache, I had to occasionally work for my bread then. I greatly appreciate being able to move it from one place to another with a phone application," he said. "Anyway, I was employed by a brothel. That is where we met."

"You were working in a brothel?"

"It is not what it sounds like."

"How is that not what it sounds like? You just said you were working in a brothel. I'm sure you were very popular though."

Asher laughed, and it was a warm, welcome sound in all the silence and seriousness. "I was not working there in that manner, though I am not surprised that is where your mind immediately went. I was acting as protection for the women working there. It was a decidedly upper-class establishment, a veritable palace where the madame was rich as a lord. I was short of funds at the time and had been offered the position simply walking by. I gather the offer was based on my size."

"How long ago was this," Hannah said, "that they were just looking for whorehouse bouncers on the street?"

"You talk a great deal."

"Yep."

"It makes it terribly difficult to tell you a story."

"No it doesn't. I want all the details and you like giving them. That's why you love me." She hadn't meant to say that last part. Fortunately he didn't seem to notice.

"If you continue to ask questions, I will still be telling this story tomorrow…"

Hannah rolled her eyes in the dark, which she knew perfectly well he could see. "Proceed," she said. "I believe we were at whorehouse security."

"My official title was something that sounded more appealing if I recall, but yes, my role was to remove troublesome gentlemen from the premises. I was trying to escort the man who would become my friend out because he was causing a scene. But I had to do it without causing offense," he said, "as he was the crown prince of the country."

"And you managed that how?"

"I convinced him to join me at a nearby drinking establishment. As I plied him with drink to keep him occupied, we found ourselves talking. He was vastly intelligent as it turned out, and strikingly knowledgeable about every subject we broached: art, politics, literature in any number of languages, history. History is always enjoyable to debate with someone who believes themselves an expert, especially when discussing events I happened to be present for. I have found a great deal of truth is lost in the recording."

The clouds that had drifted over the face of the moon moved away, and Hannah could see Asher clearly when he looked over at her and smiled thinly. "We became friends after that; as close as brothers over time. He was a good man, and when he eventually took the throne, I watched the event with pride. When he asked me to come to his court, I did from time to time.

"It was different for me there than for others. I dared challenge his opinions when I did not agree with him, because unlike the others who surrounded him, I was no sycophant; I wanted nothing from him. And there was nothing he could do to me. I had no fear of him, no awe of his position. I'd watched a hundred kings come and go before his time."

His smile gave way and his eyes shifted away from her, toward the black of the window. "But over time I watched him change. He grew paranoid, violent. If this had happened today, I imagine he would have been diagnosed with some type of mental illness and treated. At that time, in his position, however, he simply continued to grow more unlike himself. Once, when his daughter angered him over something trivial, he grabbed her and pulled her hair out by the roots. He began to have courtiers killed, along with their entire households down to the servants, for reasons that were purely delusion."

"What did you do?" Hannah said.

"I could not reason with a man who was growing mad. No one could. He was a king. Who could tell him what he might not do? Who could order his incarceration? Over time he became even more danger-ous. Not only did he order more and more executions, he perpetrated them himself, beating servants to death, chasing old men around his castle with knives."

"What happened?"

Asher didn't answer for a moment. When he finally spoke, his voice was so quiet she had to lean forward to hear. "The injuries and deaths he was causing, it was all too much. I finally intervened and gathered support to have him held somewhere until perhaps he could regain his sanity."

"Did he get better?"

He shook his head sadly. "He did not. And when I failed to have him deposed, he had me killed. Ordered me beheaded without a moment's hesitation. He had me—a man he loved like family—put to death."

Asher sat back and suddenly Hannah felt cold. "When I returned to life I went back. I intended to take his life, though the thought was abhorrent to me, because somewhere, at the core of him, was the good person I knew. But I felt I had no choice, with so many lives at risk because of the bad that had wrapped itself so tightly around the good."

"Did you?" she said. "Did you kill him?"

He shook his head. "No. Someone else did just before I arrived."

"Would you have?"

"I will not pretend, Hannah. You would know it was a lie. Somehow you always know. I do not think I could have. Perhaps that was wrong, but despite his myriad sins I do not think I could have brought myself to end his life. And though I did not cause his death, I still feel the loss of the person he was. Because in him, at one time, was such good."

"Because you loved him, or at least who he was. And that's how you feel about Amara."

"She is my sister," Asher said. "There was a time when she was just a normal, simple girl. You remind me of her, though you might find that strange. But you are like she was then, clever and kind and full of life. Amara was a beautiful girl who loved others, her family, most of all the brother with whom she shared everything, even before we were born. I do not know that I can ever entirely forget that. I do not think I would stay the hand of the person that eventually ends her, because the wrongs she has done there is no accounting for. I do not know if I could do it myself, knowing it would be for the last time, but in any case, her death—her true death should she meet it—the loss, I will still feel it."

"Because we can't help but love the people we love." He nodded in the dark.

"Do you think we'd make it?" Hannah said. They'd been sitting in silence under the weight of the conversation about his sister, and though the words left her mouth just above a whisper, it felt like she'd suddenly shouted.

Asher turned from where he'd been looking out over the window edge. Hannah had given up trying to see anything in the brief periods when the clouds uncovered the moon. Trying to stare through the shadows had given her a dull ache behind her eyes, so Hannah had left him to do the watching.

"Do I think we would make what?" he said.

"If we left, right now. Do you think we could make it out of here," she said, "if things don't go the way Joel planned?" *Or even if they do,* Hannah thought. If Joel succeeded and Amara and Roman weren't a threat anymore. "Couldn't we just climb down and leave? I could be gone, and no one but you would know where."

"Would you?" Asher asked.

Having Joel back in her life still didn't feel real to Hannah. Was this mysterious place of his as safe a destination as he claimed, or even necessary? Maybe Roman and Amara were the only ones who knew what she was. And if there were more, would they want to be anywhere near her, with her such a threat to them? Wouldn't it be safer for any immortal in their right mind to just stay far away? If she left, she might not see Joel again, but she'd never expected to anyway. The man had walked away from her, leaving her in danger only to conveniently swoop down in the nick of time to help her.

"Yes," she said.

Asher reacted, but not the way she expected. He just turned his head away, cocking it to the side. That was a little disappointing.

He reached down and pulled her up beside him. "It is too late," he said. "Yet again, it is too late." She heard the noise then as well. There was a whomp, whomp, whomp growing closer.

"It is always too late," he said.

"That must be our ride," Hannah said. But just because someone was here for them, it didn't mean they necessarily had to go. They could wave to the nice people in the helicopter and tell them to keep going. See ya, I'm going to take my chances elsewhere.

Hannah looked out the windows to try and see which direction it was coming from. Asher, however, was looking straight down. There was the sound of a vibration, and he pulled out the phone Joel had given him and looked at the screen.

"Something is wrong," he said.

"With the helicopter?"

He shook his head. "With the plan. It did not work. They have Roman. But they did not capture my sister."

"I guess it's good I didn't try to talk you into ditching the ride then," Hannah said. The helicopter was the only option now, after all, and it was close; close enough to get them out safely. She could see it—small but growing larger—a little firefly with blinking lights and the last of the moon reflecting off the rotors. "They're here."

"So is she," he said. Then Asher shouted. "Hannah, get off the floor!"

She took a step back just as a dime-size hole opened up in front of her foot, leaving a matching hole in the roof. She didn't hear the suppressed bullet or the next one as another hole appeared beside it. Throwing herself onto the cabinet, she pulled her bag open and found the Beretta. She didn't even bother aiming at anything, just tossed it to Asher. He sent a bullet through the floor; there wasn't any return fire.

"The helicopter's right here, we can make it," she said. The helicopter was about to pull level with the landing below the trapdoor. It was close enough for Hannah to see the people inside the open door. Then she saw one of them stagger backward, and it banked away fast.

There was a crash, and something swung by her head. Asher had ripped the bench from the wall and, holding it above him, was using it as a battering ram, driving it upward into the roof. A few blows pushed a jagged hole into the wood; two more and she could see the sky. Reaching up, he pulled down on the edges, forcing the hole wider with his hands.

"Hannah, come now. On the roof."

She almost made the leap off the cabinet, but another line of bullets ripped their way up through the floor, the last one catching her somewhere on the backside and sending a burning pain tearing a red-hot streak up the back of her. Hannah went down on one knee. The angle she twisted when her leg gave out was the only thing that saved her from catching the next barrage of fire.

Asher picked her up off the ground. With one hand he shoved her up through the hole in the roof, sharp edges of the wood and stray nails digging into her skin as she squeezed through. She pulled her legs up onto the roof and looked back down, just in time to see the trapdoor begin to open.

It only took him one step, and Asher was on top of the door. Strafed with bullet holes, it collapsed under him and he fell from sight.

The helicopter had climbed back up, returning for another try but hovering beyond reach of any more attacks. She could see people inside it, one on each side of the open door, two more in the cockpit. They were looking back and forth between her and whatever was going on below. Something they saw must have made them think the coast was clear, because suddenly the craft banked, coming her way.

Hannah was lightheaded, maybe from the gunshot, maybe from the dizzying height, and coupled with the wash of the approaching helicopter, it threatened to topple her, so she slid down onto her belly. Looking down through the hole in the roof she couldn't see Asher or Amara, just the empty space where the trapdoor had been.

The wind thrown off by the rotors grew more intense. When she looked up the helicopter was so close Hannah could see the bright blue eyes of the person leaning out and reaching for her, waving her over. The distance was little enough she could have made it any other day, but right now, she didn't know if she could even stand. Where she'd been shot it felt like she was being burned alive, and when she forced the legs to move, everything buzzed and went white.

With her arms she pulled herself forward, dragging herself on her stomach the short distance over the small roof. She was going to have to stand up, pain or not. There was just no other choice. Hannah pushed herself to her elbows.

In theory this whole plan had seemed ridiculously simple. Three people would leave, deceive Roman and Amara, and she and Asher would step into a waiting helicopter. Reality, as always, was turning out to be slightly more difficult.

The helicopter wheeled away again. Hannah dragged herself back to the hole in the roof but there was still nothing, no sign of Asher or Amara. She pulled herself back to the edge of the roof and peered over, stomach rolling at the height. Nothing there either.

There was a flash below her, followed by a small bloom of fire, and finally the sound of an explosion she could just make out over the noise of the rotors. Hannah jerked her head back. That was when the entire structure suddenly pitched, and she slid, skidding over the edge.

———————•••••———————

Her fingertips were the only thing keeping her from plummeting to the ground. Hannah hung from the edge of the roof, unable to pull herself up. She should have been dangling against the side of the building where she could get some traction with her feet, but the angle was all wrong. There was nothing there. Her body was flying out in a direction that didn't make sense.

Turning her head, she saw why. The tower was leaning. The spindly wooden supports were buckling like knees that had been kicked in, and instead of gravity pulling her flush against the outside of the little room, her feet were far away from it, her body hanging out over open air at a forty-five-degree angle.

The helicopter grew close again. The downdraft it made was working against her, tugging at her already precarious hold. She couldn't turn toward them to reach for the person leaning out of the helicopter to try and grab her. Hannah couldn't take a hand off the roof; she didn't dare.

"I can't let go. Can you come closer?" she said, yelling over the noise of the helicopter. She doubted they could hear; her words were whipped away as soon as they left her mouth. "I can't let go!" she shouted again. If they could get close enough before she lost her grip, just a little bit closer, she might have a chance.

The only direction she could see clearly was down, if she let her head drop toward the ground between her dangling feet. It was too far, not a fall she could hope to survive. But even if it had been, it wasn't safe. Below her was Amara.

Amara wasn't moving, just looking up, standing there and watching. Hannah couldn't tell for sure, but she thought she saw Amara smile. Why wouldn't she? She'd managed to evade capture and find Hannah. Maybe she'd even managed to kill her brother yet again, since Hannah couldn't see Asher anywhere. Amara was probably waiting smugly for gravity to drop Hannah right at her feet with a final dead thud.

There was a shudder, and Hannah sank with a jerk, almost losing her tenuous hold on the roof. The tower had canted over even further, the broken supports sticking out like so many pick-up sticks. Amara was still far below her, but not as far as a moment ago. Everything was shaking and shifting—the whole thing was going to give, and soon.

Hannah kicked her legs out, trying to swing forward so she could get her feet against the building. She managed to touch it with one foot, but there was nothing for it to catch on. She swung back out, the movement pulling against her screaming fingers. They felt like they were being torn off a little bit at a time, with all her weight dragging on them. She hitched herself up as best as she could, digging into the sharp, pebbly surface of the shingles. It wouldn't do much good. There was no way she was going to be able to hold on much longer.

With the possibility of her death a short drop away, time slowed and her mind found a moment to wonder what it would mean to be one of them, with no worry beyond the immediate pain that was coming. To feel no fear, knowing when her eyes shut, they would always open again.

To live again and again, countless lives passing by, so many they were barely remembered over time. Hannah had thought about it enough times. Did living like that have any meaning at all, if you never had to consider the end? It was better not to be like them, she'd convinced herself. Better to have one single life and make that life count for something. Besides, the responsibility of an eternity might have been too much for her. She didn't have super human fortitude—look at how she'd crumpled after one bad stretch. When she thought she'd killed Asher the first time she'd seen him, Hannah had buckled, flailing instead of coping. For all she knew, given enough time maybe she would become completely warped. She might turn out as bad as Amara.

It was easy to think that way, that it was better just to be a regular human with no do-overs, when you weren't looking directly at the possibility of dying. Staring downward at her death, Hannah fully appreciated just how much she wanted to live. When she lost her grip—or when the tower collapsed—even if she somehow survived the fall but met with Amara waiting below, Hannah was going to die.

The helicopter must have pushed forward again in an attempt to reach her, because the pressure of the wind increased. It was too much, pulling one of her hands free, leaving her swinging, dangling from one hand.

Twisting back and forth, Hannah was suddenly able to see all around her. It was lighter, the very edges of the trees starting to grow pink, colored by the shiny bulb of sun pushing its way up behind them. In a few minutes it would be a beautiful sunrise. And Hannah was going to miss it. It would all be over soon, so she resisted the urge to look down and kept looking out. Hannah might not see the sun fully risen, but she could make sure Amara was not the last thing she ever saw.

Suddenly her wrist crunched, the hand that had wrapped around it grinding the bones against each other. It happened so quickly—the rough yank upward as the building shifted downward—that for a second Hannah floated weightlessly in the air. Then her feet touched down, and for a moment she and Asher stood there, feeling the roof shudder and threaten to slide away from under them. She latched her arms around his waist.

The helicopter came closer again, and the tenuous balance gave. The tower began to fall.

She felt his hands at her waist, tearing her away from him, and then they were gone. Hannah could see him behind her, moving away. She was flying through the air, away from the crumbling tower, toward the helicopter. Asher had thrown her, launching her just as the building gave up and sank.

She sailed helplessly through the sky, then she crashed onto the floor of the helicopter and slid. Arms caught her before she flew out the open door on the opposite side and dragged her to her feet. Hannah just had time to see Asher standing there, appearing to levitate briefly in open air, before the tower dropped from beneath him and he fell out of sight.

Someone pushed Hannah into a jump seat and started to harness her in. She tore away from them and went to the side, trying to look out as the helicopter banked sharply and wheeled away. All she saw was the pile of matchsticks that had been the tower before she was pulled back from the opening.

"We need to go back," she said, trying to see through the cloud of dust rising around the splintered woodpile. She couldn't tell if anyone was standing there; if Amara was still there, or where Asher had ended up.

The blue-eyed man pulled her away from the door and pushed her back into the seat. He buckled a restraint over her and pulled the straps tight.

"Our orders are to get you out of here," he said.

"Land this thing. We need to get down there!" she yelled. Asher could still be alive, and Amara was there. She would escape again. Everything had gone to hell.

"Ma'am, we'll be out of here soon. You're injured, and we need to get you some medical attention." Hannah jerked away from the needle prick she felt on her neck. She tried to brush it away, but suddenly she felt an unbearable weariness that made even lifting her hand too much effort.

"What did you ..." she trailed off, too sleepy to finish.

"Just something for the pain, ma'am. You're safe now. We'll have you out of here before you know it."

Her eyes closed before she could open her mouth again.

8

"Let me out!" Hannah yelled. She slammed her palms against the door, but the dull metal surface seemed to suck up all the sound. She had to sit back down on the narrow bed to steady herself, closing her eyes until the fuzziness cleared.

She got up again more carefully. Pulling open the waistband of the unfamiliar gray sweatpants she was wearing, Hannah peeked down into them; there was a big pad of white bandage running from the small of her back down over her rear. Strangely, it didn't hurt, except in a far off, detached kind of way.

Everything felt slightly detached. She'd woken up groggy, bandaged and dressed in unfamiliar clothes in a small room with bare block walls. In design it fell somewhere between the worst college dorm room and the best prison cell. Besides the bed, the only other thing in the room was a tiny square desk with a built-in chair. It touched the frame of the industrial steel door she had been banging against fruitlessly.

In the bathroom, Hannah splashed some cold water on her face. She gulped some down but it didn't combat the strange, metallic dryness in her mouth. In the cheap plastic mirror set in the tile above the sink, her face was cloudy, the irregular reflection only exacerbating the cottony feeling in her head.

When Hannah laid her ear against the door she was sure she could hear the shuffle of feet and the murmur of voices. She went back to banging on the door.

"Answer me. I know you're out there," she said. "I can hear you. Let me out."

There was no response.

The door didn't even have a handle. There were no visible hinges, nothing on the surface to differentiate one inch of dull silver from the next. Hannah tried to get a grip in the tiny crack between the door and the frame, but it was too tightly fitted.

"Damn it, let me out!" Taking a step back, Hannah rammed her shoulder against the door. It swung open with no resistance, and she found herself face down on the floor.

Next to her nose, a polished shoe poked out from the hem of a crisply ironed pant leg. Hannah gathered herself together and got up, ignoring the proffered hand. She recognized the man standing in front of her; he'd been one of the men on the helicopter, the one with the bright blue eyes under the brim of his helmet. He'd been all business then, dressed for combat and armed to the teeth. Now he was so tidily buttoned up he could have passed for an accountant.

"Glad to see you're finally awake," he said. "If you're ready, I'll take you over to medical." He started to walk away, expecting her to follow. He was a few steps away before he realized Hannah wasn't behind him. He stopped and waved her in his direction. "If you'll follow me."

"Where am I?" Hannah said. She stood halfway between the room she didn't want to go back into and the hallway she wasn't sure she wanted to follow him down. "Where am I, and why was I locked in there?"

He smiled in what she supposed he intended to be a reassuring way. "Sorry about that. We brought you back and patched you up, but you were out cold, so we put you in there to make sure no one bothered you until you were up and about. Orders were to secure you and keep you safe."

"Where's Joel?" Hopefully he was around here somewhere. And Asher. What had happened to him? And to Amara.

"Joel? He's probably upstairs in the operations room," the man said. His voice was bordering on patronizing now, a little too close to the way some adults talked down to children they thought were asking too many questions. She didn't appreciate it.

"I can take you up there as soon as we get you checked out," he offered. This time he walked away from her, taking off down the hallway without looking back. She hesitated a moment longer, then took a couple of quick steps to catch up before he disappeared around a corner.

"I'm fine," Hannah said, "you can take me to Joel right now."

He slowed to accommodate her and smiled, teeth in rigid ranks of perfect white. "Sure," he said. "We'll be there in a moment."

She followed him through an intersection, down an identical stretch of bleak industrial gray until they turned, then turned again almost immediately. Hannah was quickly growing disoriented, every hallway the same interminable speckled floors and plain, flat walls interrupted only by the evenly spaced and knob-less metal doors.

"Here we are," he said. They stopped short in front of a door that looked just like every other one. He waved a card where the handle should have been and it opened with a buzz and a soft click.

"Lovely. Thank you, Davis." When they entered, a woman in a white lab jacket turned to face them. She pulled off her glasses and let them drop on a chain around her neck. "If you'll just have a seat, dear," the woman said, "we need to take a look at that injury."

She motioned Hannah toward a padded exam chair. A chair seemed a strange place for an examination of where she was hurt. Then she noticed the restraints hanging from it; that was not going to happen.

Hannah turned to leave the room, running face first into a solid wall of Davis. "I'm fine really," she said, trying to edge around him, hoping he would get out of the way. Instead he shifted, putting himself more squarely in front of the door. Hannah turned back to the woman. "Come on, what do you really want?" This was all a little too insistent for a checkup.

"Come now, it's just a simple exam," the woman said. "It's important you allow me to examine you. If you'll just put this on." She picked up a hospital gown and tossed it in the air.

The instant Hannah's attention shifted, an arm wrapped around her throat. Another clamped around her wrist, twisting her arm behind her back, forcing her to spin around. Davis pushed her backward and into the chair. "Don't struggle," the woman said.

Hannah struggled. She tried to twist her way free before the thick velcro straps were looped tightly over her wrists. Davis held her ankles together while the woman in the lab coat finished restraining her, wrapping another wide band across her ankles.

"There. That should do, Davis," the woman said. "If you'll assist, this won't take long." She reached out and he handed her something. "Thrashing around will only make this more uncomfortable." Hannah watched her tear the packaging open of a blood draw kit. Eyeing the needle, Hannah only thrashed harder, remembering the last time she'd been strapped to a chair, subjected to a forced blood donation. It wasn't any more fun this time.

"Davis, hold her still." Hands clamped down on either side of her head. Hannah felt a swab wipe at her arm. "Heavens, look at these needle marks," the woman said. She made a *tsk tsk* sound. "Sloppy. Very sloppy. Done properly it won't cause such bruising. This you won't even feel."

Hannah felt it—the sting of the needle when it slid under the skin at her elbow. There was a rip of tape and the click of a tube locking into place.

Suddenly the door flew open.

"What is the meaning of this?" an unfamiliar voice spoke. The woman in the white jacket jerked toward the intruder, her unexpected movement wrenching the needle sideways in Hannah's arm painfully and knocking the connector out of the tube.

"Stop what you're doing this instant," the new arrival said. Her voice wasn't raised, but somehow it demanded compliance. "I cannot imagine what gave you the idea this is acceptable. Leave," she said. "Now."

"But I have orders from—" The woman in the white coat reached back toward Hannah, who was leaking blood from the disconnected tube. It was dripping over her arm into a spreading red patch on her pants.

"You have your orders from me now. Leave."

Davis was already gone, the door an empty hole where he had silently slipped out. The woman in the white jacket wilted visibly in front of the figure before her. With one last look at Hannah and her leaking arm, she scurried out.

"Hold still," Hannah's rescuer said. She pressed a wad of gauze down on Hannah's arm and neatly extracted the needle. There was the ripping sound, and the restraints came off her arms and legs.

"I don't know what the meaning of this is, Hannah. This is not at all acceptable," the woman said, "and I am sorry for it." She looked up from where she was tending to Hannah's arm. "My name is Mena."

———•+••+•———

As rude as it was to stare, Hannah couldn't take her eyes off the woman cleaning the blood from her arm with deft swipes. Mena seemed not to notice the looks, or was kind enough not to say anything. Convinced everything was clean and had finished bleeding, she turned over Hannah's hand in her tiny, overly warm one.

"Do you mind?" Mena asked. She was peeking under the edge of the bandage someone had replaced over the cut on Hannah's palm. Hannah nodded and Mena peeled it back. The raised flesh had receded and only a faint pink gouge still showed. Hannah healed very quickly; it was a bonus considering how often she got hurt.

"I think it looks okay," Mena said. "Probably could benefit from a little soap and water." Hannah couldn't argue with that. All of her could benefit from some soap and water. "What about the other one?"

Hannah assumed Mena was referring to the bandage she was sitting on. Her whole rear end felt dead, and with everything that had just happened she'd nearly forgotten about it.

"It feels surprisingly okay. Doesn't hurt at all," Hannah said.

"Can I take a look at it?"

"Do you know what you're doing? Are you a doctor?"

Whether or not she was doctor was still in question, but Mena was an immortal, that much Hannah did know. She'd heard her name before, on another occasion when she'd been hurt trying to escape Amara, when Asher had been looking for someone he could trust to tend to her injuries. Still, it seemed odd Mena would be a doctor—it seemed strange any of them would have anything as mundane as a day job.

"I am a physician, among other things. Granted, I finished my medical training in eighteen fifty-eight, but I've stayed current," Mena said with a small smile.

That was good enough for Hannah, though she still felt a little strange, standing up and turning around, sliding her blood-covered sweatpants down over the bandage.

"You've been remarkably lucky. This is really more a deep scratch than a penetrating wound. The bullet must have just grazed you. An inch the other direction and it would have gone right through the gluteus maximus," Mena said. *True, but an inch in the opposite direction and it would have missed completely,* Hannah thought. She'd had a sneaking suspicion getting shot in the ass was in her future—now she could cross it off her list.

"It's going to sting a little, when the pain medication wears off," Mena said, getting to her feet.

She was close to Hannah's height, a few inches shorter maybe, her figure reedy and birdlike. Mena had that childlike build young girls do, when they've acquired their height but are still waiting for the other physical traits of adulthood. She was remarkably beautiful, of course, with a delicate, heart-shaped face and thick dark hair pulled back into a soft roll at her neck.

"I'll have medical send something for the pain to your rooms. You might want it later. I'll take you back so you can change into something less macabre." The thick brows over the enormous brown eyes were furrowed. "Where did you come from?" Mena asked, leading the way out of the room.

"From a helicopter," Hannah said. "We were in the woods in New York before that—"

"Where are your rooms?" Mena said, a laughing lilt in her voice. "Joel's not back yet, though I'm sure he will be soon enough." Her voice grew serious again. "I can't imagine who thought it was appropriate to do anything other than let you rest until he arrived, considering the circumstances."

Hannah led the way, navigating her way uncertainly back to the small room. When she stopped in front of what she thought was the correct door and pushed it open, Mena sighed at the tiny, spare cell.

"I might have guessed from where I found you," Mena said. "This is unacceptable. Come with me." She turned on her heels. "I'll be having a word with whomever was granted temporary oversight during the operation."

Hannah had to take quick steps to keep up with Mena's brisk pace. She moved remarkably fast for such a slight person, and with a great deal of haste for someone who had nothing but time.

"Why isn't Joel back?" Hannah said.

"Roman took him out," Mena said, "which was a possibility we accounted for. He hadn't reestablished contact as of a few minutes ago, but I'm sure he'll be along shortly."

The thought of Joel being killed—again—took a moment for Hannah's mind to process. She wasn't accustomed to the idea of him dying and popping up good as new. It was going to take some getting used to.

Hannah got a moment to catch her breath in an elevator, then they were off again, through a maze of increasingly less austere hallways. The floor had just transitioned to soft, silent carpet when Hannah stopped suddenly. She realized why the figure in front of her looked so familiar. Mena stopped too but didn't turn around to speak.

"Finally placed me, have you? Yes, I am. The actress." Mena answered the question Hannah hadn't asked out loud. "Come along."

Hannah spurred herself forward to catch up with Mena, who was off again. She actually had to run a few steps to pull side by side with her. When she did, Mena smiled over. "I never wish away my time, but honestly it will come as a relief when my current life is forgotten entirely."

"What made you do it? Were you bored? You were already a doctor and then you just decided to become an actress?" Hannah said. Then again, if you have forever to do whatever you want, why not? Cave diver, writer, professional beer taster … Hannah had a list she'd probably knock out too, if it were her.

"I never had an interest in the profession itself," Mena said. "But the influence being a celebrity provides is incredibly useful. I never considered it until the most recent world war." Mena's pace picked up. Hannah hadn't thought it could be any faster, and she was nearly jogging to keep up.

"I had a dear friend then and she and I loved to go to the pictures. Before the films there would be clips of actors and actresses encouraging people to buy war bonds. Everyone just went crazy for it. If Bette Davis or Rita Hayworth said to buy war bonds, people would spend their last penny at the suggestion, even if they'd pled poverty to one of their neighbors trying to sell them the same thing the day before. People could say all they wanted about patriotism, but the real driving force was celebrity."

"So you decided to become an actress for the influence?" Hannah said.

"I did, I'm almost ashamed to admit. Sounds shallow, I know, but I swear I had the best of intentions," Mena said. "I didn't do it right away. It was many years later when I had a particular cause that needed a greater amount of attention than it was getting. I decided to give it a try." She turned yet another corner, into a hallway with thick carpet and bronze light fixtures on the wall that gave off a soft yellow glow.

"I made a few movies—which is a great deal of work as it turns out. I had no idea. I wouldn't do it again, even with an unlimited number of lifetimes. But it did work, and before long I was able to use my influence to direct people's attention anywhere I wanted it."

Mena's pace thankfully slowed. "It was all very good in theory, and technically it's been very successful. A measure of celebrity does wonders for garnering support for any cause." They stopped in front of a door. "But it's sad it has to be that way really. The person who invented the polio vaccine or mapped the human genome could walk down the street naked and they'd hardly be noticed. But make a few films," she said, "and you can't leave the house without being mobbed. I may fake my death and move here permanently, just for the peace and quiet." Mena pulled a card on a silver chain from around her neck and waved it in front of the door. "Here we are."

While Mena crossed the room and began to rifle through the drawers of a lacquered chest, Hannah just stood in the doorway and stared at the room.

It was the most strangely beautiful mishmash of time periods and styles. A battered slab dining table—weathered and worn to dove gray—was ringed by heavily embroidered chairs alternating with carved stools that looked like they had been looted from an Egyptian tomb, their paint worn away by immeasurable years. Over the table a lighted orrery slowly drifted, the planets on their golden stems globular works of art in Venetian glass. On the pale gold fleur-de-lis patterned walls, dark oil paintings in fat gilded frames hung next to modern splatters on unframed canvas.

Mena stood up with a pile of clothing in her arms and looked at Hannah standing in the doorway. "Oh, do come in," she said. "I won't bite." Hannah stepped inside, catching her foot on the edge of a heavy oriental rug. She was happy Mena didn't laugh, just handed her the clothes and smiled.

"It was you Joel called from the tower, wasn't it?" Hannah blurted out, pausing next to a radio unit on a dainty writing table. Mena nodded.

"It seems Joel and I were intended to bump into each other throughout the years," Mena said. "While we might differ in the execution, we have similar goals, and a similar affinity for out-of-date technology. Which is fortunate, as it turned out to be as useful now as it was when we met."

"When was that?" Hannah said. Despite what she'd thought, she knew nothing about Joel, and had no idea how long he'd been around. Asher was nearly a thousand years old. Had Mena and Joel been on Earth that long as well?

"You'll have to ask Joel to tell you about it. He's a far better recorder of history than I am. It's a rather exciting story involving espionage and war and danger. I fear I'd never be able to do it justice." Mena waved her hand in the air, brushing away the memories like cobwebs. "And besides, it's all ancient history now."

"So you do this too, on top of being a doctor, and famous?" Hannah asked, sorry she'd have to wait to hear the story. "Joel said some of you worked together, trying to keep track of people like Roman and Amara."

Mena looked up from the small tablet in her hand. "I do work with Joel from time to time," she said. "My interests lie in a slightly different direction, but I lend my assistance on matters like this if needed. This is primarily Joel's operation." She laughed a light, tinkling laugh. "He bribes me to ensure my presence, and I generally cave to it, I admit."

Hannah wondered what you needed to bribe someone like Mena. She was trying to figure out how to politely phrase the question when Mena spoke. "I need to check on some other new arrivals, to make sure they've been properly accommodated. And to discover if Joel has resurfaced. You can come with me when you're cleaned up, if you'd like."

9

Hannah felt like a different person, scurrying down the hall half an hour later. She was clean, free of the crust of dried blood and dirt, days' worth of sticks and leaves untangled from her hair. Dressed in the flowing pants and soft yellow tunic Mena had given her, she was warm and comfortable, and the immediate fear and confusion had mostly worn off. She felt safe under Mena's wing, and since Joel had yet to reappear, Hannah had come along with her to check in on the new arrivals, whoever they were.

"Is Asher one of them?" Hannah said. She'd been hesitant to ask, knowing Mena and Asher had spent a great deal of time together in the past but having no idea where things lay between them now. Still, her desire to know where he'd ended up overcame her hesitation.

Mena shook her head. "I only know he was at the scene after you were picked up. He was injured, though not fatally, but chose not to come in with the returning team, or so I was told. Shame, it's been some time since I've seen him."

He hadn't been killed then. And he had chosen not to follow Hannah here. Maybe his sister had gotten away and he was once again after her. That had to be it, otherwise why wouldn't he have come? If Amara was still on the loose, Hannah wondered if she was safe, even here. The sooner Joel arrived and she could find out what was really going on, the better she would feel.

"Anyway," Mena said, showing her card to the sensor on the door.

"He's not the kind of guest we're here to see about." There was a buzz, and the door clicked open.

Inside, an armed guard was standing rigidly at attention on either side of the doorway. Mena nodded and they stepped aside, returning to their statue-like stances as soon as they passed. Down a short, empty hallway Hannah could see two more guards in front of another door, this one made of glass webbed with wire mesh. They eyed Hannah but Mena ignored them, swiping her card again and pushing the door open. She walked through and Hannah started to follow, but the guards closed rank in front of her.

"Let her pass," Mena said. There was an ancient gravitas in her tone, with an undercurrent that made it clear obeying her wasn't optional. She waved them out of her way lightly, shooing away a nuisance with the tips of her fingers. Grudgingly, they moved aside. Hannah stepped past them, then turned back and watched them through the diamond pattern of wire as they secured the door then slid silently back to their places.

"They shouldn't have stopped you," Mena said. "If anyone has a right to be here, it's you."

Hannah wasn't sure where exactly *here* was. The room they'd stepped into was long, and narrow enough from one side to the other that it looked like another colorless hallway, except off in the distance it ended in a rectangle of concrete wall. On her right was a block wall painted a shiny institutional gray, bare except for a narrow strip of recessed lighting along the top. The light gave off a sterile hospital glow and reflected a thin blue line on the opposite side of the room, which was made up almost entirely of glass.

The glass doors ran from floor to ceiling with slim metal dividers between them. Most of the panes were dark, except for the two nearest them, and another, far down the room. Hannah took a step closer to the glass and understood where Mena had brought her. It was a prison.

Behind the barrier of glass, in the far corner of the stark cell, someone was curled up on a narrow metal cot. Their legs were pulled close to their chest, arms tightly wrapped around their shins. A sheet of dull, honey-colored hair hung down lank and greasy from the head resting on top of the knees. Hannah would know that shade of hair anywhere.

Amara. An involuntary gasp slipped out. But it was relief, not fright. They *had* captured her. She wasn't out there, regrouping so she could come after Hannah again. And this wasn't the monster that had been haunting Hannah.

She was different. Diminished—that was the word that came to Hannah as she looked at the creature behind the glass. Matted hair, bony limbs outlined through the baggy sweat suit, visible blue veins in the thin, clasped hands. An undeniably human Amara.

"They were able to capture her after you were evacuated. Asher had her incapacitated," Mena said, looking at the figure behind the glass. "Despite her myriad sins, I would prefer she not be kept like this, her or anyone else." Hannah detected a hint of something she couldn't place in Mena's tone. Concern? Pity, maybe? "There isn't another clear alternative right now though. I daresay she's nearly as dangerous as she's always been—to herself and others—despite the change. And Amara may be human at the moment, but we know nothing about the permanence of the change your blood brought about."

Mena took a last long look through the glass at Amara, who hadn't moved, and stepped in front of the next cell. "This one," she said, "his situation is slightly more complicated." Hannah managed to peel her eyes away from the unmoving Amara and look into the next cell. She reeled backward as far as she could go, flattening herself against the wall behind her.

"Hannah," Mena said, "meet Roman."

She'd heard him described, the little boy who had died and come back over many years, growing more vicious over time. She'd seen him in her nightmares, a tall, sinewy monster with sharp teeth, wiry arms wrapped around his victims. Days ago, she'd even seen his actual figure in shadow. But never face to face. Hannah was immensely pleased he was behind glass, now that she was finally seeing him.

At first glance Roman appeared to be standing squarely upright in the center of his cell. A second look revealed he was restrained that way, pinned down like an exotic moth. His arms were secured above the elbows and at the wrists with thick black straps. On his legs, what looked like metal braces ran from hip to ankle, locked to the board behind him.

Despite the manacles and being behind six inches of glass, Roman terrified Hannah. He was staring right at her, unblinking, boring into her head with lashless eyes made of ink, so dark they lacked an iris. Sharp black eyebrows were lowered over them in a scowl, and the intensity of his glare was at odds with how eerily wide and childlike his eyes were.

His skin was luminous and white, but somehow less perfect than the others of his kind—like cream, but on the verge of spoiling, a decomposing swirl sitting just beneath the surface. Roman's top lip was thin and bloodlessly pale pink; the bottom was probably the same, under the blood covering it, trickling down from somewhere inside his mouth. A pink tongue like a snake's darted out and licked away some of the blood before disappearing again.

Mena cleared her throat. "It seems obvious Amara is entirely human," she said. Hannah turned toward her, keeping one eye on Roman. "When she was sedated she went down easily and completely under an average human dose. And physically, you can see she just isn't …" Hannah nodded. It was clear enough.

"He's more difficult," Mena said. "We think Paige managed to dart him with one of your cartridges when he was captured, but we can't know for certain. All we can do is hold him until we know, or until his nature takes its course—god forbid—and he vanishes again."

Hannah thought she saw Roman smile, his thin lips twitching, lifting slightly in the corners. "Can he hear us?" she said. Mena looked at a series of buttons on the panel next to the glass and shook her head.

"Not unless the intercom is turned on," Mena said.

Maybe he can read lips, Hannah thought, because she felt like he knew exactly what they were saying. Something had changed in his expression. She would have sworn he was laughing silently, mocking her.

Mena didn't seem concerned, casually turning her back on him and leaning against the glass. "Did the others who encountered your blood change quickly?" she asked. "Most of the information I have is conjecture. There are very few people who can really say what happens when your blood turns one of us human, and two of them are in this room." She looked back toward Amara's cell.

Hannah considered for a moment and decided it couldn't hurt anything to fill Mena in. What she had to tell wasn't much more than Mena had already heard.

She knew Mena had known at least one of the men Hannah's blood had made human. But if Mena felt anything about Gabe's death, her expression didn't betray it when Hannah told her the story. Mena seemed slightly more interested in Michael, Hannah's father, the first person to find out firsthand what her blood could do.

"And he was visibly aged?" Mena said.

Hannah nodded. "Gray in his hair, crow's feet. He was definitely older, and not as—shiny—as the rest of you." It had been Michael who brought Amara into Hannah's life, to track her down and retrieve her blood. "He thought it would change him back. But Amara killed him first, without waiting to test his theory. Instead she injected Gabe with the blood meant for Michael. Gabe tried to make a run for it, but she killed him before he made it through the door."

Mena frowned, processing the information, filling the gaps in what she knew. Hannah kept her face turned toward the cell Mena had her back to. She didn't like the idea of them knowing what she was saying, despite Mena's insistence they couldn't hear her, but she liked the idea of having her back to either of the people behind the glass even less.

"And then I bit my tongue hard enough to draw blood and took a chunk out of the hand Amara had over my face," Hannah said. "She didn't wait around long enough to see if it worked or not. I don't know if you've ever seen how fast she is, but she was gone in a blink. This is the first time I've seen her close up since then, though I've thought about her every five seconds."

"So we know that much then; it only takes a very small amount of blood, and the effects are nearly instantaneous," Mena said. "It appears the physical changes are slower. I hope not too slow. We'll have to wait it out, observe Roman and hope the dart didn't miss. If it did, he may simply disappear."

Mena turned, looked into Amara's cell one last time, then took a step toward the exit. "Who's in the other cell?" Hannah asked.

Mena turned back and looked in the direction of the other glowing rectangle. "There shouldn't be anyone else here." Consulting her tablet, she didn't get the answer she was looking for, so she walked toward the third lighted pane with Hannah close on her heels.

The window was opaque rather than clear like the others, the light behind it only able to force a dull glow through the panel. Mena pushed a button, then pushed it again, shaking her head. "Guard," she called down the hallway, motioning to one of the frozen figures behind the glass. When he reached them, Mena pointed to the door.

"Did we bring someone else in?" she said. "There's no one logged into the system."

The guard shook his head. "No, ma'am. The smart glass is malfunctioning. Security is aware of the problem, but since everything else is operational they thought it would be safer to leave it this way until the cells are empty. Didn't want to risk accidentally compromising security while it's being fixed."

Mena nodded and he trotted back to his post.

Hannah cupped her hands against the frosted glass, trying to peer through, but it was like staring through a dense mist. The glass felt oddly warm against her hands and she pulled them away.

Mena took one last ineffectual poke at the buttons and they turned to go. Almost to the door, Hannah caught movement out of the corner of her eye a split second before the body impacted the glass. She jumped away, barreling into Mena.

Amara had thrown herself face first against the glass. Now she was just standing there, staring at them. She was a withered and shrunken skeleton in baggy gray, but her eyes hadn't changed. They were still the same iced-over blue, flinty and cruel. They looked at Hannah over the smear of blood her split lip had left on the surface of the glass. Hannah saw Amara smile through the film of red.

She didn't want to be in here anymore. Hannah didn't have to double step to keep up with Mena's pace now. She was right behind her, happy to put some space between herself and the prison.

———•••••———

"Joel!" Hannah took the few shorts steps to him and threw her arms around his neck. He grabbed her by the waist and spun her around before depositing her next to him, keeping an arm around her shoulder. Mena gave them a smile and slipped out the door she'd just ushered Hannah through.

They were on the top level of an arena-size room. It was tiered like a lecture hall, each level lined with workstations, all facing a giant screen. The middle of the screen showed a map peppered with different colored dots. In the borders around the central image were strips of scrolling text alternating with live news reports and what looked like surveillance camera feeds. Altogether, it was a dizzying rush of information.

The equipment around the room—racks of electronics, computers everywhere—filled the air with a kind of static, an electricity that was being swirled around by the men and women buzzing back and forth across the levels. Everyone was busy and focused, except for those immediately around them. Seeing all the nearby eyes turned their way, Hannah shrugged out from under Joel's arm and ducked behind him.

"What is this place?" she said into the back of his shirt, and he pulled her back beside him to join him where he was leaning against the metal railing overlooking everything going on below. He raised an eyebrow, and every staring figure immediately returned to work.

"This is the central operations center. Ops," he said. "My headquarters."

"When you said you had some super-secret group and it had grown, I didn't picture something quite this big," Hannah said. "I was envisioning you and a man cave full of your military buddies. What is all this?"

"This," Joel said, "is what happens when you spend enough lifetimes trying to protect the population from people like Roman and Amara. Welcome to Cosmos."

Hannah laughed out loud, the sound echoing back to her in the cavernous room. "Cosmos? Sounds like the evil organization from a movie. Or was that what you were going for?"

Joel smiled the wry, lopsided grin she remembered. "I founded it before there were movies, or evil organizations probably," he said. "I might call it something else now, if I had a do-over, but I only get those with life." Hannah followed when he walked along the railing toward the far side of the room. He motioned to a man standing by one of the doors, not visibly armed but carrying himself in a way that made her fairly certain he had a weapon tucked under each arm of his jacket.

"It may sound funny to you, but it's a fitting name," Joel said. "Cosmos, the order of the universe. The opposite of chaos." He called over the guard. "Kirk, can I see your hat for a moment?" The man rushed over and handed it to Joel, who motioned him back to his station.

Turning it to face Hannah, she saw the emblem on the front. The word *Cosmos*, each of the Os a tiny snake eating its tail. "I know what a nerd you are, so you know what an ouroboros is. It's always been a meaningful sign for me," he said. "A symbol of constant rebirth, of life out of death." He raised a hand to Kirk and threw the hat, making it sail across the room in a perfect arc to where it was caught.

"After I found out what I was, and that there were others like me, I discovered some of them were bringing chaos into the world rather than order," Joel said, his voice serious now. "These people, they destroy the balance. They threaten human life, and they could never be neutralized, at least not for long."

Joel waved away a few starched individuals that had gathered around them, work in hand for his perusal. They dispersed immediately.

"I made it my mission to try and keep them in check, protect humankind from them. Over time, we developed tools to help us track them more efficiently and hold them longer. Some of those tools actually turned out to be pretty lucrative. The medical and defense applications and arms technology that came about are what funds all this."

He stopped and turned, shrugging away the seriousness. "The goal didn't change," he said, "but along the way we developed into a multinational corporation. Now it's actually Cosmos Research and Development Technologies, Inc., at least that's what is says on paper. Sounds slightly less cheesy."

It did sound less cheesy—slightly. It also sounded incredible. This had all been somewhere under the surface of Joel's life while he'd been playing single uncle and raising her.

"It's amazing. So how do you—"

"Joel. You're back!"

They both turned in response to the woman walking through the door behind them.

She was taller than Hannah and willowy, with one of those exquisite faces where every feature was perfectly balanced, from the wide-set eyes to the perfect bow-shaped lips. Her white-blonde hair was pulled back from her face into a sleek bun, and her skin was tan and flawless—perfect—but not quite as perfect as Joel's. From a distance, Hannah might have mistaken her for one of them.

The way she was moving forward made Hannah think she was going to throw her arms around Joel. At the last minute, she pulled back and coolly offered him a hand. When he dropped it fairly quickly she looked at Hannah and stepped back.

Maybe the chilly reception was because Hannah was a plain old average human. She wasn't going to be mistaken for immortal in any kind of light. Regular people were probably not terribly impressive if you were used to spending your days around the extraordinary, like

Joel, or Mena, or any of the other obviously different people Hannah could see scattered throughout the room.

"Charlie, this is Hannah," Joel said. The woman nodded, only slightly less icily.

"What was the delay?" Charlie asked Joel. Her expression had transformed back into a captivating smile.

"I think my tracker must have stopped working slightly before my heart. We'll have to look into calibrating them differently," he said. "It threw off our projections. Wouldn't have been that big a problem if I hadn't ended up on top of a mountain. Naked frostbite is exceptionally unpleasant." Joel grinned at Hannah and winked. Charlie looked slightly flushed.

"Projections?" Hannah said. "You can predict where you come back? I thought it was random."

Charlie rolled her eyes and quickly jumped in to correct Hannah's ignorance.

"With global positioning technology it's not that complicated," she said. "Ballistic re-entry is very basic, conceptually. Taking into consideration orbital speed and easily quantifiable outside influences—"

Thankfully, Hannah wasn't the only one who decided they'd already had about enough of Charlie, because Joel cut her off with a severe look.

"Could you please get me the operational reports and the progress files for anything upcoming," he said. "Have them brought up to my residence." He gave Charlie a dismissive nod and she scurried off, a blank look on her face.

He turned back to Hannah. "We can predict a lot of things," he said. "It appears random when you experience it, starting out in one place and popping up in the middle of nowhere and so far from where you started. But there's a pattern behind everything, and this is no exception. I tracked where I started and ended up until I found a trend."

He pointed toward the screen, at the large map in the center, then leaned over the railing to the woman sitting directly below them. "Shannon?" The head turned up toward them. "Can you pull up the last A to B we've tracked?"

"I can do you one better," Shannon said. "We have one about to go in half a minute. I was just about to change the screen view."

With a few clicks, the map on the screen started to rotate. It panned across water, then back over land, zeroing in on a blinking red dot. Hannah watched it flicker, the blinks growing short and closer together.

"Three, two, one," Shannon said. Her countdown was only off by a second. The flickering red dot went black, and suddenly the map moved, the surface scrolling by while the dot stayed in place. When the movement halted, the dot turned blue and became solid again.

"What was that?" Hannah asked, staring at the blue dot. The view zoomed back out to what it had originally been, a map showing a scattering of other dots in varying colors and patterns of pulsation.

"That," Joel said, "was an immortal. What you saw was the track from where they started and where they ended up." He leaned over the railing.

"Thanks, Shannon."

"Welcome, boss."

Joel took Hannah by the elbow and they moved on. "I can't take all the credit. I saw the trend, but Mena figured out the math. It's been a game changer really, as far as keeping track of immortals. We found if we considered Earth's rotational speed and the latitude a person was at when they died, accounting for our planet's movement around the sun of course—"

He must have noticed Hannah's eyes straying somewhere after rotational speed and started again.

"Basically, it's like someone picks me up and holds me just beyond Earth's atmosphere," he said. "Between when they let go and when I hit the ground, Earth moves out from under me. How far depends on my original latitude and longitude, obviously. Rotational speed is quicker the closer you are to either of the poles. If we know where and when an immortal dies, we can figure out where they're going to land."

Joel stepped back from the railing. Once again there was a group of people beginning to accumulate, tablets and folders in hand. He ignored them.

"Picture a globe. Remember the one you had when you were little," he said, "the nightlight one that spun all the time?" She nodded. "Imagine a penny on the surface. If you were to pick it straight up and then drop it again, it wouldn't hit in the same place it was picked up from, because what was underneath it will have moved. It's like the world moves out from under us before we land. I say land for lack of a better word, since I can't prove there's any real falling involved. Though some swear they feel like they've been dropped before they awaken, so maybe it's an appropriate description."

Hannah pictured him plummeting to Earth from the sky, comet trail behind him. "Maybe that's where all the clothes go," she said, "burning up on reentry."

He laughed out loud. "Another of the great mysteries of the universe solved."

"So it works like that every time?"

"Every person, every time," he said.

That was strange. Strange because Hannah knew it wasn't always the case. She remembered the times Asher had materialized right next to her.

She also remembered Asher's words, and something made her keep it to herself, though she was positive Joel would have been very interested in the information.

"And you put a tracker in yourself?" Hannah asked. "How does that work? How long does it stay charged? It doesn't work after you die, does it?"

"Questions, questions," he said. "I swear I'll answer them all. Just give me a couple minutes to tie things up here and get this circus under control. We'll go somewhere we can talk."

He motioned her over to a narrow bench against the wall. The minute she was away from him, he was swallowed up by tablet-wielding people.

10

Hannah observed it all from her perch, the hushed scurrying back and forth, the click clack of shoes and keyboard keys, and the flickers and flashes of changes on the giant screen. She tried to unobtrusively weed out the exceptions from the normal humans in the crowd; there were a few. She probably could have picked them out based on the way they dressed alone. They looked like they were on vacation, compared to their buttoned-down human counterparts who were clearly here for business.

"Hello again, Hannah." She looked up at the source of the deep voice. A wall of a man had appeared in front of her and Hannah jerked back, smacking the back of her head against the wall. He laughed a gravelly laugh while she rubbed her head.

"We haven't been formally introduced," he said. "I'm Noble."

It was the man who had briefly popped his head up through the trapdoor of the fire tower before heading out into the darkness posing as Asher. Hannah could see how he'd been able to play the role, and why he hadn't attempted to squeeze through the trapdoor. Noble wasn't quite as tall as Asher, but he was quite possibly even broader. Based on his slightly luminous skin, he was clearly like Asher in more than just scale. Without the stocking cap, he had a gleaming bald head, and she wondered if the lack of hair was something he needed to maintain, or if he came back that way each time.

"Thank you," Hannah said, standing and stretching out a hand. Noble smiled widely and gave her a slight bow, but didn't take her offered hand. Hannah dropped hers awkwardly back to her side. Thankfully Joel appeared next to Noble.

"I see you've officially met my Hannah," Joel said.

"Like I told you before, I expected the person able to take me down once and for all to be much, much bigger." Noble winked at Hannah and walked away.

Joel took her elbow and propelled her toward the door. "Let's get out of here," he said, leading her out of the room into an empty corridor.

"So you can predict where you end up. Is that how Noble got to the tower last night?" Hannah said. It made more sense now, knowing that. It explained not only how he'd appeared out of thin air but also what Joel had dropped through the trapdoor. Noble must have been out there stark naked.

"Exactly. Clever girl. Mena was needed here, and we didn't have another immortal around who could pass for you, so that's why Paige had to parachute in. We couldn't exactly bring her in the same way. Noble though, he popped up right on schedule."

Hannah didn't know how she felt about that. Noble had just ended his life—or had someone end it; she wasn't sure she wanted to know the details—just so he could appear in the right place at the right time. She couldn't get used to their cavalier approach to their own deaths.

They stood waiting in front of an elevator door. At least, Hannah thought it was an elevator, because when Joel waved his card in front of it, it hadn't opened, only made a muted ding. Apart from that ding, it was exactly like the last door they had come out of. In this place, one door was very much like the next.

The door slid open. Its only occupant stepped out, nodded to Joel, and walked away down the hallway. Hannah leaned backward, staring, until the man disappeared around a corner. She said, "Tell me that wasn't...?"

Joel tugged her gently into the elevator by the sleeve. "Long live the king," he said, laughing. "I can't convince him to keep a low profile. Someone recognizes him every other day."

"How do they do it?" she said. "The ones like him, and Mena. Don't people notice that they don't ever get old?" There was a soft whir and her stomach tugged as the car lifted. A thin line of colored light representing their movement traced its way upward along the side of the door. They had either been very far down, or were going very high up. Hannah was shaking her head, still thinking about the man she'd just seen.

"Faking your death is far easier than you would think," Joel said. "But if you have the means, you don't even have to do that. You can just fake your life instead."

"Fake your life?"

"Easy as pie," Joel said. "When it's time to move on, all you do is find someone who looks like you and convince them to step into your life. Most people jump at the chance to walk into the fame or money someone else built up." The elevator slowed to a halt. "All we do is hand it over and slip away. On the off chance they change their mind or someone suspects, well, who'd believe them?"

The door slid open.

"And here we are," he said, holding the door open for her.

Joel's living quarters were enormous. Where Mena's had been soft and warm, filled with pieces of the past tucked together in strange coherence, the room they'd just stepped into was bright, austere, and strikingly modern. Everything was made from glass and stone, or matte burnished metal. It was beautiful, but it was unfamiliar. Nothing in it reminded Hannah of any of the places the two of them had lived over the years. She didn't know why she had expected something that felt a little more like home.

The only nod to color was a bowl of perfect green apples on the table. Joel picked one up and tossed it in the air. He added another, then another. Juggling them a few rounds, he passed them back to the bowl, except for the last one, which he caught. He gave a mock bow before he bit into it.

"Since when do you know how to juggle?" Hannah asked. Add it to the growing list of things she didn't know about him.

He took another bite and smiled. "It's amazing what you pick up when you've been around long enough," he said. He lobbed the core easily into the trash can at the same time her stomach growled. His smile dropped and he looked at Hannah. "Did anyone think to offer you so much as a cup of coffee at any point since you arrived? I heard you weren't welcomed with the greatest respect."

That was a bit of an understatement.

"I read the report on my way back," he went on. "It said you were sedated after evacuation so your injuries could be tended to, kept in a secure location, and then sent to medical for a follow-up examination. I just read Mena's closing notes on the operation. Her take on the report reads a little less clinically."

"Does it say I was stabbed in the neck and knocked out in the helicopter? I woke up locked in a cell, and then someone strapped me into a chair and tried to steal my blood."

"I'm so sorry, honey. That would be Charlie's doing," he said. "Don't hold it against her."

That was easier said than done, especially with the icy reception she'd gotten meeting the woman. Joel saw the look on Hannah's face and shook his head.

"Really, it was all a misunderstanding. Charlie is absolutely brilliant, but she tends to be very literal. The orders were that if I was held up, to find you a safe place to stay and make sure you weren't injured."

"Um, what part of that translated into tying me up and trying to drain me dry? If Mena hadn't turned up—"

Joel pulled her into a crushing hug. "I truly am sorry," he said. "I expected to be here to welcome you properly. I didn't think for a moment anyone would be looking after you but me, or I would have been more explicit. The staff that treated you harshly—I'll dismiss every one of them immediately, and I'll reprimand Charlie."

Based on their first encounter, she was fairly sure Charlie wasn't going to take too kindly to being scolded on Hannah's behalf.

"It's fine," she said. "Don't bother." There was no real harm done, she guessed. While she'd been petrified at the time, it didn't seem like as big a deal now that she was safe and not scared. It had happened because Joel wasn't here, and he was here now.

Disentangling herself from him, Hannah walked across the room. He followed her to stand in front of a bank of windows that made up the entire far wall. The landscape outside was unfamiliar.

"Where are we? You never told me where we were going," she said. "Since I was out during the helicopter ride, I don't even know what state I'm in." Or country for all she knew.

They were high up, so far off the ground they were even with the tops of the rocky peaks poking their way up from the stretch of forest. Joel pointed at a tall, flat-topped formation in the distance. She squinted at it, unable to make out what he was pointing toward.

"Here, try with these." He pulled open a drawer and handed her a pair of binoculars. It took a moment of adjusting the focus until she saw it.

"South Dakota?" She looked at him with raised eyebrows, adjusting the dials again to bring the carved faces into better focus.

"I'll bet you can't guess which one is still alive," he said. "I'll give you a hint. He's not facing this direction. I moved the whole apartment because I couldn't stand him staring at me all day."

Hannah looked over the area again, this time without the binoculars. They were floating above an ocean of green, broken only by islands of stone.

"What happened after they picked me up? How did you catch Amara?"

"You know me, Han, I like to cover all my bases. There was a second team on standby not far away, on the off chance she slipped our grasp. They were en route to you the minute we knew Amara hadn't taken the bait. When they got there, the tower was down and she was unconscious. Asher was babysitting her, to make sure she stayed that way. They just loaded her up and brought her in."

"Why didn't they bring him?"

Joel shrugged. "He didn't want to come. I wasn't there, but I'm told he said, 'Amara's finished. Tell Joel I'm done with all this,' and then he left. I don't think we'll see him again."

That didn't sound like Asher, but maybe those weren't his exact words. Their point was clear enough. He must have known then that his sister was human and the threat to Hannah was gone. His job was done.

Hannah's face must have fallen, because Joel picked up her hands. "I know he seemed gallant, showing up to protect you from his sister. But he doesn't need to protect you anymore. You don't have to worry about him popping up again."

Of course he'd gone. Asher was only ever in her life because of his sister. Now that Amara was human and captured, she wasn't a threat. His self-imposed mission was accomplished, and he didn't have to feel responsible for Hannah anymore. He could go live however he wanted.

She was happy for him. Hannah wanted him to be happy; truly she did. She pinched out the little spark of childish hope. When Joel had told them there wasn't a chance of her making Asher human acciden-tally, she'd thought maybe—well, she wouldn't even admit to herself what she'd thought. It didn't matter now. He was gone, and she might never see him again. She understood, and she didn't blame him, but she would have liked to say thank you, and goodbye. Now she'd have to pull up her big girl panties and quietly nurse her bruised heart alone.

There was a soft tap on the door.

"That's dinner," Joel said, "and after that, a good night's sleep somewhere safe. There's absolutely nothing for you to worry about, for the first time in what must seem like forever. You're here now, and it's just you and me again from now on."

———◆·••◆———

They left the pile of dishes on the table. From the couch, Hannah watched the last of the day fade away over the jagged tops of the hills. The remaining sunlight was a thin orange line against their rim, like the burning edge of a piece of paper. She felt Joel sit down beside her and they watched the line of fire burn away.

"A toast," Joel said. He had a bottle in one hand and glasses in the other. Setting the glasses down with a clink, he began to work the cork from the bottle.

"I don't think I have enough room left," Hannah said. They'd lingered over their meal. Sitting at a table like that, with Joel, was something she hadn't imagined doing again, and she'd drawn it out.

There was a soft pop as the cork released.

"Find some room," Joel said, pouring a glass and handing it to her. He filled his and raised it. "Here's to you." The glasses clicked quietly together.

Now that the sky was fully dark she could see the two of them in the window, and Hannah watched Joel refill his glass in the reflection. They could pass for the same age, now that he'd done away with all the artificial maturity. But the difference in him went further than skin deep; it was something in the whole way he carried himself. The steady uncle, walled up inside functional flannel and rough, working man's movements, was missing. This Joel was sleek and sanguine, more tightly drawn. When Hannah looked at him, it was like the faded, used-up person on top had been peeled away, leaving a sharper, unworn man underneath.

Sitting next to him she was a dark little scrap. Outmatched and in over her head. It was how she felt next to every other immortal she'd encountered. Now Joel as well. Seeing her frown in the reflection, Joel threw his free arm around her shoulder.

"What is it?" he said.

"Mind still swirling, I guess. It's this world of yours. Now that I'm not busy running for my life, it hit me there's no going back. I can't ever un-know about it. My life is never going to be normal again. Everything I had is gone. Everything I know is gone. I have to start all over again."

Hannah watched his face break into a smile, and she twisted around so she could look at him. "I might have been wallowing in the self-pity a little bit there, but it wasn't that amusing," she said. She tossed back her champagne in one angry gulp and started to get up off the couch. Joel reached up and pulled her down by the back of her shirt.

"I'm not amused," he said. "I'm just extremely happy. I've been alive for a very long time, and this is without a doubt the best day of my life." Joel put his arm back around her shoulder. "Hear me out," he said, seeing the disbelief on her face. "This life, the people you're afraid of, you've been dealing with them how long? A year, almost two?"

She nodded. It felt like an eternity, but yes. He reached over and refilled her glass.

"I've spent my entire lives—plural—worrying about them," he said. "The man strapped to a board forty floors below us, he's like a poison. Evil just leeches out of him. Believe me, I know. I've had a front row seat for a big chunk of his horrifying existence." Joel jumped up suddenly. "This conversation requires something stronger." He poured himself a few fingers of amber liquid from a decanter on the sideboard. "Bear with me, there's a little bit of dark and dreary before we get to the happy part."

He held the decanter toward Hannah, but she shook her head. Joel threw back his drink and refilled it before he sat back down.

"The very first time I encountered Roman he was living like he was the son of the devil himself. He was called something different then, but the name makes no matter." He waved the digression away with his hand. "He had amassed a band of followers and they only added to the terror he caused. They'd watched him disappear and return like black magic, and they worshipped him. And they emulated him. Together, they left a wake of death across Europe."

Joel was staring forward at the window glass. The expression on his face was tortured and far away, lost in history.

"They killed hundreds of people, Han. Hundreds. Pregnant women, babies. Brutalized. Cannibalized even. He didn't even try to hide it," he said. "He didn't need to. He was tried and found guilty, jailed, hanged, again and again." He turned to face her, back in the present. "You know how it works. Poof. Gone. Then right back at it."

Joel paused to tip back his drink, a wry smile on his face. "When I first discovered what I was, I thought it was the greatest gift god had ever given a man. For some reason I'd been chosen—me—selected above all others to live endless lifetimes. I studied, I wrote, I traveled.

You can't imagine now, the world is so changed, but I went to places that weren't even known to exist, places beyond belief at the time. And all I had to do was accept my most recent death and open my eyes in a new and wondrous world." The empty glass hit the side table with a hard click. "But there's always a balance," he said. "The scales always have to be evened; all gifts have strings attached. I discovered the price for my extra time."

"Roman," she said.

Joel nodded. "I found out before too many lives had passed that I wasn't the only one." Joel looked at her and smiled, shaking his head. "It was pure hubris on my part. I thought it was just we two—he and I—good against evil. I thought it was my god-given duty to stop him. And I tried. I swear to you I gave it everything I had. I tracked him down, held him in chains as long as possible, even tried to show him the error of his ways and convert him from his evil path … that part was probably more pointless than trying to keep him contained. In any case, you know how futile an effort it was."

She knew. Roman's lives were brief, the shortest of any of their kind. He could never be kept long.

"It saved a few potential victims maybe, and it was more effective than hanging him, as far as keeping the population safe, but it was a Sisyphean effort," Joel said. "He'd been terrorizing the world for two hundred years before I came along, and he'd be doing it forever."

Joel paused and sloshed some champagne into his rocks glass, then reached over to upend the rest of the bottle into her flute. Hannah stared down at it, rotating it and watching the swirling design chase itself around the gold rim, the pattern repeating again and again.

"So you've been chasing him around endlessly this whole time, for how long?" Hannah said. It made her feel a little whiny about running from Roman and Amara for such a relatively short time.

"Hundreds of years. And I'm still at it. Though soon, it wasn't just him I was after. I found out there were more of us, so many more. And he's not the only one of us to go bad, as you well know. I often wonder if there's an even split. Maybe there's a good one for every bad one. The universe is always seeking balance."

It was a chilling thought, that for each of his kind there was a terrible counterpart out there somewhere. For every Joel, a Roman. For every Asher, an Amara.

"It's gotten easier," Joel went on. "Technology is extraordinary. I can't sedate one of us indefinitely, but it works for longer periods now at least, so I can hold them more securely. I can put a tracker on someone they won't even know about. It'll transmit their location, vitals, everything, up until the second they die. And I can predict where they'll end up next." He raised his glass. "Which brings me back around to our toast."

Hannah shook her head. "I've had way past enough. I don't have your undead tolerance."

"I insist," he said. "Just one more. We went the long way round, but we've finally got to what we were supposed to be celebrating in the first place. The other reason why having you here is so special."

She sighed and relented, clicked her glass against his. "Okay. Toast away."

"To you, Hannah Eve Cirric. You're looking at this like it's a loss. But starting over isn't losing, it's gaining. It's getting a new life, the real one you were meant to have, the best one possible." He smiled at her. "Now I know why all this happened. There was a reason for everything. Fate put me in the right place just in time to save your life. I was meant to be there; to raise you and protect you and even to let you go," he said. "Otherwise, you never would have found out what you are. It's no coincidence we were put together. Today is the happiest day of my life because you're here, and you were designed to be here, to help me bring my work to a close. You—your blood—is going to help me put an end to them, once and for all."

11

The unsettled thoughts and foreign surroundings couldn't keep her awake. All the food and champagne hadn't helped either. Hannah fell asleep almost immediately, burrowed under the sheets in the bedroom across from Joel's. But it was a disjointed sleep, muddled with disturbing dreams.

Hannah dreamt of a hooded figure winding its way over old cobbled streets, creeping around tight, dark corners like a mist, cloak flowing behind like a black river. It left a slime of fear and panic as it went, and everything living scattered from its approach, until the streets were silent and dead.

The demon stopped and turned in a swirl of dark fabric to look back on its handiwork. There was a trail of bodies laid out in its wake, floating on top of a slick of red. Every one of them was impossibly beautiful, with eerily perfect, liquid skin and achingly lovely faces. But only for an instant. At once, they began to show signs of rot and decay. Dark veins spidered across their faces, contorting their features, creeping into the whites of their eyes. Their bodies blackened and deflated, collapsed with purification, melting into dirt.

Laughter rang out from under the hood. The body under the black cloak shook with it. The hood slid back with the movement, and Hannah saw herself, mouth thrown open with elation, happy red tears leaking from the corners of her eyes.

Hannah sat up, entangled in the sheets, nightgown plastered to her with sweat. She was trying to catch her breath when the door opened a crack and Joel peeked his head inside. Seeing her awake he came in, coffee mug in hand.

"Finally, you're up, you lie-abed," he said. He saw the expression on her face. "You look like you've seen a ghost."

"Bad dream," she said. "No more champagne before bed for me." He handed over the coffee and sat down on the edge of the bed.

"I hope you like your room," Joel said. "It's been here waiting for you for quite some time, just in case."

She took a moment to examine it more closely. It had seemed entirely new to her when she'd crawled into bed last night, but in daylight it was strangely familiar. The sleigh bed was made up with soft flannel sheets, and an artfully faded patchwork quilt was folded over the footboard. The bright blue sky outside the wide windows was framed with lace curtains, and in front of her, over an antique chest, was a large oil painting of a pine forest done in broody greens and dark blues.

Hannah recognized the room because it was a close relative of one she'd slept in before. Her own—in the house that she and Joel had last shared. The house Amara burned down. Except this version of the room was richer and finer than the original. Or maybe this was the original, and her own had been a cheaper imitation.

"Sorry to leave you to your own devices so soon," Joel said, getting up from the bed. "I have to take care of some of the usual business." He paused in the doorway. "Push six on any phone if you need me. I left something for you out on the table. I think you'll enjoy it."

Hannah thought he meant the breakfast. There was a plate covered with a silver dome, a carafe of coffee, and a pitcher of orange juice on the dining table when she finally made her way out of bed. She picked up the pitcher and wiped away the ring it had sweated onto the surface of the table before it could run onto the book lying next to it.

It was a thick volume—dictionary thick—bound in rich, brown leather. Hannah ran her hand over the heavily embossed surface, feeling the symbols and swoops. There was no title, no writing on it of any kind. She pushed the domed plate aside and pulled the book in front of her.

There weren't any empty front pages or wasted filler leaves. The writing started promptly with a column of words at the top of the first righthand page. The text was arranged like a table of contents, but without any page numbers. And it was all names. The list started with Alethea. Underneath that, Amara. Under Amara, Asher.

When Hannah paused on the name she felt a strange tug and turned her head as though he should be standing behind her—which of course he wasn't. She ran her finger down the rest of the page, skimming over a few names she recognized, and many, many more she didn't. It continued onto the next page, and the next. At the end of the ninth page, halfway down, the list stopped with the name Zoa. It was a list of the people who died and returned again and again; an index of immortals.

Hannah turned to the first entry and started to read, but a faint streak of yellow showing through the onionskin distracted her. Turning a handful of leaves brought her to Amara. Where the first entry had been filled with close black print with no images or color, Amara's had a yellow band inked across the bottom.

Tipping the book to the side, Hannah could see a few other places where bits of color showed. She paged through until she got to the next one. Gabriel. There was a red stripe running across the bottom of his. The entry for Michael was the same. The book was conveniently color coded.

"Yellow for human. Red for dead," Hannah whispered to no one.

She noticed another difference between entries when she went back to the beginning. The top corner was clipped off some of the sections, like index notches in a Bible. Except these cuts weren't lettered, and they were spaced unevenly throughout the thick book. Hannah stopped to read a little from the first notched page. After the second, it was clear they weren't random at all. Torture, murder, arson, insanity; the words jumped out at her. The cuts marked the entries for the worst of the worst, like a most wanted list of the perpetually living.

Hannah turned back to the very first entry. Resisting the urge to skip ahead, she read carefully through it. While the book looked like an extravagantly bound novel, the entries were businesslike, efficient, like a biographical study, a concise record of facts and statistics. The clinical way they read didn't do anything to lessen the impact of the content, and when she began the second entry she was doubly glad Amara was currently human and in a box. If she'd known half of what the woman had done in her many lifetimes, Hannah wouldn't have slept a night in the past year. Reading it gave her chills and she was glad to finish it, turning over the yellow striped page to the third entry. *Asher.* She brushed away the strange feeling, like he was hovering behind her, and began to read.

Asher

Origin: Exact date of birth is unknown, though it has been confirmed to be no later than 1100 A.D. Place of birth in England, believed to be somewhere near Ely or Cambridge.

Given name was likely adapted from the Norman/Germanic Ansger, given the time period and location of his earliest appearance. Known alternate appellations used in previous lives include Ashar, Aescher (various spelling of the same), Ancel, and Axel. More recent aliases have included Andrew and Aaron with various generic surnames. Any number of additional convenience identities have been in use and are relevant only in tracking his movements.

The subject's actual surname is believed to be Jacobson. This is suggestive of parentage, though this cannot be fully substantiated. Historical evidence of the use of Jacobson by his sister is more reliable and appears twice in documentation extant from the period, in the instance of her first marriage and after the events of her execution.

Physical Description: Hair, blond. Eyes, blue-gray. Fair skin. Muscular build. Height based on photographic comparison calculated at approximately eighty-two inches.

Note: Asher is the elder of a set of fraternal twins. This is the only known instance of this regenerative abnormality being hereditary.

Historical Data: Due to his extreme age and the paucity of written records in the subject's earliest lifetime, very little is known about Asher's movements until the sixteenth century. He may have made an appearance in various military engagements dating back as far as 1199, but these cannot be substantiated, and having had no significant impact on the outcomes of the conflicts, are left as conjecture.

A brief appearance in the Swedish court (circa 1560s), can be positively attributed to Asher but is irrelevant historically.

Asher's role in the attempted escape and death of Anne de Chantraine (Belgium, circa 1622) is verifiable though of minor importance to the greater events occurring—the witch hunts of the 17th century. They were, as were nearly all previous such periods of moral upheaval and mass hysteria, the result of unexplainable disappearances and reappearances of various immortals being construed as the work of the devil.

In the case of de Chantraine, Asher's appearance comes into play as a side note to the events already in motion. De Chantraine was accused of communicating with beasts, cursing her neighbors and various farm animals, and having illicit congress with the devil, very much in line with the witch hunt hysteria of the period. De Chantraine was incarcerated and interrogated.

Primary source material refers to a giant man alleged to be the servant of the devil attempting to release de Chantraine from imprisonment. Witness statements regarding his attempt to free the accused from confinement agree his actions resulted in his death at the hands of the accused's jailers. After witnessing his death, it was recorded the man known now to be Asher Jacobson miraculously reappeared nearly a week later. He followed his first attempt with a second, which again resulted in his death. His reappearance was taken to be proof of the accused's satanic sympathies. Anne de Chantraine was summarily strangled and burned at the stake.

No other notable or verifiable appearances. Modern occurrences appear solely as a footnote to the actions of his sister. Asher Jacobson does not appear to pose a direct threat to humanity on a meaning-ful scale, however, indirectly he has been linked to the deaths of as many as fifty women. Fatalities occurred as a result of his habit of forming close relationships with members of the human population, possibly for the sake of companionship or for physical purposes. The last confirmed appearance, circa 1915, ended in the same manner as all previous instances, with his sister ending the life of the human companion and a number of collateral relations as a matter of course.

This willingness to endanger humans by proximity, despite the knowledge of the expected outcome, appears to be an indication of either disregard for the human race beyond personal comfort, or possible mental/emotional deficiency.

Known associates:
Gabriel - US, NOR (Deceased)
Jeffrey - HOL, BRA
Dashiell, Lord Warrington - UK
Jeremiah - UK, US
Philomena - US, SWI, JAP
Amara Jacobson - US, RUS, IRA (Human)

One short page. That was it. And most of it a sidebar to his sister's violence. A hundred lifetimes condensed into an efficient little block of text, with an ending that made Asher sound like a sick, lonely man.

Hannah thought what Joel didn't know about Asher could fill the book. At least now, with Amara human and behind inches of metal and glass, there was a chance the rest of his story could continue with some happiness.

Speaking of Joel, she thought. Hannah skipped ahead. Jane, Jeffrey, Lucas. She went back, to see if she'd missed it. She went to the very front and ran her finger down the alphabetical list again. There was no entry for Joel. She wondered why the pages bound to be the most accurate and complete were missing.

Joel found her still bent over the book, breakfast long since cold and forgotten, feet tucked up under her wrinkled nightgown. Hannah sat up bleary eyed when the door opened, a crick in her neck from spending the morning—and part of the afternoon—face down in the close print.

He shook his head in amusement. "Get dressed, lazy pants. Let's go get some lunch." She obliged him and got ready, but eyed the unread part of the book when they walked out the door.

In the elevator, Joel pulled a chain of gold links from his pocket, far too rich for the plain plastic keycard attached to it. "This will get you through any door here, without exception. Not that you'll need it, if I'm always going to have to convince you to get out of your pajamas and leave the room."

He looped the chain over her head and had his arms around her, pulling her hair out from under it, when the elevator door slid open. The maître d looked away discreetly, as did a few of the diners at the small tables near the door. Hannah stepped away from Joel, sticking the card into the neck of her dress. He caught her hand and tucked it under his arm, pulling her into the room.

Joel led the way, the maître d falling in behind them. They wove their way to a small table in the farthest corner, and Hannah slid gratefully into the chair pulled out for her, happy to sink out of sight. The tuxedoed man slipped away and another quietly took his place, showing Joel the label of a wine bottle.

"I hope you don't mind," Joel said. "I took the liberty of selecting our meal in advance."

She didn't mind. Hannah wouldn't have minded sliding down under the table, hiding behind the cloth to avoid the eyes sneaking glances—and some not so subtle stares—in their direction. Why was everyone looking at her like she had horns?

"Very fancy place," Hannah said, watching the waiter pour a small amount of blood red wine into Joel's glass. Before coming here she'd never seen him drink more than a single beer in a day, usually during a football game. Looking at this Joel, rolling the wine around, eyeing it as it clung to the sides of the glass, she had trouble believing he was the same person. This was the man who raised her, and it felt like she knew less about him by the hour.

Joel must have found the wine acceptable, because he nodded, and their glasses were filled before the waiter silently disappeared.

"This is the fancy-pants dining option here. I wanted to impress you right out of the gate." He raised his glass and grinned, pinky sticking out affectedly. "Most of the staff live here full-time so there have to be some options besides the cafeteria, otherwise there'd be mutiny. Especially for people like me. When you're old enough, you get to be a food snob."

It was an impressive place, all gold leaf and oversized light fixtures dripping cut glass. But it was hushed and uncomfortable, and every time she turned her head, Hannah caught people staring in their direction.

Suddenly all the eyes went somewhere else, and Hannah was staring as well. The maître d was escorting a man through the dining room. He was tall and lean—and probably very handsome—but it was difficult to tell for sure because a clown mask had been poorly tattooed over his entire face. Based on the red, raised outline, it was a very recent acquisition. When he passed by their table the man waggled his eyebrows, which were clumsily circled in thick black ink.

Joel burst out laughing, shaking his head. "I've told him a hundred times not to make bets with the staff down in scientific. They're literally the smartest people on the planet. You'd think after this long he'd have learned." He wiped tears from his eyes with the corner of his napkin. "I won't even pretend I haven't done it," he said. "Once I got *Harriet till*

115

Death tattooed across my chest in big block letters, daisy chain around the whole thing. Proof I'd love her until I died. I won't insult you by pretending it was an accident when I got hit by a buggy two days later."

He was still grinning when the waiter appeared with their plates and set them on the chargers with a flourish. "Thank god bodily modifications disappear with the pants and wallets. I did have a rather dashing earring for a while. But it was just too much of a nuisance, piercing it over and over."

With his dark good looks and mischievous smile, Hannah could easily imagine him with a piratical gold hoop. It was entirely possible he'd actually been a pirate, now that she knew he'd lived countless lives. Her life so far must have been just a tiny sliver of his.

She let Joel do the talking, through the soup, and the fish, and the fussy, flowery dessert. Hannah didn't do more than nod or smile until coffee was poured into delicate china cups. She heard a great deal about his organization and about the people who worked here. He pointed out some of them as they came and went, both the extraordinary and the regular human variety.

Who she didn't hear any more about was him. She'd hoped after the bit about the tattoo and the earring she might be able to fill in some of the gaps. Hannah took a sip from her coffee and looked at him over the rim. Something made her hesitant to ask for more details. She wasn't sure what. The old Joel—her Joel—had questions thrown at him fifty times a day since she'd learned to talk. He'd never shied away from answering then.

She decided just to ask; it was the quickest way to get an answer. He'd taught her that.

"Joel, about your book …" she said. He nodded for her to go on. "Once I got started I couldn't stop, but I got to the—"

"They're here, Joel, if you have a moment."

Hannah jumped when Charlie spoke over her shoulder. Her coffee cup tilted and sent a milky brown wave over the white cloth. Hannah mopped at it ineffectually with her napkin, ducking her head too quickly to see if Charlie was smiling smugly.

"Leave it, Han. It's fine," Joel said. "What is it, Charlie?"

She handed him a tablet and a stylus. "The next of kin is here. The forms are in order to turn over Paige's assets. All you need to do is sign so we can release everything."

Joel took the stylus and scribbled across the screen. "Give me a moment. I'll be down momentarily."

"Paige's assets?" Hannah said. She stared at the irregular coffee splotch spreading on the table, tracing the border with her eyes.

"Remember her?" Charlie said. Her voice was clipped and unkind. "Didn't anyone tell you? Not everyone who went out after you came back."

"I said give me a moment." Joel's voice didn't rise, even slightly, but the hard edge in it made Charlie pull back the tablet she had thrust in his face. She slipped away without another word.

"Joel?" Hannah's voice was a whisper.

"The agents here go into the field to retrieve people like Roman all the time. It's a very important and potentially very dangerous job. While we plan for every contingency, there's always risk." Joel reached out and picked up Hannah's hand. She couldn't bring herself to look up at him. "Paige did what she was supposed to do, but Roman didn't go down as quickly as we anticipated. He managed to get ahold of her first."

Paige was dead. She'd been out there as a decoy, to get Hannah out of danger. Paige had only been in danger because of her.

Joel didn't let go of Hannah's hand when she tried to pull it away and sink back into the chair. He pulled her forward.

"Look at me," he said.

She couldn't. Joel gave her a sharp shake and she opened her eyes, hot tears pooling in the front of them and making her vision blurry.

"I said look at me," Joel repeated. "Like every human being in this organization, Paige was a highly skilled asset. It wasn't her first mission and she knew exactly what she was walking into."

It didn't make Hannah feel any better. She swiped a hand across her face. One more person was dead because of her. One more body on the pile. At night the faces of the dead ran through her head; some nights she just watched the ghost-reel instead of sleeping. Now there was one more. Maybe that's why everyone was staring at her.

"It's a terrible loss. She was a good agent and a good person. She'll be missed. But this is not about you," Joel said. "Paige was the first agent ever to go out there and truly and completely achieve her goal. They went out to bring Roman in and they did. He was brought in, and for once he's going to stay put. Roman is never going to get the chance to kill another person. Paige saved lives. Hundreds, probably thousands of lives. Lives of people who haven't even been born yet."

Hannah sucked in a deep breath and tried to give his words some weight inside her head. She hoped it was true at least, about Roman. "You think he's done?" she asked. "Did she get him with my blood?"

"He's human now," Joel said. "I'm sure of it."

He pulled her to her feet and led her toward the door. One of her feet caught on nothing and she stumbled. Hannah dragged herself along on feet made of wood.

Call it self-pity, call it weakness, but Hannah didn't want to be who she was. She just kept handing out death, no matter which way she turned. Joel might talk about all the lives Paige was responsible for having saved, but Hannah was responsible for deaths. Paige's, along with all the other people who'd died protecting her, and the innocent collateral damage as well. She was also responsible for the deaths of the immortals she made human. They would eventually die, if she changed them. But if she didn't, was she then complicit in the deaths of the humans they might kill, even into the future, on and on even after her own life was over? Right now, she felt the weight of all those lives on her. Hannah remembered her dream. She really was going to be the demon responsible for an endless trail of dead bodies, no matter what she did.

12

"Thirty-two, thirty-three, thirty-four."

Hannah counted the doors quietly under her breath, stopping at the intersection of two identical hallways. On the small tablet in her hand she used her thumb and forefinger to enlarge the diagram of the floor she was wandering around. She spun the image with her index finger and it shifted into 3D, the angle change making the doors visible in the diagram, each one numbered and labeled. Swiping ahead, she counted how many more she had to go—a lot—and backward, because somehow she'd taken a wrong turn and needed to backtrack yet again toward her destination.

Hannah had sunk into silence after lunch, shaken by the news of Paige's death, the unbearable weight of it. Joel must have had enough of her staring blankly out the window and had the tablet brought up from ops for her. He set a red blinking dot flashing over a point on the map program and told her to go find it and blow off a little steam.

She started walking again, eyes flipping back and forth between the screen and the floor, trying not to end up on her face. The digital map she was swiveling and rotating was absolutely necessary. If she was struggling to find the location with it in hand, she would have been lost for a week trying to find anything here on her own.

Cosmos wasn't just a building, she'd quickly discovered. It was an enormous sprawling complex made up of a large number of interconnected facilities. From the central building Cosmos snaked outward like the roots of a tree crawling away from the trunk, reaching out far enough to carve itself into the granite hills around them.

Hannah wasn't prepared to venture farther from the center than she already was, and stopped to orient herself once again. She was currently lost in one small portion of a single level of one building. There were a hundred more.

The main building itself was laid out simply enough, and so vast from top to bottom Hannah doubted she would have a need to go beyond it any time soon. She'd looked at the diagram; floor upon floor of levels, starting far underground. The lowest levels were secure floors with descriptions that didn't pop up with the touch of a finger like the rest. Hannah wondered if she had been down there when she'd gone with Mena to where Amara and Roman were being held.

Above the subterranean levels, floors were strictly business, divided between research and laboratory spaces, offices, and training facilities. Resting on top of everything else were the residential floors, growing increasingly more luxurious as they neared the top, ending with the highest level where she and Joel were housed.

"You're supposed to be right here," Hannah said, speaking to the tablet, poking at the red dot. The tablet did just about everything, but responding to frustrated comments clearly wasn't one of its functions.

Suddenly her face collided with a glass panel and she bounced off, landing painfully on her still tender backside. Hannah picked herself up and rescued the tablet, then jumped back when a pair of figures flashed by the window, laughing at her as they ran by. Hannah scowled and looked through the glass into where the map had led her.

Like everything else in the complex, the fitness center was enormous. She could see down to the floor below where people were working out in a weight training area that took up most of the lower level. Above them were banks of machines; treadmills, ellipticals, rowing machines, all being pounded away at by determined staff members. Through a wall of glass on the next level up were courts for basketball or squash, lined up one after the other, parquet floors gleaming.

Another figure passed in front of her, a second close behind, groups of figures running by on the elevated track far above the main floor.

----•••••----

Hannah was disappointed at how beat up and slow she felt, but she fought through. A little physical discomfort was worth the mental relief. She settled into an easy trot and kept it, ignoring the painful twinge every time her injured leg hit the ground, and trying not to be intimidated by the pace set by the other occupants of the track.

While they were all dressed in the same uniform gray with the omnipresent snake logo from the supply in the locker room, that's where the similarities ended. Everyone here was on a different level, both the humans and otherwise. Young, attractive, obviously fit, they blew past her easily at the dizzying height of the elevated track. Oh well. Hannah might not be fast, but she was persistent. She tuned out the world and just kept circling.

It wasn't a normal oval of track. Lanes dropped away or swooped upward from the main level, creating sharp inclines and headlong dips. She peeled off into the left lane and took the decline downhill. It leveled off for a moment at the bottom, then she doggedly made her way back up, panting by the time the path rejoined the main track.

One by one the people running alone or in small groups dropped off and disappeared, eventually leaving only one other figure on the track. At the tightest part of the turn she could see Noble running half a track's length behind her.

When she went low, he went low, taking the swoop downward on the opposite side. If she increased her pace and stayed level, he did the same. They played the game for a long time, and she kept running until she reached a point where her legs had taken about as much as they were capable of. When she couldn't stomach the thought of taking the dip downward again, she slowed. Hannah felt the track shake when Noble drew closer.

"I've seen better runs in my shorts," he said, pulling up beside her.

"Yeah, well, I was shot yesterday. Shouldn't you be faster after a couple hundred years?" Hannah said, out of breath. She'd liked Noble immediately, even if he wasn't willing to shake her hand. He had an easy manner that wasn't the least bit superior and a genuine smile. Right now he was looking down at her, lips pulled into a gleaming grin.

Hannah had read his section in Joel's book and it hadn't changed her original opinion of him. Noble was incredibly charismatic, and it wasn't a new development. It had served him well enough in the past for him to found a religious group that still hailed him as a prophet, and he'd started political uprisings to topple cruel dictators not once, but at least three times in history; and those were the ones Joel knew about. He had an impressive list of accomplishments spread over his series of lives.

They did a few slow circuits side by side, cooling down. Hannah had to push herself to keep pace with him because she was tired and feeling the sting of the flesh wound, and because she had to concentrate on not tripping from laughter. Noble had no trouble talking a blue streak at the pace they were moving.

"… that was before Joel had the railings put up on the roof," he said. "Lucas and me, we had this race going for like four years straight." Noble turned around to run backward so he could face Hannah. It didn't slow him down a bit. "Headfirst off the top floor to dead on the ground, then back here from wherever we ended up. Whoever made it first won."

Noble boomed out a laugh that bounced around the cavernous empty space. "I lost my island, a vintage Bentley I'd had since it was new, and a date with Norma Jean on her last night before checkout," he said. "Somehow, Lucas kept beating me. Of course it turned out he was cheating."

Running backward at her pace must not have been challenging enough for him. Without missing a step Noble turned and leapt on top of the narrow railing around the edge of the track. "Nobody told me Mena figured out how to calculate where we'd come back. If she wasn't such a saint I'd have sworn she was in on it," he said. "Lucas was making sure we went off the roof at just the right time. He had a private jet waiting to bring his ass back here."

Hannah laughed, losing her breath, then pushed to catch back up with him. It took another lap of chasing the bright white shoes on top of the thin railing before she could get out a winded question.

"Is Lucas here?" she said. "Can I meet him?" Maybe she'd have to bone up on the details of his life in the book beforehand, read the crib notes.

"Nah. Lucas cleared out yesterday. He's not the only one." Noble raised his eyebrows. "Not too many of the regular people here know about you, but rumors have spread with my kind. Guess I'm one of the few not afraid of you."

Hannah sped up, legs keeping pace with her sudden anger, indifferent to what was either blood or sweat trickling down the back of her leg. "Why would anyone leave because of me? It's not like I'm contagious," she said. "I'm not hiding behind doors with a needle out to get everybody."

"Maybe *you're* not," he said. At least that's what she thought he said. It was spoken in nearly a whisper. Then he was back to booming. "Like you could sneak up on anyone anyway. You run so heavy it's like you're pissed at the floor."

It was pretty clear Nobel had a death wish. He turned in his narrow track on the top of the railing and began running backward. "Don't take it personally," he said. "People here come and go all the time anyway, even without you running around like some kind of midget of death. There's only a couple of my kind that keep a permanent residence here anyway."

"So you live here? Have you been here for a long time, working for Joel?" Hannah sucked in a breath.

"*With* Joel. I don't work for anybody and I don't answer to anybody," he said. "I started out under another man's foot and I'll never forget it. After I died the first time, I came back full of righteous anger."

Her angry energy, on the other hand, had quickly run itself out and her pace had slowed back down. Not his. Noble sped up, moving faster backward on the rail than she could run facing forward on the track. "I tried to change the things that are wrong in the world with violence. That didn't work," he said. "The next time I tried to change things with peace. That didn't work either."

She was fighting to keep up now, listening to his voice. Noble was practically skipping backward. "I figured it out after a while; it takes a little bit of both. That was something Joel and I could agree on," he said. "In exchange for my help with things like picking you up or manhandling the Roman types out there when needed, Joel helps me. If I need someone to strong arm a policy through the pipes to eliminate some of the injustice in the world, he puts on the pressure. If I need a small army and a nuclear warhead to wipe some subjugating asshole off the map, Joel gives me that too. We have a mutually benefi—"

The track split. She didn't see it until the last second. Noble didn't see it at all. Before she could open her mouth to warn him, he missed the shift in the railing that divided the lanes and dropped like a stone, disappearing into the open air.

Hannah heard a sickening thud. She looked over the railing, trying to see where he'd fallen. Noble was on the ground, splayed out, both his legs bent at impossible angles. Tearing down the ramp, Hannah screamed for help on the way down. The sound just washed away in her wake. She skidded to a halt at the bottom of the final incline where he was lying.

A thick black pool was spreading out underneath him. The shape of his head was wrong—flattened. His eyes were wide open. One of them twitched.

Hannah reached a hand out toward him.

Except he wasn't there. The only thing in front of her now was a single white running shoe.

It didn't matter that it was almost certain Noble was alive somewhere in one piece, or that he'd ended up a splattered mess on the floor because he'd thoughtlessly thrown away another life. It didn't matter that it wasn't the first, second, or even third time she'd watched someone die in front of her and disappear. Watching someone die was horrifying. She leaned over and threw up.

——•••——

Her leg was asleep. Hannah had been sitting on the unforgiving floor without moving, just staring at the large white shoe, smelling the sour vomit. It was the pair of lean, pressed employees that walked by, looking down at her like she was on display in a freak show, that made her finally get up.

She was calmer at least. Joel would be back in their rooms by now, and he could probably assure her Noble was fine and tell her where he'd ended up. Hannah hoped it was smack in the middle of a field of cactuses as payback for showing off and making her witness his horrible death.

Grabbing a carton of water from the cooler to wash the foul taste from her mouth, Hannah looked for the closest way out. She brought up the map on the tablet and followed it toward the nearest elevator, which took her through the maze of a locker room and out the back.

She hadn't realized the lower floor of the fitness center was on ground level until she made a turn into a short stretch of hallway that ended with the elevator. On one side of her there was a wall, on the other a tall bank of windows with a door in the middle that led outside.

Pushing a shoulder against it, the door didn't budge. Pulling out her card, she waved it near the handle, grateful to hear it click. Nudging the door open with her hip, she stepped out.

It was warmer than she expected, with a breeze that smelled clean and fresh from being swept through the green trees that made a fence in front of her; she could hear the breeze rustling past the leaves. It helped clear her head, a little air that moved for a change, with no ceiling overhead.

"Freeze! Don't move!"

Hannah dropped the carton of water in surprise. Ignoring the order without thinking, she spun around to face the person who had barked it at her.

"I said freeze!" There was a man standing in front of her. He had a very large gun on a strap over his shoulder. It was leveled at her. "Now move."

She wished he would make up his mind before he shot her for not being able to move and stand still at the same time. Hannah took a slow step in the direction the ugly-looking muzzle was gesturing.

"Inside, now!" Lowering a hand slowly to the door handle, Hannah pulled on it. It was locked. She reached a hand toward her neck to pull out her card.

"Freeze! Keep your hands in sight!"

"You don't need to yell. Which do you want?" Hannah said. "If I can't get my card out, I can't get back inside."

"Freeze." He didn't answer her question, just kept the gun pointed at her midsection. She slowly dropped her hand back down to her side. He leaned his chin over and nudged a radio on his shoulder.

"If you just call—" Hannah reached for the door.

"I said freeze." His hand reached into his pocket and came out holding a thick black zip tie.

"No way. I don't think so. Just call—"

"Hands behind your back, now." He waved the gun, speaking into his radio again. "Restraining subject now. Security section 4, level main. Hold to open exterior door." He listened for a response, then turned to Hannah.

"Name and designation." *Was he talking to her?*

"Name and designation," he repeated.

Apparently he was.

"Hannah, Hannah Cirric."

"Designation?"

"I don't know, I just came out for—"

"Put your hands behind your back." He didn't wait for her to comply, just reached for one of her arms and twisted it behind her. She tried to stomp on his foot, but her running shoe hardly made a dent in his heavy boot.

"Security section 4, breech by Cirric, Hannah," he spoke into the

126

shoulder radio. There was a crackly confirmation on the other end. "Standing by." He held her arm painfully behind her for a moment, waiting for an answer. He got it quickly, though she couldn't make out the words. She heard him curse quietly, and her arms were released. There was a click as the door she'd been pushed up against unlocked.

"Ma'am." The man reached toward her, and she jerked away. "I'm so sorry, ma'am. Let's get you inside." His hand went past her to the door handle, pulling it open. "My apologies, ma'am. I'm very, very sorry. If you wouldn't mind just stepping inside, please." He held the door open, waiting for her to pass. "For your protection of course. Can I escort you back to your residence?"

Hannah got a look at his face when she scooted past him. He looked twice as scared as she'd just been. Good.

He bustled in behind her, letting the door close with a snap of the lock. She was shaken, but she wasn't going to wait around for an explanation, whether it was for her protection or not. The guard was still calling apologies after her when the elevator door slid closed.

———•••••———

"I was just about to come find you, you were gone so long." Joel was standing just outside the elevator door when it opened. "Noble called me as soon as he popped back up. He didn't give me the details, but he said that was the most exciting run he's had in a long time. Wants to go again tomorrow when he gets back." Joel held the door open for her and she slid past. When they were both inside, he closed it and leaned against it.

"You always hated to run when you were younger. I'm surprised you've taken …" His words trailed off when he saw the expression on her face. "Sweetheart, what's wrong. Was it that bad? Noble didn't give me the details, but he really didn't seem that upset."

She ducked into him and he wrapped his arms around her. At least she had that, after a day like today. "It was horrible, Joel. Noble fell and died right in front of me. It was one of the worst things I've ever seen," she said, talking into his shirt. "I was upset and I just wanted to

127

get some fresh air. I only went about two feet out the door and some guy with a gun started screaming at me to get back inside. He had my arms behind my back and he was going to handcuff me."

Joel's face darkened. "You were outside? I never imagined you would just walk out like that. I didn't even bother to warn you, it seemed too obvious. It's not safe." He pulled her arms from around his waist so he could look at her. "Roman and Amara aren't the only threats to you. Inside this compound is really the safest place for you to be."

Hannah frowned, stepping away from him. "I felt super safe with a man pointing a gun at me, yanking my arm out of its socket."

"He was just doing his job, making sure there was no one on the premises who shouldn't be. He didn't know who you were." Hannah wasn't convinced, and it must have shown on her face. "I'll admit," Joel said, "his reaction was extreme. I can have him terminated if you wish."

"What's the extension for the firing squad? Do you want to call or should I?"

"That's my girl, gentle as a lamb." Joel cracked a smile, but it fell quickly at the look on her face. "I'm sorry it upset you. Be angry at me if you want, but I'm doing everything I can to protect you. The security here is as tight as I can make it because I just got you back and I don't want anything to happen to you."

Hannah took a deep breath and tried to let go of some of the irritation. Joel looked so sad and concerned, and it was because he cared.

"Han, inside here is the safest place for you."

"Fine then. I'm super safe. And I'll be sure to file a request before I walk past any doors or windows, in case I accidentally get some fresh air on me. You might have to have me shot." She said it, but with fake attitude she knew he recognized.

"Don't be a smartass." He leaned over and gave her a kiss on the forehead. "I want you to be happy here. And I'm not going to keep you cooped up indoors. In fact, we have somewhere to be."

Hannah raised an eyebrow. "Where?"

"Grab a shower and get changed and you'll see. I have a surprise for you."

Hannah relented and went to get ready. She was still upset, but she wasn't really angry at Joel. She did appreciate that he'd brought her here and wanted to make her as safe as he could. It was good to think she might actually be done trying to stay out of harm's way. But something needled at her, because wrapped up in all the concern for her safety was the thought that her stay here might not be entirely voluntary.

13

"**C**lose your eyes."

Hannah had been tugging irritably at the hem of her dress, the extra fabric getting caught between her legs and tripping her. It had been waiting for her when she stepped out of the shower, laid out on the bed, the dark blue fabric like rippling water. But it was fussier than anything she would have chosen for herself and she'd been wrestling with it, not paying attention to where they were going until the elevator slowed to a halt. Joel stepped behind her and put his hands over her eyes. She heard the door slide open, and the still, canned air was spun away by a gust of wind. It was heavy with the scent of sweet clover, and it whipped the offending dress up around her knees.

"Surprise!"

Joel uncovered her eyes. They were on a terrace, high above the ground, in a niche carved from the side of the main building. In front of them was a pergola made from carved wood, rounded like a tunnel. Flowers and fairy lights dripped from the edges, over the small table and two chairs underneath.

"What's all this?" she asked.

He grabbed her hand and pulled her toward the table.

"Happy birthday," he said.

Hannah frowned. "I would say it's not my birthday, but since you're the only person who knows more about me than me, it probably is." She lowered herself slowly into the chair as he pushed it in.

Joel took a bottle of champagne from an ice bucket and unwrapped the foil from the neck. "It is your birthday. Your real birthday."

"What is today?" she said. "I don't even know what the date is. I feel like I've been living in a time warp."

"It's October the first." Joel held the bottle away from them. "We'll do this in the less sophisticated but way more celebratory manner." He pushed his thumbs against the cork and sent it flying with a pop, over the end of the terrace into the dark. Hopefully her favorite guard was still down there and it hit him in the eye.

Joel filled their glasses and sat down across from her. She looked up at the twinkling lights and inhaled the scents from the blanket of flowers woven together overhead. She took a deep breath and tried to process the information. Joel had just handed her another readjustment of everything she knew to be certain. She'd thought the world was moving along in a predictable direction, but once again, she was being made to look at everything differently.

Not that it's all bad, she thought, looking at Joel. He reached down to pull a shoebox-size container from under his chair, and when he came back up she reached out a hand and touched his arm. He might not be exactly the same, but Hannah thought she'd lost him for good, and she didn't know what would have happened to her if he hadn't turned up again like he had. Everyone else in her life was gone, but she had him back.

"Eager, are we?" he said.

"No," Hannah said. "It just hit me again. Seeing you alive."

"I'm going to have to spend a great deal of time making up for that. But as you're here, time is what we have."

She reached for the box but he held on to it, not letting her take it from his hand. "This gift, it's not an entirely happy one," he cautioned. "I'm sorry for that. But it's one you deserve. I just couldn't give it to you before now."

The box was light, made of tin, the dented surface covered in chipped, jade paint. The lid was outlined in faded gilt, and she set it aside and picked up the small stack of papers inside. She fingered the end of the frayed ribbon that held them together before she pulled it free from its neat bow. The section of the ribbon that had been under the stack was stained dark brown.

"It was in your hair when I found you," he said. Blood—hers or her mother's. She knew almost nothing about the night her father would have killed her if Joel hadn't intervened. Hannah gently set the ribbon aside.

On top of the pile was a slip of newsprint. The headlines screamed through the faded ink.

Brutal Double Murder Rocks Town, Infant Missing.

The article that followed was short, devoid of names and details. There was a grainy photo of an apartment building ringed with crime-scene tape. She set the clipping aside.

The next one felt like a blow to the chest, seeing their faces laid out in flat gray in front of her. Hannah had to force herself to let go of the breath she was holding in. Her mother and aunt. They had been murdered trying to protect her. Their images stared at her in faded black and white, looking like the ghosts they were.

There had only been a single photo of them in the house while she was growing up. It had been a happy one, her mother and aunt smiling, arms intertwined. The women in that photo were not the same as the ones in the clipping in her hand. Hannah looked at Joel.

He sat back and scratched his head. "I'm sorry, Han. The people in the picture you had, they came with the frame. Even if I'd had real photos besides these, I couldn't have given them to you."

"Why?" Hannah tried to absorb the faces in front of her. He'd had these all this time, while she'd created a picture in her head of her family based on a stock photo.

"Please listen." Joel gently took the picture and set it in front of her so he could take both of her hands. "Someday you were going to try to find out if you had more family out there. If you'd had their real pictures and started spreading them around, your father would have figured out who you were."

She stared down at the small, square photos, the faces in them so young they might have been taken from a high school yearbook. They were perfectly identical, that part had been true at least. It was nearly impossible to tell them apart, and the poor quality of the image had her straining her eyes for details that probably weren't there. They both had black, almond-shaped eyes under full eyebrows and thin, oval faces. Hannah found a little of herself in the straightness of their dark hair and the fullness of their lips.

"Which one was she?" Hannah said. Joel reached across and laid a finger on one of the faces. A stranger's face.

The champagne lost its bubbles, untouched while Hannah read through the short stack of articles, filled with every painful detail of the murders. The horror didn't end with the two deaths. In the months that followed, there were more deaths, and a number of unexplained disappearances. She turned the pages, not sure how they related to the original crime.

"He tried to find you," Joel said, "through their friends. And their family." Through *her* family. Trying to find Hannah, her father had tracked all these people down and killed them, one by one. She sat back, letting everything slip back into the box.

"I didn't give you this to hurt you, or break your heart. I just wanted you to know that you had family, roots."

"Roots? They were pulled up pretty thoroughly." Picking up her champagne glass, Hannah looked at it, then threw it as hard as she could against the waist-high railing that separated them from the darkness. Joel handed her his, and it followed. Joel picked up the glass charger in front of him and handed it to her. It went crashing into the brick and tinkled to the ground, all of it piling up in shiny shards.

"Do you want to do a chair through the door next?"

"Maybe in a little bit." Hannah slumped back into her chair.

"You have every right to be angry and hurt and throw things. You can't change the past. But you've changed the future, do you realize that? Michael will never do to anyone else what he did to you."

Hannah just stared at him for a moment. "You kept all of this from me and I get why. But everything about my life is different than what you made me believe. Was anything about my life real? Is Hannah even my name?" The expression on his face told her it wasn't.

"What is it then?"

"Lila," he said. She rolled it over in her head. Her name, but not her name at all. He was suddenly smiling an embarrassed smile.

"What?" she said. He leaned back and waved his arm. She saw a distant figure move and the door open.

"We're going to need another bottle."

Hannah waited impatiently while the table was reset and another bottle was opened. The waiter looked at the pile of broken glass but didn't say anything, just slipped away as silently as he'd come.

"Okay, out with it," Hannah said, sitting back and crossing her arms.

"I named you after a horse," Joel said. When she raised her eyebrows, he grimaced. "I probably shouldn't have led with that part. I had to give you a new identity to make you harder to find, so I changed your name and your date of birth. My meeting to arrange your new documents happened to be at a racetrack. I looked down at the program and there was this horse at ten-to-one odds."

"Because I was a long shot?"

Joel rolled his eyes at her. "Ten one, ring a bell? It caught my eye because it was your actual birthday. The horse's name was Hannah's Perfect Palindrome, out of Cirric Stables."

He looked at her. "In my first life—lives—words were more powerful. There was strength and magic in the balance. Words like that—palindromes—were more like spells; they provided protection. You needed all the protection you could get."

Looking past her, out into the night sky, Joel smiled. "I guess it worked, because here you are. And there was a little more magic in you than anyone expected."

———◆•◆•◆———

Hannah didn't feel very magical. She'd read through the gritty newspaper scraps of her life over and over again, all through the night.

Conceding defeat when the sun began shining insistently through the window, she dragged herself out of bed and was sitting drowsily on a bar stool, face buried in the book, when a quick double knock sounded on the door.

"I'll get it," Joel said, walking out of the office where he'd been closeted over his computer. He opened the door to let Mena in. "Morning, Mena. Hannah, I'm going to run down to ops for a while. What do you have planned for the rest of the day?"

What did she have planned? Not much, other than running endlessly around the track and possibly some more serious moping. "I'm going to head down to the fitness center, I guess."

"Sorry I've had to be in work mode so much. It'll be done soon, I promise," he said. "I'll be back for dinner. Call me if you need me." With a smile for Hannah and nod to Mena, he was gone.

"Is that Joel's mysterious book of the undead? He's always badgering us for information and trying to run down documentation about our previous lives. I gather it's quite the historical record by now."

Mena stood on her toes to look over Hannah's shoulder at the open book. Hannah reddened. It was currently open to Mena's section, and Hannah felt like an invader, reading about her life. Mena didn't appear to be bothered in the least.

"I should really find time to read it one of these days." Mena pulled the book over in front of her and turned to the beginning. She paused for a moment at the top of the list of names on the first page. Then she gave a little shake of her head and ran her finger down the list. "Heavens, I haven't seen her in ages," she murmured, stopping over one, "and him? No wonder. He always was up to no good."

Hannah got up to refill her coffee. When she sat back down Mena was reading through a page somewhere in the A's. Hannah guessed it was Asher from the location. Mena flopped a chunk of the book forward when Hannah came close.

"Is it all true?" Hannah said, looking at the curtain of dark hair falling down over the unlined face, struggling to believe the person standing next to her—if what she'd just been reading was indeed true—had been walking the earth for more than three hundred years; which, incidentally, made her a baby by immortal standards.

Mena turned the pages until she reached her own section and began to read, eyes ticking back and forth as she made her way speedily through the text.

"Well, let me see. It must be fairly accurate, because as you can imagine, Joel does very thorough research. Likely he's dug up things I don't recall myself. There are probably lives in here I've entirely forgotten."

Imagine having so many lives they'd cease to exist even as memories, Hannah thought, considering Mena's perfect profile while she read.

Mena's lips pulled up into an amused smile. "The most recent parts are surprisingly accurate, and certainly the parts Joel was around for. Though I only played a very small part in the death of the mad monk, and while we got up to all sorts of mischief in World War II, he's been far too modest and given me a great deal more credit than I deserve for the whole Hitler thing. I'm sure you suspect as much as anyone else it wasn't really a suicide. But really, I only theorized the most efficient delivery system. I didn't actually do the work."

Hannah just shook her head in amazement while Mena continued to scan the pages. "It's rather embarrassing really," she said, turning to Hannah and giving her an impish grin. "Now you know I'm a great big liar. I'm not actually a saint, and I had to tell a nun a little fib to explain a 'miracle' I may have performed. One should never lie, especially to a nun. But in my defense, it served a good purpose. I was able to save a man's life, and after, it was much easier to hand out medical assistance as long as I gave the credit to divine intervention. I'm really not as beatific as I'm being made out to be."

Somehow Hannah had a hard time believing that. She'd returned to Mena's pages because she had a face to put with the name, and because Mena was—by all Hannah's personal observations—an incredibly good person. Hannah had also been looking for signs of Asher, but that, she admitted only to herself. She was disappointed in that endeavor. Mena's story made no mention of Asher, except as an end note in the list of known associates. Maybe the romantic entanglements of immortals weren't interesting to each other, unless there was some great historical significance. Napoleon and Josephine had merited a great many pages.

Mena paused in her reading to turn to Hannah. "My original life deserved little attention, because it was far less nobly lived than this implies. I told you I'm no saint, but nor was I a great sinner. I lived a very average life." She looked up and smiled, but not at Hannah, more through her, peering off into the past. "I was lucky enough to be born with a measure of wealth and beauty that left me with no cares beyond where the waistlines were falling for the season and the availability of French silk. Until the smallpox epidemic began.

"Hannah, do not read these pages and draw the conclusion that I'm a noble creature," Mena said. "I did not venture out to help my fellow man in their suffering. I didn't even dare enter the rooms of my own parents or my little brother when the dread disease came to our door. And even then, when they were dead and I fell ill, at first I was more concerned about the possible damage to my complexion than anything else."

She was still smiling, but Mena's lips were frozen in place, as though they had stuck that way while her thoughts were wandering. "What a callow child I was; so very far gone before I even considered I might actually die. What a wasted life I had led. What foolishness and selfish pursuits had filled my days. I had not appreciated the immense value of a single day of life until then."

Her eyes flicked back to the page, then up to Hannah, Mena's blank stare now focused again. "And I did what all foolish children do. I tried to bargain with god. I swore if I was given another chance, I would not waste it. I wouldn't throw away the mind and body I had taken for granted. I would use every moment to help others."

She laughed then, a dry, short laugh that still managed to sound lovely, like wind chimes. "I really did think for a period my pleas had been heard and my prayers answered. And I strove to fulfill my end of the bargain. Now that I had my second chance, I used each moment. Funny, how having eschewed the schoolroom in my first sixteen years,

I found myself starving for knowledge so I could help better the world around me. I was hungry to enact change in my borrowed time."

Mena flipped idly through the pages, her voice dreamy. "I felt like I accomplished a great deal in that next life. I can tell you honestly that I was just as surprised the second time it happened, when I was granted yet another. But I stayed my path, deciding it was a blessing rather than a bargain I needed to fulfill my end of. I strove to do the same again—I've done the same each time. I still do; try to use each day as profitably as possible. Though I admit I've become selfish about it after so long. I love the knowledge that comes with time as much as the good it can bring to the world. I decided long ago that my condition, it wasn't anything as implausible as a miracle from above, but I feel the same need to try to ..."

Mena didn't say what, just trailed off and flipped the book closed with a thump. "I don't know why this was given to me. But this world, I devour it; the knowledge, the ability to fix the things that were thought to be unfixable, solve what were god's own mysteries, and mend everything that had been cracked. I'll do this until I'm gone. I know someday I will be. Nothing is meant to last forever."

Her pages don't do her justice, Hannah thought, watching Mena, her eyes now frozen on the scrolled cover of the book. Mena slid it back in front of Hannah, then reached down to her side and tossed something to Hannah. Not expecting it, Hannah didn't catch it, of course, and it tumbled to the ground.

"All water under the bridge now. I didn't stop by to rehash the past anyway. I just came to return this," Mena said, leaning over to retrieve the small black bag from the floor. "They finished processing the equipment from the mission to collect you. This was left over when they logged all the inventory."

When Hannah saw what it was, she laughed. "You're brave, bringing me this." It was her air pistol, in its bag with the dart parts and blood draw kits. She unzipped it and began to empty it.

"Brave?" Mena said. "I hope you wouldn't put a dart in me without asking, but then again, would it be the worst thing that could happen?"

Hannah paused in placing the dart gun and spare CO2 canisters on the countertop and looked at Mena, who was staring out the window toward the naked stone peaks. Today the mountains were hiding, tucked away behind a tonsure of wispy clouds.

"I wouldn't," Hannah said. "And couldn't anyway. I'm short on supplies. Do you think there are any aero darts around here somewhere?" They seemed to have everything else. "I swear I won't poke you with one."

"I believe you," Mena said. "I'm sure there are some in munitions or medical. You know, I hadn't thought about it much for a very long time, the possibility of growing old and dying. I don't think I'm wired to dwell on unlikely scenarios. But recently, I've considered it." With that her attention snapped back. "But not today anyway. Unless you're in a particularly bad mood. Anyway, I have work to do."

Hannah picked up the air gun and opened the chamber, looking straight through it, seeing only empty air. "This was loaded. I gave two darts to Paige and Joel to use on Amara and Roman. That left me one in the chamber. It was a little old, but it was the only one I had left."

Mena looked down the empty barrel Hannah was holding out and shrugged. "Maybe they got rid of it when they broke down the equipment that came back. Old blood can be dangerous. It was probably discarded as medical waste."

Maybe. Hannah pulled everything out of the bag. She tipped it upside down and gave it a shake. Maybe the missing cartridge had worked its way to the bottom.

There was no dart, but something else slid out and landed in her lap. It slithered over her leg and onto the floor, landing on the tile with a clink. Mena reached down and picked it up—a teardrop-shaped pendant on a thin silver chain. Looking at it for a moment, Mena handed it over to Hannah.

"How did this get in here?" Hannah ran her thumb over the surface, feeling the gentle irregularity of the worn design. This was Asher's necklace, the one he'd given her. It had belonged to his wife, long long ago in his first life. It had originally been part of a cup, the valuable silver shaved away a little at a time until the oblong in her hand was all that remained.

Hannah had left it behind when she walked away from his house in Savannah. Fumbling slightly, she undid the tiny clasp and put it on, tucking it into her shirt. It felt like a lead weight resting directly over her heart.

"It must have come in with the bag," Mena said. "After an operation everything relevant is retrieved and sealed, then brought back here to be cataloged. Nothing would have been put in the bag after that. Whoever processed it must have assumed you put it there for safekeeping and left it."

If that was true, Asher must have slipped it in at some point when they were in the tower.

"That belonged to Asher, did it not?" Mena said. Hannah ducked her head instead of answering, busying herself with putting everything neatly back into the little bag. She knew about Asher and Mena. They had a past—a very long one she couldn't compete with—having only one short little life. "Maybe it was fate the two of you should meet," Mena said.

"Fate?" Hannah said. "You don't seem like the type to really believe in fate."

Mena's chair scraped out and she stood up next to Hannah. "True, maybe fate is too unscientific a term. Maybe it's a natural predetermination of sorts. You are aware Asher is the first of us?"

Hannah looked up. "He isn't though, is he? I've heard him mention at least one of you that's from before his time."

One corner of Mena's mouth pulled up into an entertained grin.

"Walks on water, loaves and fishes, funny sandals?" Mena said. "An entertaining theory. Entertaining enough I spent a great deal of time trying to verify it, and I assure you, he wasn't one of us. Though I guess if my own existence is an indication, anything is possible in this wide world. But from what can be empirically proven, Asher is the oldest being on Earth—by minutes only, of course; Amara was close on his heels. But it's interesting you and he should have met, since he was the beginning, and you, it seems, are the end. Maybe Mother Nature has finally decided to close the loop. She doesn't tolerate loose ends."

"But I'm not really the end," Hannah said. "I'm human and I'm only going to live so long. Even if every one of you that's around now decided you'd had enough and asked for a blood donation, there would just be more after I'm gone. I'm not really the end, more like a hiccup."

"Since there hasn't been a new occurrence of someone like me in more than a hundred years," Mena said, "I think it's a safe bet this is it. There's no way of knowing what the future holds, but it appears to me something put you and Asher together, and for a reason. No loose ends."

"You really think that?" Hannah said. Something about how they'd met, the way they kept meeting, was definitely more than just chance.

Mena shrugged. "It makes as much sense as anything else, more than a great deal of other lines of thinking I've considered. People like me are an anomaly. You—you're also an anomaly. We are both a serious diversion from mankind's regular path. Divergences from the path are always corrected eventually."

Hannah, weighing the bag that held the dart gun in her hand, wondered if it was the case. Her blood changed things; that much was true. But was it really a correction? Yes, it could undo bad things. But it undid good things as well. People like Mena and Asher and others Hannah had read about but hadn't met, they didn't need to be undone. It wasn't that simple. Hannah couldn't just chalk it up to nature, being the one responsible for which lifetime would be someone's last.

"I can stabilize that for you, if you'd like," Mena said. Hannah looked up at the quick change of subject.

"Stabilize what?"

"Your blood. Whole blood outside of a temperature-controlled environment is only safe for around twenty-four hours. I can't speak to the effectiveness of yours because without a chance to study it, I honestly have no idea how it works." She grinned at Hannah. "That is absolutely a hint. I would like nothing more than to find out what allows it to do what it does. But for your purposes—assuming it needs to be medically useable and in a liquid form at the very least—it's a reasonable supposition it wouldn't pose a threat to anyone beyond the twenty-four-hour mark."

She looked at Hannah's arm, the elbow still mottled with green bruises and a constellation of indifferently healed needle marks. "There are compounds that can extend its shelf life," she said, "at least keep it from coagulating for as long as a week. It would cut down on the needle damage."

Hannah couldn't argue with that. And while she didn't feel like she was in immediate danger here, she was still uneasy. This was a strange, sometimes violent place. Some of the people here had nothing in the world to fear but her, and she *was* in the same building as Roman and Amara. She wouldn't say no to a longer lasting way to keep herself safe in her pocket. Hannah nodded.

"Stop by my lab tomorrow morning." Mena pulled out her tablet and tapped at it. Hannah's vibrated on the counter. "I sent you the location and what time to come by. I'll draw some blood and process it for you. Maybe I'll be able to talk you into giving me a sample—for my own personal edification of course."

At least she'd asked first. It had been a forced donation situation up until this point. Maybe Hannah would. "If I give you a sample, maybe you can find out why I'm such a weirdo."

Mena laughed. "Weirder than whom? I got hit by a bus last month in Rome and came back to life in Detroit."

Hannah smiled but didn't offer up the oddity she was thinking about, which was why Asher came back near her. But she threw out some of the others. "We can have a weirdness contest if you want," she said. She told Mena about how she tended to heal quickly, and how not a single animal had ever done anything but ignore her.

"If you heal a little faster than ordinary, it might just be part of the DNA you inherited from your father. People like me, we have an unfair advantage. If we're injured badly enough to expire, we come back. When it isn't terminal, we regenerate and repair nearly eighty-five percent faster than the average human. It might not be technically miraculous, but it's definitely accelerated."

Mena looked puzzled. "As for the animals, that is something new. I'd love to find out what causes it. If I had to hazard a guess, I'd say it's probably a natural defense of some kind. A great many species have developed ways to blend in with the world. It's a less violent, biological method of self-defense. Maybe it's a little something from Mother Nature to keep you safe from the world around you. The greater your chance at survival, the greater the chance you can deliver the payload nature intends."

It was all theoretical, but it was the best explanation Hannah had heard so far. Except Mena's whole theory made Hannah sound like a ticking time bomb, or a deadly virus.

14

Asher's necklace slapped against her sternum with every step, clapping against bone each time one of her feet hit the track. It felt like it was pounding itself into her skin. In the locker room, when she reached up to touch it, she was surprised when it lifted easily on its chain.

She was still idly toying with it as she walked through the rear of the fitness center and turned the sunny corner toward the elevator. Through the glass Hannah could see two figures in black fatigues facing the trees, both with a gun slung over their shoulder. Careful not to draw their attention, she crept up to the door and pulled out her card. When Hannah waved it by the handle she didn't hear the telltale click. She tried again. Silence.

Before the guards turned in her direction she slipped out of their line of sight. Maybe it was for her safety, but she felt like she was in a well-appointed cage. She found the nervous energy she'd burned off circling the track returning. Hannah turned to go.

Not back to the residence. She wasn't ready to return to bouncing around idly and staring out the windows. Hannah turned on her heel instead of getting in the elevator and started to wander aimlessly around the building. She didn't even look at the tablet, just shoved it in her pocket and walked. She wound around corners, went up and down levels. Maybe this would be her new activity of choice; seeing how lost she could get before Joel sent out a search party to bring her back for dinner. It would be like when she was a girl and he would shoo her outside to play, telling her not to come back in until it was time to eat.

Roving around the maze of hallways, taking elevators whenever they crossed her path, Hannah's seemingly random journey came to a halt outside a door. Giving in, she pulled out the tablet and looked at her small blip on the map, tapping it to bring up the location. Level 5 Detainment.

Pulling out her card and waving it in front of the door, she doubted it would get her in. Joel's original profession that her card would give her the run of the place had proved to be hollow. It no longer got her through every door; at least it didn't get her through some of them. It was a surprise when the lock disengaged.

Inside, the first pair of guards simply nodded, letting her pass by. Her card opened the second set of wire-webbed glass doors as well. The same guards who had stopped her stepped together, but one held out a screen for her to wave her card in front of. He looked at her, then back at the screen in his hand. Hannah started to retreat, but he nodded to his partner, and they stood aside to let her pass.

Hannah wasn't sure why she'd come here. It was like something had coaxed her to where she stood, reeled her in slowly on a string wound around the corners and down the long hallways. It led her in slow and silent steps until she came to a halt in front of Amara's cell.

It hardly seemed possible in such a short time, but Amara looked even more emaciated and insubstantial than she had a few days ago. Her lank hair had grown more dreadlocked and tangled and her cheekbones jutted sharply, dark hollows beneath them.

She was no longer huddled in the corner.

Amara was staring straight forward at the glass, into the darkness of the hall beyond her enclosure, like she hadn't seen Hannah step in front of her. Amara stood completely still, not even appearing to breathe. Neither of them moved, Amara's silvery blue eyes just drilled holes through the bulletproof glass without blinking. The expression was the same as she remembered, icy and cruel.

Hannah backed up involuntarily into the wall when Amara's lips suddenly pulled up into a smile. Her hand reached up, absent-mind-edly twirling a knotted strand of hair around her finger. Amara's lips formed a word Hannah couldn't hear. When Hannah shook her head, Amara stepped closer to the glass. She pointed to the buttons on the wall.

"No way in hell," Hannah said.

Her lips moved again, making words Hannah couldn't make out. Amara pointed again. Hannah's eye looked to the buttons. One read in clear, unmistakable print *Intercom.*

"Not going to happen." Hannah sat down on the bench against the wall and stared back at Amara. Amara, who was behind glass and now a frail, sick woman. One who had a lot to answer for. Hannah got back up slowly and looked at the buttons. They were very clearly labeled, and none of them opened the door. She couldn't accidentally let Amara out. She reached up and pushed the button.

"I wondered when you'd come visit me. I wouldn't have been able to resist seeing me in this state, if I were you," Amara said.

"Yeah, well I'm not you," Hannah said. But then again, here she stood.

"How is dear Joel keeping you? He and I go way back. I'm put out that your cage is so much larger than mine." Amara must have seen something in Hannah's expression, or she was simply toying with Hannah for her own amusement. "Oh, did that hurt?" she said.

Hannah reached up to hit the button again and turn off the syrupy voice.

"But don't you want to know what he said?" Amara said, her face contorting into a smile. Her lips were cracked and dry, raw bloody strips showing between the dead white parts of her skin. They hadn't lost their cruel twist. Hannah slowly dropped her hand.

"What who said?"

"Joel. Joel and his pretty little friend, when they came to visit my next-door neighbor. You do want to know what they said, don't you? When they came down to give Roman your little present, a little double tap to the veins to make sure it took." Amara returned to twirling her hair. When her finger caught in a knot she yanked it, jerking the hair out at the roots. Her insane smile didn't falter when she dropped the hank of hair with a bloody chunk of scalp attached and found another piece to twiddle with.

"Roman said 'thanks very much'," Amara said. "Then he laughed for about an hour because … well, he's crazy. And then he said something like 'nice try, since I'll never, never, never ever die.' Oh, and then he said he's going to get out of here and come find you and eat your face."

Hannah's eyes flicked over to Roman's cell, but she couldn't see him from the angle she was standing at. She didn't move to change that, turning her eyes back to Amara.

"Though I would say he's maybe just a teensy bit delusional. I'd say Roman's probably done for, if all your previous work is any indication. Don't tell him that though, I'd hate to burst his bubble."

Amara took one slithery step forward. Hannah tried not to react, but she felt her whole body leaning back, angling away from Amara.

"I didn't believe it either if I'm being honest—which I rarely am. It all happened so slowly. After a while the bruises don't heal quite so quickly, and you don't have quite as much pep in your step. Next thing you know, you start looking like shit." Amara tilted her head, smiling at Hannah with sickly false concern. "You look confused, honey. Are you disappointed it doesn't work faster? Did you think you could just send Joel down here to give Roman a shot, and the next day he'd look like me? Good things take time. You don't start looking this fabulous for months."

Amara twirled around in a circle like a little girl playing ballerina. The bland gray shirt, identical to the ones Hannah took from the gym to run in, filled with air and blew out around her shrunken frame like a tutu.

"Are you going to do the mystery guest next?" Amara spun to a stop and wobbled back to her position in front of the glass. "I bet you'll be surprised who's behind door number three. I'd say do him yourself, but I doubt you'd deny Joel his greatest pleasure. Being a buzzkill is his life's work, after all, and the reason he's keeping you here like a prize pig. It's pretty clear you're toeing the party line, what with sending a little bloody present down for Roman."

Amara suddenly went very still, standing straight and rigid like she had been when Hannah arrived. "Don't be such a pushover, Hannah Banana. Play hard to get and maybe you can get him to put you down here with me. Then we can be roomies. You can braid my hair and paint my toenails. And then—when you're sleeping—I'll snap—"

Reaching forward, Hannah slapped the intercom off. She stumbled backward when Amara lunged, throwing herself against the glass again, leaving another smeary pink film of blood. Amara was laughing, and even though the intercom was off Hannah could almost hear it, deep throated and rich, the way it had been when Amara was immortal. Amara smiled, then went still, staring blankly into Hannah once again.

Quickly, Hannah stepped forward and pressed another button, the one above the intercom. The glass went opaque, hiding Amara from sight.

Turning, Hannah found herself looking directly into Roman's face. He was no longer restrained and was standing on his own. Just standing, ramrod straight, arms at his side, staring forward.

"Finally, finally, finally we meet," he said.

Hannah jumped, and he grinned. She realized the most frightening thing about Roman was that he managed to appear completely endearing and attractive from a certain angle, until she turned her head just right and saw the wrongness in his skin and his eyes.

"We'll see, we'll see, we'll see. We, we, we, will see, see, see." His childish, cooing voice came sing-song through the intercom. She reached up to flick it off. Then she paused.

"What will we see?" Hannah said.

"How many of us will die, before he drains you dry. Die, die, die till you're dry, dry, dry." Roman smiled again, a cherub, then a demon, then a cherub again. She hoped to god he was human. But even if he was human, he was still the most frightening thing on Earth.

"You and he and a little friend. Which will come to the quickest—"

She slapped the intercom off and whited the glass. That was enough of that. Hannah made her way back out quickly, turning one last time to look behind her, seeing the two lit cells nearest her and the lone far-off block of light from the broken cell still burning beyond them. Something was still pulling at her, but she pulled back and left as quickly as she could.

* * *

Hannah stood under the scalding spray until her skin was a boiled-looking red. The feeling of disgust, the crawling sensation Amara's words had left, the sliminess of Roman's looks, they just wouldn't wash away. When she couldn't stand the heat any longer, she got out and ferreted a long cotton shirt out of the dresser. Hannah burrowed under the blankets even though there was still daylight peeking through the lace curtains. She heard the door open when Joel finally returned and came in to check on her, but she pretended to sleep.

When the door clicked shut and Hannah heard the footsteps fade away, she reached for the drawer of the side table and quietly pulled out the book. She looked for Joel's chapter again, knowing it wouldn't be there. She read Roman's and Amara's. She read Asher's again. There wasn't anything new. She knew there wouldn't be.

Eventually she really did fall asleep, drifting off with the book open over her chest. That night she didn't dream, to her relief, but she heard things; whispering in her ear, voices from far below her drifting up from underground. The words themselves were unintelligible—murky and mumbled—but almost close enough that if she could stop her breathing and pause her heart to dead silence, she could make out the words. She awoke in the dark of early morning, feeling haunted.

Even though her hair was still damp from her last shower, Hannah turned the water on and stepped in again, this time standing under a freezing spray until she couldn't take the cold. When she stepped out, she was shivering but clearer headed and resolved on speaking to Joel.

Her life might have been short compared to his, but in her relatively brief time she'd always been able to trust Joel. He clearly cared about her, or he wouldn't have gone to such great lengths to raise her and take care of her and bring her here to safety. She'd just ask him. What could it hurt? And anyway, the things that seemed so ominous in the dark were simpler in the light of day.

"Come on, sit. I made you breakfast," Joel said as soon as she padded into the kitchen, hair still dripping. "Voila!" He set a plate down on the table.

She couldn't help but break into a smile. "Overcooked scrambled eggs and burned home fries. Your specialty."

The familiar meal and Joel's inability to cook helped to loosen a little bit of what was so tightly wound. As poorly made as it was, the food in front of her smelled like home, like waking up in her bed in the house that was just a memory to the smell of butter browning and potatoes charring in cast iron, eaten sitting across from the same— mostly the same— face.

"Are you feeling okay? I was worried you were sick when you were in bed when I got in. I was going to send down for the doctor," he said, sitting down next to her.

"I'm fine. There's just a lot on my mind." Hannah picked up her coffee, soaking in the warmth against her palms. "I have a whole lot of questions."

"Then ask," he said. His smile was reassuring and she wondered again what was making her so hesitant. Still, best to start with an easy one.

"So the book, why aren't you in it?"

"Why am I not in the book?" Joel was looking at her intently, studying her eyes. "You never knew I was a writer, did you? And not just that book."

She shook her head no. While she was growing up he'd been a voracious reader, but she'd never seen him set a pen to paper for more than making a grocery list.

"I've always been a writer, since my very first life. I'm more or less prolific at any given time, depending on what my life permits. I had actually been thinking about taking some time away from here and starting something new while you were settling into life without me. The cabin— the one you went to with Asher—did you know it was mine?"

Hannah paused, fork in midair. She remembered it very clearly, the cabin not far from her home, the one Asher had rented after she'd hit him with her car, so he could keep an eye on her. It was where they'd fled to; not that it had done them a great deal of good. His sister had burned Hannah's house down and killed a dozen innocent people to flush them out.

Joel speared a forkful of potatoes, gesturing with the fork when he continued. "I swear to you, it was sheer coincidence he rented it. I built it after I had to leave you so I could come back and watch over you from time to time. I was going to fill the shelves up some more in my spare time."

"In the cabin," Hannah said, "you didn't write those ridiculous vampire and werewolf books, did you? Please tell me that wasn't you."

He frowned in mock consternation. "Laugh all you want, those books have been incredibly lucrative—though I didn't really write them for the money. I wrote them as a bit of a joke. I've always been amused by the way people will read things like that and let the characters worm their way into their head until they all but exist. They wouldn't blink if a good-looking vampire walked over and bit them on the neck, but not one of them would ever believe the truth about the person who wrote the book, even though the author is as unbelievable as the content."

"But that doesn't answer why you didn't write about yourself in the book," Hannah said.

Joel put down his fork suddenly and took the coffee mug out of her hands, gathering them in his. He turned them over to consider the palms, running his thumb over a thin scar, one of the many fading marks she'd accumulated in the time she thought he was dead. He reached over and touched the divot on her arm, where the bullet had torn away the flesh and skin the day Amara had nearly ended her life for good. His hands were unnaturally warm, but she still shivered at the thought.

"It never really felt right, I guess. I think it's because the lives in that book have always been never-ending stories until now," he said. "Over time I've added lines or chapters to the sections, changed names, updated last known locations. But they never felt like rounded out, full stories. Mine wouldn't be any different, and I could never bring myself to sit back and record my history with satisfaction, because a life that doesn't have an end will never have a real high point, or even an ultimate low. Or at least that's what I thought until recently."

He let go of her hands and sat back. "The greatest change could always be right around the corner. When I got wind of what was happening to you—when I rushed back and saw Amara standing in the middle of that snowy road, staring down the barrel at you—that was the lowest low, the thought I might not make the shot and she would kill you. Now, of all my lifetimes, this is the greatest height. You're sitting here, and we have the ability to permanently close the chapter on so many things. Maybe I'll write my own story down after all."

Joel got up suddenly and walked to the window to look out. Hannah spoke to his back.

"Some of the chapters are closed for good, or will be. Like Roman's. Did you go down and give him my blood again, to make sure he was human?"

"What makes you think that?" Joel turned around.

"I went down to the prison."

He shook his head, but he didn't look surprised, or angry. Instead he broke into a thin smile. "I give you free run of the place and you choose to go hang out in a prison. You haven't even tried the pool yet."

Joel shrugged it away, like none of it mattered. "I won't deny it. I did. I'm surprised it bothers you. It was what needed to be done; what was going to happen one way or another. Amara's capture didn't go the way it was planned, but she was clearly already human when we caught up with her and brought her in."

He came and sat down again. "You gave me your blood willingly enough when you were trying to get away from them. I just used the dart meant for Amara to guarantee Roman stayed where he was. It seemed a shame to waste it, and since there was no way to be sure Paige got enough of your blood into him to seal the deal, I didn't waste the opportunity. Now it's mission accomplished, and those nightmares down there, they're going to face their crimes. And someday, eventually, they're going to wink out of existence and hopefully be forgotten, all without harming another person."

It was true. He was right. Hannah had handed over the darts to save her own skin once already. And Roman was dangerous. For him to finally be human and behind glass was the way it should be, wasn't it?

The thought of him down there made the other question about the prison that had been in the front of her mind fly out of her mouth before she could stop it. "What about the other cell?" she asked.

"What other cell?"

"The lit-up cell. The third one. Who's in it?"

Maybe she was completely wrong and it really was empty and mal-functioning. The last person in the world she should probably believe was crazy Amara. But it wasn't just what Amara had said. It was what she was hearing, the urge she kept having to go there. Hannah just wanted to know.

"No one," Joel said. "What would make you think that?"

"The cell with the light on. Is there someone else in there?"

"Let's go." Joel stood up, motioning to the door.

"Go where?"

"Down to detainment. Or better yet, I'll save you the walk." Joel strode into his office and came back with the laptop in his hands and set it in front of her. He brought up a camera feed of the hallway of cells and made a call on his phone.

"Vicki, it's Joel. Could you please put me on a visual call."

Joel turned the screen toward Hannah and it flickered, the black screen going to an image of a woman's face, the gridded glass of the prison doors behind her head.

"Can you please turn your camera the other way and do a slow walk through of the cells. Make sure they're all set to transparent so I can see in."

The guard nodded and the view turned and began moving forward, the picture bouncing up and down with her steps. In the feed on the laptop, she saw the guard come into view, the phone in her hand pointed toward the cells. She watched the screen pass Amara, then Roman. It went by one empty cell after the next, all clear glass, all the way to the end. At the block wall, the view flipped.

"Thank you, Vicki." Joel turned off the feed. He didn't look upset, which made Hannah feel even more flushed and guilty. "I've kept plenty of the bad ones in there over the years, but right now it's just those two. Who did you think I was holding? Maybe Santa Claus down there without cause?" He laughed. "Believe me, when he's here, there's plenty cause. Sneaking into people's houses like that? Really."

She laughed, feeling foolish. "I'm sorry, Joel. I can't believe I even asked. It was just something Amara said that got to me."

He shook his head. "Amara is the last person you should be listening to. I won't keep you from going anywhere you want in here, but I wish you wouldn't go down there. Amara may be human, but she's not going to stop doing anything she can to hurt you and anyone else she can, as long as she's alive."

Joel was right. And what had she really thought? That Joel had Asher down there in a cell? She couldn't believe she'd even considered it. Maybe it was the crazy part of her that couldn't accept the fact that Asher was gone for good.

"No, I am sorry."

"There's no need to apologize. But I want you to think about it. There are going to be others down there, and soon. Bad people like Roman and Amara. Some of them even worse, if you can wrap your mind around that. When the time comes, are you going to be willing to do the right thing? Beings like that, they can't be allowed to continue on. And you're going to be the one to stop them."

He smiled when he said it, like it was light conversation, an easy decision such as what to wear or where to go to lunch. But he was telling her he wanted the same thing Amara had wanted, only with a shinier veneer. Joel was going to keep turning other immortals into humans. And he expected her to help him.

15

Joel disappeared after breakfast, leaving Hannah to spend most of the day sitting on the couch facing the windows. He'd returned to find her staring out, watching raindrops spatter against the glass, gather together, and trickle away in snaky lines. The dark clouds inched across the tops of the mountains but never completely cleared. Hannah felt hemmed in by the stormy gray that blocked out what little sun was left in the sky.

"I wish I could go outside," Hannah said, not turning when he sat down next to her. She'd run out the closest door into a torrential downpour, just for a breath of air and a chance to gather a little head space.

"Of course you can go outside," Joel said. "I hope you wouldn't want to go roaming around outside the ground floor where you might be in danger, but I can have your meals brought out to the terrace while I'm gone." She saw his smile drop in the reflection on the glass. "I just came up to tell you that I'm leaving soon. I'll be gone for a couple days. We picked up some information on a pair of really bad characters, and I want to act on it while they're in a good position to be intercepted."

He'd said there were going to be more people like Amara and Roman here soon. She just hadn't thought it would be this soon.

"Who is it?" she said. "What are you going to do with them?"

"Well, that was something I was hoping you'd help me with. You have to have thought about it." He turned to look at her and waited for her to face him before he spoke, his bright green eyes unusually serious. "These are bad people, Han. The two I'm going after, their names are

156

Delphine and Jeremiah. You have the book. Read about them. I think you'll understand what needs to be done."

She pulled her knees up to her chest as the rain began to hammer harder against the glass. The view grew muddied, blurring into a drab gray watercolor. Joel slid over and put his arm around her. She was tense, but she didn't pull away, giving in and settling her head familiarly against his chest.

Joel reached over and turned her chin up toward him. "These people have used their lives to bring nothing but hurt and pain to humanity. If you give me your blood, I can bring them back here and actually hold them until I know they won't just slip away again. They'll never have a chance to hurt anyone else, ever again. When I know they're human, I can turn them over to the proper authorities and justice can be served—at least for some of those they've hurt."

Hannah frowned. Her father, Gabe, Amara, Roman. She'd handed them all their deaths, indirectly at least, whether it happened immediately or was going to sometime in the future. Now she was being asked to do it again. They had all been dangerous people—she'd witnessed that firsthand. But what about these next ones? She didn't know anything about them. Was she supposed to just let Joel decide, be the executioner to his judge and jury?

He was still looking at her face expectantly. He grew stern when she didn't immediately answer.

"Think about it," he said. He looked away, staring out at the storm. "I know you'll come to realize what needs to be done. We should change them as soon as I get back, rather than risk losing them and having to start all over again. Remember, this isn't about you and your tender conscience. Lives are at stake. Innocent human lives. It's not a hard decision. It's not really a decision at all."

She got up and stood in front of the window, only able to see a smudgy version of herself. He came to stand beside her. "We won't be killing them," he said, "if that's what you're worried about—even though maybe they deserve it. We'll just be making sure they don't get another life after the one they're currently living, another life they could use to do more horrible things. It would make them the same as everyone else. One life is all any being should ever have."

Hannah wondered if he felt that applied to him. Would he be willing to end it all, grow old knowing when he died this time it was going to be for good? She opened her mouth to ask, but Joel shook off the seriousness with a toss of his head, like shaking off the rain outside.

"I'll speak to Mena," he said, walking across the room to leave. "She should be around, since she's not playing an active role in this mission. I'll have Noble stop by too, as soon as he gets back, to keep you occupied. The staff will get you whatever you want. Just page Charlie on my number." Hannah was sure Charlie was just waiting around to eagerly fulfill Hannah's every wish. "Just keep your card on you so you can come and go inside the buildings. I'll call you when I can."

Joel opened the door and started to step into the hallway but ducked back in.

"While I'm gone, think about it. Read the book. I expect you'll come to the correct conclusion before I get back." He clicked the door shut behind him.

———◆◆◆◆◆———

Hannah spent plenty of time thinking about what he'd asked. Too much time, and there wasn't a way for her to just turn off her thoughts. She settled for pacing a track in the carpet in front of the bank of windows, then gave up and got dressed.

Despite having been there for a few days, it still took a great deal of pulling out drawers and rifling through cabinets in the marble-covered bathroom for her to find everything she needed. It took just as long in the giant walk-in closet to find something to put on. Though every one of the neatly hung items was her size and clearly meant for her, they weren't anything like the things she usually wore; the sweats she'd been putting on from the locker room were the closest to anything Hannah would have picked out for herself. She'd decided to resort to putting on the clothes she'd slept in last night, but while she'd been running they'd disappeared from where she'd draped them over the bed, along with everything that had been stuffed in the hamper.

Giving up on finding a pair of sweatpants, she put on the softest thing she could find, pulling a stretchy navy shift over her head and going on the hunt for something to get her hair out of the way. A trip through the bathroom drawers revealed a single sprung blond bobby pin. She resorted to the fussy enameled hair picks she'd found on the dresser and jabbed one through her knot of hair.

She bobbled the second one and it cartwheeled out of sight, disappearing under the bed. With an exasperated sigh Hannah got down on her hands and knees and poked around for it. Reaching her arm out, she swatted the pick out from underneath the bed and jammed it into place.

When she brought her arm down there was something stuck to it, near her elbow. She brushed away the triangular snip of paper and headed out of the room. Something made her stop, and she bent down and picked it back up. Holding it on the tip of her finger, she eyed it, then with a shrug, flicked it away again and walked out of the bedroom to scare up something to eat.

"What are you doing here?" Hannah said, freezing in the doorway. The refrigerator door was hanging open, the top of a white-blonde head visible just above it.

"Wasting two doctoral degrees filling the refrigerator so that—god forbid—you don't have to go without disgusting animal products for five seconds while Joel's gone."

Charlie jammed a carton into the door and shut it with a little more force than necessary. Hannah had no idea what she'd done to Charlie to rate this kind of attitude.

Hannah's eyes narrowed. "Were you in my room?" The missing laundry wasn't the only thing in her room that seemed just slightly off. Nothing but the contents of the hamper were missing, but she got the feeling things were the slightest bit shifted, like they'd been rifled through.

"Your room?" Charlie gave a thin-lipped, false smile. "Why would I want to go into *your* room? Probably just housekeeping coming through to pick up after you. Can't have you overexerting yourself."

"What's your problem?" Hannah said.

Charlie didn't bother answering, just turned on her heels, yanking the grocery cart angrily across the room and out the door, slamming it behind her. Hannah shook her head in disbelief. She only stopped when there was a ring from her tablet. Hannah answered the call and Joel's face materialized on the screen. She could hear a loud engine and the chop of rotors in the background, but only darkness was visible around him.

"Joel, where are you?" she said.

He pulled back the camera a little and she could see the dim insides of a helicopter, maybe the same one she'd been rescued in. There was a line of seats along the wall, people in black fatigues strapped in. She recognized a familiar set of blue eyes. Davis waved. Hannah scowled and resisted the urge to give him the finger. Joel turned the camera back on himself.

"We're refueling and then we're leaving. Just wanted to check in before we took off. How are things there?" He took it off speaker so they could speak privately.

"I don't know if you've noticed, but Charlie is kind of a dick. I also think she might have a bit of a thing for you, since in your presence is the only time I've seen her display a human emotion," Hannah said. "Based on her attitude toward me, maybe a lot of a thing for you. I really don't need her to do things for me, especially if I have to worry about her stabbing me with a butter knife every time I turn around. I mean, she does realize you're my uncle, right?"

"Well, I'm not really your uncle. And I imagine she's just curious," Joel said. Curious? Murderous maybe. "She's one of the few people right now that's party to what you're capable of. Your presence is really going to change everything for Cosmos. It's a lot to take in for someone dedicated to what we do."

"Yeah, well, if she's all bowled over, she's got a funny way of showing it. Charlie really doesn't need to be waiting on me. I'm perfectly capable, and she's made it clear she's overqualified."

"She's completely loyal and I trust her implicitly. While you might not find her the warmest and cuddliest of people just yet, when you get to know her, I think you'll find her perfectly friendly. And I know you're entirely able to take care of yourself, but you don't need to anymore. No need to worry about laundry," he said, "or cleaning, or cooking unless you feel so inclined. I won't object to that if you feel like it—I miss your cooking, but otherwise, leave a list on the counter or ask Charlie and the staff will get you anything you ask for. Anything."

"Cushy lifestyle. Why did you make me do so many chores as a child? I feel like there should have been at the very least more allowance involved." She said it jokingly, but it was strange. She'd enjoyed their life; the rough, outdoorsy, self-sufficient style of it all. This place was as far as you could get from the kind of life she knew and loved and had always thought was just the way Joel was.

He laughed over the increasing background noise. "I made you learn how to put in a day's work because I didn't want you to grow up to be a brat. Obviously a failure on my part. I gotta go. I'll call you when we're bringing them back. Love you. Talk to you soon." The screen went black.

Ducking back into her room, Hannah immediately flung open the closet door and pulled out the shoes she had hidden Asher's necklace in. She panicked momentarily when she shook the wrong shoe and found it empty. When it was safely back in her hand she considered it for a moment. She'd tucked it away from Joel's notice. Hannah wasn't certain why she felt the need to hide it, or why she even cared, but something had made her take it off and keep it out of sight. She slipped it over her head now, holding it in her hand for a moment before dropping it into the neck of her dress. Her head jerked toward where she thought she heard something, a whisper or a low voice somewhere, but it was nothing at all.

———•◆••◆•———

Her meeting with Mena had slipped her mind. If she'd remembered before the tablet beeped to let her know she had an appointment, Hannah would have given herself more time to get there. Even with the map on her tablet painting her a red path from point A to point B, finding her way through the labyrinth of corridors had taken longer than she'd expected. She was huffing and puffing when she finally reached her destination, another unmarked door like all the others.

The door's appearance did nothing to prepare her for what was inside. The minute she entered, Hannah was suddenly disoriented, shrunken against the vast cave of a room in front of her.

The ceiling reached up to cathedral heights, and the room was longer than she could easily see, stretching back and out of sight. Compared to the dull gray of the hallways it was blindingly bright, the sterile, brilliant light bouncing back and forth through a grid of hundreds of rectangular glass cubicles stacked two-high, filled with equipment she couldn't begin to identify.

Figures in white coats were everywhere, heads bent low, deeply entrenched in their tasks. Hannah felt very awkward and out of place.

"Hannah! There you are. I was afraid you'd gotten lost."

Mena materialized from between a block of cubicles, waving Hannah forward and down the central aisle that ran between the workstations. As she ushered Hannah along, the people they passed either didn't notice them at all or looked up only briefly, nodding to Mena before diving back into what they were doing. It was pleasant to be completely unnoticed. She might see if she could start hanging out here.

"This place is enormous," Hannah said, looking above the second tier of cubicles at the humming blocks of equipment suspended from the ceiling. "What is all this?"

"My lab, though the word lab seems very tiny for a space like this. Laboratory is better, but that makes me sounds like a mad scientist," Mena said, grinning. "What it really is, is Joel's way of keeping me here as much as possible, so I can be convinced to get done all the things he wants me to." She laughed lightly. "It's flat out bribery, and I'm ashamed to admit, it generally works."

She pointed toward a glass cubicle filled with clear tubes emitting a strange red light, gesturing as though Hannah should know what it was. Hannah had no idea.

"If there's a piece of equipment I want," Mena said, "he gets it, along with the people who know how to use it. The only thing he's ever said no to me on is building a Hadron Collider underneath the place, but I'm still working on it. I'll soften him up eventually."

Mena paused and smiled at Hannah. "Both of us think we have the upper hand in this deal, but the truth is, we're both winning. A great deal of good gets done. He gets his nano locators and tranquilizers, and I get my vaccines and advancements in disease detection and prevention. This place has all the benefits, with none of the usual red tape associated with research and development."

Hannah's attention was pulled away by a flash of blond hair above a white lab coat in the corner of her eye. Her face pulled into a scowl. "Charlie is everywhere," Hannah said under her breath. Of course under her breath was like yelling to someone like Mena.

"Oh, Charlie has lab space here, though I'm not sure what she's currently working on. Heaven knows we have the room, and she's certainly brilliant. I'd love to steal her away to my staff, but she'd never leave Joel's side. She's wasted there really."

Hannah looked the direction Charlie had gone, less impressed with her brilliance in light of her general crappy demeanor.

Pausing before one of the workstations, Mena opened the door with her card and ushered Hannah inside. She pressed a button on the inside of the door to make it and the surrounding walls opaque. "Here we are, have a seat," she said.

It was a tiny office, no larger than any of the other cubicles. Nearly every surface was bare, except for a computer on the desktop and a paperweight holding down a precisely squared stack of paperwork. The paperweight was an oval of clear glass, in its very center a small ring of intricately braided hair, like a piece of old-fashioned mourning jewelry. It was a shade of honey blond Hannah would recognize any-where—the color of Asher's. Something twinged inside her.

She turned toward where Mena had opened a drawer and was pulling out a large plastic bag filled with sterilized blood draw equip-ment. "This won't take long," Mena said, "and I know you aren't afraid of needles. I'll just draw a couple of vials and have you out of here so you can get on with your day." She smiled, though Hannah thought her expression was tighter around the mouth than it was a moment ago. Maybe she was just imagining it. Or maybe Mena was vexed by the effort of finding a decent vein in Hannah's mangled arm.

Hannah watched the needle slide in. There was only a brief pinch, then a steady stream of blood filled the line and began to make its way into the tube. Mena stared at the red as it moved from Hannah's arm.

"Did Joel mention anything to you, about him giving Roman a dose of my blood, in case he's still … like you?"

Mena wasn't like Roman—that didn't sound right—but the com-parison didn't faze the figure in front of her.

"No, he didn't, though if I'd been paying attention, I could have saved him the trouble. Roman's human, has been since the moment they brought him in."

"How could you know that?" Hannah said. It had taken a lot longer to be certain in Amara's case.

"Temperature. If you weren't aware, people like me tend to run hot. We always register well in excess of a hundred degrees. I've never once encountered an exception, and we record the biological metrics on everyone from the time they're captured." Mena switched out the vial. "Both Roman and Amara have been showing a normal human temp the entire time. It didn't jump out at me until I was running over all the data collection on the cells. I'm sure Joel will be relieved to know. I'll tell him when he gets back. It will save a lot of guesswork and effort in the future."

"And it stayed that way, their temperatures?" The two in the cells were the first immortals introduced to her blood who had lived long enough to tell about it. She had a horrible fear it would wear off

164

sometime, and on a random morning she might wake up with Amara looking like her old inhuman self, bending over her bed with a knife and a smile.

"Worried about something other than their temperatures going back to abnormal?" Mena asked, reading Hannah's mind. "Granted—like I've said before—none of how your blood works makes a great deal of sense, but if Amara hasn't turned back after this long, I can't imagine what would alter that. And look how many years your father lived as a human before he died." That was a reassuring point. Speaking of Michael. "Do you think my blood works in reverse?" Hannah looked at the dark head bent over her arm. Mena sat there frozen, with the needle she'd just removed from Hannah's arm in her hand, staring off toward her desk. When a small drop of Hannah's blood leaked out, falling to the white tile in a perfectly round red dot, she jumped.

"Heavens, I'm sorry," Mena said. "In reverse?" She reached down with a piece of gauze to carefully mop up the dot of blood.

Hannah nodded. "Michael seemed to think it would turn him back into what he was before, though maybe it was just desperation. Do you think there's any truth to it?"

Mena didn't answer. She seemed to have become the slightest bit distracted, or was deep in thought.

"It's an interesting idea, isn't it? I would say there isn't any reason to think it would work in reverse, but because I can't know why your blood does what it does in the first place, there's no real way to know. I won't pretend I'm not curious about looking at your blood to see if there's any discernible difference between yours and any other person's," Mena said.

"So your guess is as good as mine?"

Mena smiled, recovering her usual cheer as she stuck a bubble gum pink Band-Aid on Hannah's arm. "Exactly. The only way to know for certain would be to inject someone who has already been in contact with your blood and is now fully human. Maybe I'll ask around for some volunteers."

"It would have to be a volunteer," Hannah said. Finding one of those didn't seem likely. "As glad as I am Roman and Amara are regular old humans, I'm not sure how I feel about all this turning people against their wishes. Not everybody deserves that, and I don't like the idea of being the one ending someone's run at being immortal."

"Immortal?" Mena bagged the vials and sealed them, tucking them into the pocket of her lab coat. She hadn't bitten on the part Hannah was hoping, fishing for a little direction from someone who had a bit more invested in the eternity thing and was doing good deeds with all their bonus lives.

"I've never been able to agree with the word immortal," Mena said. "The definition of immortality is the ability to live forever. But we don't live forever. We die all the time."

"What would you call it then? Reternal? Remortal? Nobody seems to have a better word for it, except maybe Asher," Hannah said, sliding out of her chair and standing while Mena hit the button to make the glass transparent again.

Mena let out a girlish, contagious giggle, making Hannah smile. "Asher with a better word than immortal? He must be waxing poetic in his old age. He never had an extra word for anything, or anyone, that I recall. Never was much of a talker. And what pray tell does Asher, in all his ancient wisdom, think?"

Funny, he seemed to talk enough, but maybe it just appeared that way to Hannah, who was not incredibly verbose herself. She could still picture him very clearly telling her all about what he was, sitting in the tiny house that was no more. Her smile faded, thinking about him. It was a strange feeling, knowing she might never see him again, yet feeling like he was looking over her shoulder.

"Asher thinks you're like an echo," Hannah said. "After the original person, you're only versions of yourself, becoming less distinct over time."

"Well, I give him points for imagination," Mena said, "but he is absolutely scientifically incorrect. An echo loses energy. Echoes decay. They're a single sound that's slowly reflected back at the sender from a great distance." She looked at Hannah and smiled. "An echo is only

166

a poorer, fainter version of the original, and I don't think that sounds like us at all."

She stood up and leaned against her desk, looking down at the paperweight. "If you're inclined to use sound as a metaphor, we would be more like a reverberation. Reverberations are a prolonged sound, the original sound mingled with its reflection. The end result is richer and fuller."

"Doesn't have the same ring to it though."

Mena rolled her eyes. "You're as bad as he is. I don't know about Asher, but I don't feel like I'm decaying and becoming less distinct with time. Quite the opposite," she said. "I feel like the layers of time have allowed me to gain more knowledge and flesh out my ideas. Besides, an echo insinuates a longer period before it returns to its point of origination. A reverberation is quicker, more confined. And we come back in an instant."

"Fine, smarty pants, you're a reverberation." Hannah smiled as Mena held the door open for her. She turned to look back as she wove her way out of the maze of glass cubes, to see Mena still standing— deep in thought—hand tucked in the pocket that held the vials of Hannah's blood.

16

Hannah's pocket vibrated as she stepped out of the elevator at the top floor. She pulled out the tablet and saw Joel's name scrolling across it.

"Just checking in." He waved in the video that opened up on the screen, somewhere outside this time with bright blue sky framing his dark hair, a palm tree poking into the picture on one side. She wondered where he was; clearly nowhere nearby, compared to the foggy grayness outside the windows where she was.

"Everything is going like clockwork," he said. "We have a little more work to do wrapping things up, but as long as everything continues to go as planned we'll be heading back soon." The sound of a murmured voice in the background of the call drew his attention. "Shoot, I have to go. See you soon." The screen went dark.

His face had been so bright—Joel looked elated. Hannah was struggling to share his feelings. She flopped down on the couch and stared up at the ceiling.

Joel seemed to think the whole reason she existed and could do what she did was to end the existence of people like him. Hannah could try to convince herself to agree with him all she wanted, to believe no one really deserved more than one life, but what gave her the right to play god and hand out arbitrary justice one vial of blood at a time? But being so hesitant to make the choice for the people Joel was bringing in made her feel like a hypocrite. She'd been willing to give up her blood readily enough to save her own skin.

It was hard to believe the continued immortality of someone like Amara was anything other than a curse on the world. So maybe it wasn't the bad ones that were giving her pause; maybe it was the good ones. For every Amara, there was an Asher. For each Roman, a Mena or a Noble. What about them?

Where was the line, if she started handing over her blood for use on anyone Joel deemed dangerous? Where did it stop, and who got to pick and choose who received—when all was said and done—a death sentence?

Getting up, Hannah went to her bedside table and pulled out the book yet again. It seemed abnormally heavy in her hand, and she brought it out to the kitchen and dropped it on the table with a thud. Flipping it open, she paged to the first of the names she was looking for. She found it easily, with its clipped corner. Delphine, who was possibly on her way here right now.

Hannah had read the pages the first time she'd plowed through the book. Even though she knew the people listed inside were all real, the ones she didn't know had seemed more like fiction and hadn't stuck as well in her memory. While she vaguely recalled the horrors on Delphine's pages, Hannah hadn't read it focusing on having to possibly end her.

Reading it now more carefully made Hannah shudder. The woman described was a monster, there were no two ways about it. She'd been responsible for the deaths of hundreds of people, nearly all of them young women she'd tortured and murdered, starting as early as the sixteen hundreds. And that was in Delphine's *first* life, before she even knew what she was. She hadn't needed years beyond measure to warp her mind—she'd started out that way.

And she never strayed from her bloody path. As soon as Delphine returned to life she began again, turning up in Russia in the seventeen hundreds, this time killing more than a hundred people—probably more, since those were only the ones that could be proven. She disappeared from her incarceration yet again, this time appearing in the United States where Joel had caught up with her.

The final paragraphs of her story were more of the same, filled with cruelty and lacking in remorse.

> *As had been her modus operandi in her previous appearance, Delphine used the wealth she had accumulated over her long lifetime and the power it bought her to hide her murderous inclinations. When an attempt to intercept and contain her once again was made, her unwillingness to comply and the consequent struggle resulted in a fire. At this point her crimes were publicly discovered, as a number of her victims were still contained on the premises in various states of decomposition, all having been subject to varying degrees of torture. It was a habit she had repeated, either unconcerned about the discovery of her deeds or because she drew some enjoyment from proximity to her victims, a trait seen in similar instances of serial murder, both in human and non-human perpetrators.*

> *The subject has since this time been under near-constant surveillance, which has not prevented her from carrying out crimes against the population but has mitigated the impact on humanity, by preventing her from establishing a base of operations from which to continue her habitual path.*

If even a fraction of it was true, could Hannah question the need for Delphine to be stopped? Getting up from the table, Hannah stalked her way around the island to pour herself a glass of water and pace while she drank it. Maybe she needed to get over her righteous indignation, let Joel do what he wished.

Sitting back down, Hannah found the next section she was looking for—Jeremiah. The name only stuck out for her because he was listed as one of Asher's known associates. That didn't make him good; Gabe had been on the list as well, and he turned out to be a grade-A psycho. Maybe Asher had very poor judgment when it came to his friends.

She was only a paragraph in when the door flew open, making Hannah jump, her elbow hitting the glass of water and knocking it over. She quickly shoved the book aside, only narrowly avoiding dousing the pages.

"You could knock first," Hannah said. *Or not come in at all*, she added mentally, scowling at Charlie who had walked in without speaking, coming to stand in front of Hannah. Charlie looked disapprovingly over Hannah, still in the sweatpants she'd worn to the gym, hair in a tangle over her shoulders. Charlie was neatly dressed in crisp, head-to-toe black, from the stiff collar of her shirt to the pointy tips of her polished boots. Her hair was scraped back so tightly Hannah wondered if it was responsible for the jut of her cheekbones through her skin.

"Joel insisted I check up on you periodically and escort you to the dining room if you choose to eat there. Though I'd recommend putting on something a little more—well, a little more anything if you're going to leave the room, so they don't mistake you for a homeless person and have you removed." Charlie sneered at Hannah's rumpled appearance.

"No thanks. I think I'll stay here." Hannah sat back and crossed her arms. She had no desire to sit in the fussy dining room and eat, especially if it included the pleasure of Charlie's company.

Charlie looked down at the puddle on the table, then walked into the kitchen and opened a drawer. She came back and snatched up the book, wiping every trace of dampness away with a dish towel before setting the book gently back down.

"You seem to know your way around here pretty well," Hannah said, watching Charlie take the wet dish towel and hang it precisely on a little drying rack that folded cleverly out from the end of the island.

She ignored Hannah's remark. "How about you show a little more respect for the great deal of work that went into this volume, and don't treat it like some trashy romance novel of the variety I'm sure you probably live for."

Taking one last pinched look at Hannah, Charlie turned to go. Hannah resisted the urge to reach out and pull a smile onto Charlie's face by yanking as hard as she could on the tight knob of hair at her neck, kept in place by an annoyingly neat rank of blond bobby pins.

The door slammed shut and Hannah returned to the book with a sigh. Charlie's arrival and the growing suspicion there was more going on between Joel and Charlie than she was party to had distracted her momentarily. Hannah pulled the book in front of her and found the entry for Jeremiah.

Once again, Hannah didn't remember the exact details clearly from her first reading. There were a great many people in the book, both good and bad, but still she was surprised nothing of what she was reading now had found its way permanently into her memory. Maybe some pages had stuck together and Hannah had skipped over it; it was a thin section after all. She read it through carefully now.

How did I not remember someone so absolutely crazy? she thought. She must have missed it somehow. Brutal, random murders scattered across place and time. Intentional fires set at factories packed with workers, more at a string of orphanages. Six more at churches, all with people intentionally trapped inside. When she turned the page, Hannah blanched at the description of the murder of a young woman in California, brutally killed, mutilated, bisected. A paragraph later, information pointed toward Jeremiah being the Zodiac Killer.

It was disturbing, frightening that Joel was bringing in such a clearly dangerous man, and dangerous in the present, not just in history. Not that crimes in the past made a figure any less horrifying, but the knowledge they were almost certain to continue if he wasn't stopped was chilling. *How had she missed him?*

She turned his last page and the leaf fell in place. Hannah flipped it back and forth again, looking at the paper. There was a difference in the edges of the pages in Jeremiah's section, only the slightest bit; maybe it was nothing. Getting up, she carried the book to the window to compare the pages again in a different light. The tips of the pages—where they were clipped to mark his terrible tendencies—were angled just the slightest bit differently than the other sections like it. In the light, she noticed something else. There was a subtle difference in the inks. Flipping back to the beginning of Jeremiah's section, comparing it to the pages before it, she ran her finger up the page to the triangle snipped from the corner that marked him as evil.

Holding the book open, she took it with her to the bedroom and lay it on the bed, then got down on her hands and knees and ran her hand across the carpet until she found it. A tiny triangle of paper in front of the dresser where she'd brushed it off her arm. Picking it up between two fingers, she laid it against the corner of the page. Hannah could see immediately this was where it had been cut from.

She picked up the book again and looked at it, turning it over in her hands. Maybe she hadn't remembered Jeremiah's section of the book clearly because it hadn't been there before, at least not like it was now. Jeremiah had been marked as one of those who absolutely had to be made human for the sake of innocent lives, at the same time as Joel was bringing him back and convincing Hannah to hand over her blood to end him.

There were so many things going on that weren't exactly what they seemed. Hannah was being manipulated, that much was clear, but she didn't know why. But without a doubt, for whatever reason, Joel was lying to her.

<hr />

Hannah let the hot water soak into her bones, floating weightlessly in the enormous marble tub, trying to unravel things in her head. It wasn't working very well. She'd picked up the tablet a dozen times to call Joel and ask him what was going on, but each time she'd put it down without pushing a button. She very, *very* briefly thought about paging Charlie and getting her to come up under some false pretense so she could fish for information, but Hannah wasn't that desperate. And Charlie might be a jerk, but she was a smart jerk; chances were she'd see right through anything Hannah said.

Finally Hannah had called Mena's lab. Mena seemed trustworthy, and she had a blunt, businesslike honesty. She might be willing to shed some light on things, at the very least confirming Jeremiah was or wasn't what his entry in the book now portrayed.

After countless rings the call had finally been answered, but not by Mena. The harried assistant who picked up the phone had no idea where Mena might be—she had just missed a meeting, which was unlike Mena—but he promised to relay Hannah's message. She had the tablet propped up on the side of the tub in case Mena called back.

Suddenly Hannah was slammed from above, held down in the tub by an immense weight. Her mouth opened and she gasped for air, sucking in a mouthful of hot, soapy water instead. She pushed against what was crushing her into the marble, desperately trying to claw her way toward the surface.

All at once the weight lifted. She felt herself being dragged up and out of the water. Then she was crushed again. This time by two giant arms.

Hannah knew it was him before she could blink the stinging soap from her eyes.

"Hannah, thank god," she heard Asher say through the sound of her sputtering.

He was naked.

While Hannah was accustomed to him showing up that way, she wasn't generally in the same state when it happened. Asher must have abruptly realized the same thing because he let her go for a moment. He was giving her a damp, towel-wrapped hug a moment later. In very un-Asher-like fashion, he didn't let her go quickly but held on to her tightly, squeezing her against him until her ribs protested.

It was like letting go of a breath that had been held too long, seeing him again, watching his blue-gray eyes as he examined her. He reached down and pulled his necklace out from where it was tucked under the edge of her towel. "I am glad you found this. I did not get a moment to speak to you and return it in the way I intended," he said. "There was too much scheming and subterfuge going on, and then, there was no time. I slipped it into your bag at the last moment."

"Ash, what happened?" Hannah said. "Why are you here?" His eyes narrowed and she quickly defended her words. "That's not what I mean. God knows I'm so glad you are, especially now. I just didn't think I'd see you again after you decided not to come with me." She pulled her head away from where it lay against his chest and leaned her head back to look at him.

Not that he had a choice in coming here now. Happy as she was to have him here, his showing up so suddenly and stark naked meant something had gone horribly, fatally wrong. At least he didn't look upset to be where he was.

"I was not given the choice not to come anywhere. The last thing I remember clearly was lying on the ground after the tower fell, keeping watch over Amara and hoping I could manage to stop her if she got up and tried to escape again. After that, nothing. I have no idea where *here* is."

He pushed Hannah away to arm's length, looking her over. Asher was probably searching her for any new injuries, which she usually had. He noticed the old divot on her arm from where Amara had shot her and rubbed his fingers across it, frowning at the memory.

"We're in Joel's facility in South Dakota," Hannah said. "But how is it possible you're just showing up here now? If you died at the tower … that was days ago?"

Asher shook his head. "I do not know. It is all a muddle. Sometimes everything was bright, and I thought I heard your voice. I considered maybe I had finally passed on for good. Then the light and your voice would fade out, and there were ghosts of people in gray and white. And snakes, always snakes." The look on his face was confused, pained. "I was frozen, Hannah, and I could not move, but it was all so indistinct and outside of time. I cannot recall any of it with clarity, until a moment ago when I found myself here with you."

Hannah put her hands on her temples, rubbing them, thinking. She rescued her towel when it started to slide. "Hold on a second." Opening the door, she rummaged around and threw on a shirt. There wasn't anything that would fit him, so she tossed him a blanket then sat down on the floor, leaning against the footboard. Asher slid down beside her, familiar and warm against her arm. A second later he drew away and looked at her, confused and horrified.

"What is this?" he asked, pointing at her.

"Um, it's a T-shirt. Did you hit your head on the tub or something?"

"What is this?" He stabbed a finger into the ouroboros logo on her chest.

"It's an ouroboros, you know the—"

"Snakes. The ghosts in gray and white, they were all wearing this. This same snake."

Hannah's eyes widened, her hand clapped over her mouth. "Oh shit," she said. "Oh shit," she said again, unable to cobble together anything more succinct until she took a deep breath and shook her head. "You were here. Damn it, I think I knew you were. I couldn't explain it, but I knew. There's a prison here. Your sister's in it, and Roman too. There was another cell they said was broken, and Joel swore there was no one inside. He even showed me a video to prove it was empty."

It must have been a lie, a setup to fool her. How hard could it have been, with all the technology at Joel's disposal, and her, trusting and gullible when it came to him. Another lie on the layers of them Joel had built up. But why?

Maybe to get her to do exactly what he wanted her to do, and to keep anything or anyone from getting in his way. Now that Asher was here, and she was sure he had been all along, Hannah had no more doubts about Joel's falseness. It was like being kicked in the stomach, and she had to force the hot bile back down into her throat.

"I should have never believed him," she said. "They must have picked you up at the same time they did your sister." Hannah sat back, leaning her head against the wooden bed with a clunk.

"I must have been kept under sedation for some days," Asher said. "You know how difficult it is to keep us in that fashion indefinitely. Since I am here now it must have finally been too much, and it killed me."

Hannah didn't understand it. Joel was supposed to be a good guy, keeping the world safe from bad people. He'd always been. She'd known him her entire life. He wouldn't do something like this. Asher wasn't a threat to anyone.

She didn't want to believe Joel would be responsible for something like this, but clearly he was. This was a lie, like her entire life had been.

Hannah's eyes widened. "Ash, we have to get you out of here. If Joel has been keeping you here, he'll throw you right back in if he finds you. He'll be back soon, maybe even tonight. He went out to bring in two more of you."

"Who has he gone after?"

"A woman—Delphine—and someone named Jeremiah."

Asher's eyes widened. "Delphine, she is nearly as bad as my sister," he said, "but Jeremiah, I know him. He is a good man."

"If that's true, why would Joel be bringing him here? He swears he's trying to protect the world from the bad immortals, and there wasn't any reason for you to be here, since your sister was contained and not a threat to anyone anymore."

Asher shook his head and scowled. "I would not have just abandoned you, Hannah. I never would. I am sorry you would think that." None of it mattered now. They had more pressing matters to deal with. Hannah got up, went to her closet, and began pulling on clothes, the modesty of a moment ago out the window as she struggled her damp self into her pants.

"We have to get you out of here." She fished around in the pile of dirty clothing on the floor and pulled out her key card, retrieving the tablet from the bathroom.

"Me? *We* have to get out of here," Asher said. He looked toward the window for the first time and saw their location, high in the air behind the thick, protective glass. "Which will not be possible from this room, I see."

She opened the map on the tablet and tossed it to him. "There's cameras wherever you look in this place, except in here. We could try to make a run for it and bulldoze our way out, but I don't think there's a chance in hell that will work. If you walk out that door someone is going to see you, and I imagine the first thing they're going to do is call Joel. Best-case scenario, one of the million armed guards will shoot you. But for all we know, Joel will come right back here and give you a shot of my blood purely out of spite."

"He has your blood?"

"Maybe not in his back pocket, but it's floating around here. And even if he didn't, what's to keep him from taking it any time, if he really wants to? If he'll keep you in a cell and lie about it, then there's an even chance he'll figure out how to take it whether I'm willing or not, isn't there? And clearly now we're past the willing part. All the wanting me to decide, it's bull. I don't think he intended me to have a choice, when it came down to it."

No, they had to try to get Asher out before Joel returned. "Maybe if we can get close enough to an exterior door and then you …" What was the right way to say it? "You could take yourself out, and if I'm right next to you and we're close enough, maybe you'll end up on the outside."

"Do not be asinine, Hannah. That is not an option. Even if it did work, you would still be in here."

"Ash, this whole situation, it's not simple, and it's not safe for you. Why would he even be keeping you here? Joel's all bent on taking out the bad immortals, or at least the ones he wants me to believe are bad. A couple hours ago I was beginning to think I was on board, that I could trust him, and that everything he was doing was for good. Now I'm just afraid. For both of us."

Hannah slumped forward, trying to think. She had to get Asher out of there. Even if she couldn't make it out the door, he could. The rest—well, she'd cross that bridge when she came to it. Getting him out, that was the key.

She sat up so quickly she thumped the back of her head on the bed again. There was going to be a good-sized lump.

"You might not like this," she said. "But I have an idea."

17

"**A**sh, what are you doing?"

He turned around when Hannah spoke, and she could see the shirtless upper half of him over the kitchen island, light from the open refrigerator shining off his hair. She looked out the door she'd just come in, and up and down the hallway outside the residence before she closed it behind her.

"You shouldn't be out here. What if someone else had come in besides me?"

He shrugged his shoulders. "I am sorry, but when I die I always come back voraciously hungry."

"You're always voraciously hungry. Hurry up then," Hannah said. "And put these on." She should have been irritated at his lack of concern about being discovered, but the familiar old-fashioned cadence of the words in his low, rumbly voice made her smile instead. She pulled the gray T-shirt and sweatpants she'd taken from the locker room out from under her shirt and tossed them to him. "We can't wait too long. If we get moving before Joel gets back, maybe you can just walk right out."

Looking at her sternly, he stepped around the island. "You persist in saying *you*. *We* need to go, Hannah. Both of us." He stopped in front of her, towering over her. "I am not going to walk away and leave you behind. Even if you did leave me."

Hannah's grin sank into a scowl. "They aren't going to be on the lookout for you the way they are me. There's no way I'll be allowed to just waltz out the door. Joel's made that abundantly clear, even though it turns out he's been a little muddy on his motivation for keeping me here. I'm starting to think it's not entirely for my protection after all." Hannah stuck out her chin stubbornly. "And I left you in Savannah because you made it pretty clear you weren't interested in my cramping your immortal lifestyle. You would have just up and left after a while anyway." She stared him down. "And put some pants on."

Maybe it didn't seem like a big deal to him, but Hannah remembered it clearly, the night he'd taken her to the secluded bowl of stars in the woods, with its constellations of dancing fireflies. Asher let her know that even though he now had the opportunity to be human again and possibly spend one last life with her, he had every intention of continuing as an immortal. Hannah dropped her head so he couldn't see the blush, remembered how embarrassed she'd felt—still felt—that her feelings were so off base, and unreturned.

Asher pulled at the blanket kilted around his waist. She rolled her eyes and turned around when it dropped and he began to put on the clothes she'd thrown his way.

"Just because you left without a word," Hannah heard him say, "should not make you think I would ever do the same."

"It doesn't matter now anyway," she said. "And that was different. You showed up again because you knew your sister was coming to kill me. Now she isn't a threat anymore. You're off the clock, so there's no sense in you hanging around here and risking getting killed for good."

Asher put a hand on her shoulder and spun her around to face him. "Since the moment I told you what I was, have I ever once left your side willingly?"

She didn't want to look up, but he put a hand under her chin so she had to.

She saw the intense stare that had unnerved her so much in the beginning.

"*You* left me. *You.*" He picked up the necklace from where it lay against her chest. "And you left this behind like it meant nothing. Did you even look at it?" He turned it over in his hand, holding it up for her. There was a faint inscription on the back that hadn't been there when he had given her the necklace the first time.

Without Fail.

She didn't understand. "You took me to that place, and then you said you intended to be around forever. To me that sounded a lot like, 'See you later, don't plan on joining you while you grow old and die.'"

Not that she wanted him to ever die; she just couldn't bear the thought of spending the rest of her comparatively short life in love with someone who would at best watch her get old and die and forget she'd ever existed. It had seemed better to leave and try to forget she'd ever met him. That hadn't worked out so great.

Asher put a hand around her arm, fingers encircling it. It burned through her shirt and into her skin, and he pulled her toward him. "Hannah," he said. She looked up at him, seething with frustration. She picked up her foot but put it back down, resisting the urge to stomp on his, mostly because with her bare foot she'd probably break her toes and he wouldn't even feel it.

"Hannah what?" she said, "Hannah nothing. We need to go."

"Do you even remember what I said to you?"

Did she remember? Every single bit.

"Something about you being around forever, until the last light fades. Which would be way past the point where you forgot I existed," she said. He didn't need to know she could probably write out the whole conversation word for word.

"Is that what you thought?"

She pulled herself away, cold where his hand had been. "What was I supposed to think, Ash? Seemed clear enough. You pretty much came out and said you weren't interested. I appreciate the pity rescues from your sister, but since she's about as threatening as I am right now, you really don't have to worry. Joel might be up to some shady shit, but even if he doesn't actually care about me, he needs me too much to hurt me. You need to get out of here before the last light you see is the one inside that cell. You need to leave."

"I do not need to leave. I need you."

Hannah froze, eyes narrowed. "Since when? You told me you had no intention of doing anything other than living your never-ending life, so what was I supposed to do, just hang around and do the cooking until you needed to put me in a nursing home?"

Hannah was what the old Joel would have called spitting mad.

Instead of firing back, Asher just sighed.

"How is it you are clever enough to figure out everyone else and survive all you have survived, but you choose to willfully misunderstand me?" he said.

"Well then enlighten me," Hannah said, turning away to pick up her key card and tablet from the counter, and to hide the rim of burning tears welling up in her eyes. She blinked them away and collected herself. All the standing around hashing things out was wasting time they didn't have.

Asher grabbed her arm again, both of them, forcing her to face him, towering over her. "Do you not think I would be happy to have you make me human like you?"

"Um, no, I do not think that at all," she said, "because you literally said you intend to be around until at least the firefly population is extinct. I'm obviously not going to last that long. Plus, you'd been avoiding me like I had the plague, so no, I didn't really get the impression you wanted to be human, or at least anywhere near me."

He pulled her closer again, placing his burning hands against her cheeks. "Hannah, wanting to be immortal and needing to be are not the same thing. If you made me like you, my sister or anyone else could have killed me two minutes later, and after that, you might not have lasted the week. Hannah, I need to be as I am. Otherwise, how can I keep you safe?"

His hands were still on her face and he gave them the lightest shake. "I would risk being trapped in this endless godforsaken cycle forever, if it would ensure you a long life. I would do this, even if it meant missing my chance of finally being human again."

It felt like all the oxygen had been vacuumed from the room.

Hannah twisted her head away and took a step back so she could try to draw a full breath.

"But you chose to leave me," he said. "I was forced to follow my damnable sister to make sure you were safe from her, because you walked away from my protection."

"But why, Ash? I don't understand. None of it was your fault, about Amara trying to kill me. You don't need to be worried about the guilt. I'm fine."

He shook his head. "Hannah, I love you."

"What?"

"That is not the reaction I was anticipating."

"I'm sorry. I don't think I heard you right."

"You heard me."

"Can you repeat it?" Hannah's face had dropped, and it was burning. But when he lifted her chin with his hand, it was glowing. He broke into a glorious smile when he saw her face.

"I love you, Hannah. And I need to be as I am because it is the only way I can protect you. I will not watch you come to harm. I do not care if you feel the same, but I will not leave here unless we both go."

"Why?"

"Why?" he said, laughing out loud, the sound bouncing around the glass windows and the high ceiling. "You have always asked so many questions. I will happily revisit every moment since we met. But truly, it is because we are meant to be together. We always were. Could you not see it, even when we were apart?"

She nodded slowly. "I swear, I could feel you were here. I knew you were. And even before I came here, I thought I would see you, even though it didn't make any sense. It felt like every time I opened a door or turned a corner you would be there."

He wrapped his arms around her and pulled her against him. "I could hear you. I could always hear you, every day since I found your necklace lying there. No matter where I was, your voice was always there, whispering in my head."

Hannah didn't give him much time to stare down, to drill what he was feeling into her brain. Hannah threw her arms around his neck, pushed herself up onto her toes, and kissed him while she had the chance.

"You've been around awhile. Does anything good ever happen at the right time? Like when you can enjoy it?" she asked when she finally let go.

"Never," Asher said. "Absolutely never."

It was a strange feeling, to be very happy and very frightened at exactly the same time. Hannah was cycling back and forth between the two emotions so quickly it was making her head spin. Asher, on the other hand, was managing to appear strangely unbothered, except for the slight grin on his face.

"Okay, so *we* need to get out of here," she said. "The beginning of our plan still works. We're just going to have to get creative with the rest." As soon as the words left Hannah's mouth there was a knock on the door. She felt guilty already.

"Get over there," Hannah hissed at Asher, jerking her head toward the door. "Hold on, I'm coming," she said brightly the minute he was in place. She unlocked the door and pulled it open. The poor guy didn't see it coming.

Noble was big and strong, but Asher was bigger. And they had the element of surprise. One solid blow to the back of the head and Noble hit the ground like a bag of rocks.

"I feel very bad about doing that. I will have to find him and explain someday and make my apology. Though not soon," Asher said, poking the other man gently with his foot to make sure he was out. "Not anytime soon."

Hannah felt pretty bad about it herself, lying to get Noble to come up here and take her for a run, and then knocking him unconscious, but there hadn't been a less painful option.

"Alright, he's passed for you once," Hannah said. "Let's hope it works the other way. Help me get his sweatshirt off." Hannah reached down into Noble's pants pocket and pulled out his key card. A moment later they had him tied up and wedged in the coat closet. He was crammed in so tightly she doubted he'd be able to get out without help when he eventually came to.

"Once we get out of these rooms there are cameras everywhere," Hannah said, watching Asher pull the hood of Noble's sweatshirt up over his head. "Make sure you keep your head down and your hands in your pockets. My key card only works on the inside, but his should work everywhere. We better hope it does."

It wasn't a very complete plan—in fact, there were any number of ways it could go wrong. But getting out of the building was the most important thing. If there were guards they couldn't talk their way past, they'd have to worry about it when the time came.

There was a creak from the coat closet. She hoped Noble wasn't coming to already. She opened it a crack—Asher looking over her shoulder—then swore loudly. The closet was empty.

"I must have hit him a little too hard," Asher said with a shrug. This was not a helpful development. The first thing Noble would do when he popped back up was find a phone and call Joel. They needed to get out, and quickly.

Another option occurred to her. "How much do you trust Mena? You guys were—um—close, right? Do you think maybe she would help smuggle you out? Unless you think she really did know you were in that cell."

Asher's eyes widened. "Mena is here?"

Hannah nodded. "Yeah, she works here, has a big lab and every-thing. She was the one Joel called on the radio to have them come rescue us. You didn't know?"

Asher grabbed Hannah's arm. "I would not have believed it. Mena is here, and my sister as well."

"Yeah, I told you, she's in one of the prison cells," Hannah said. "If you were down there, you and Amara were probably fifty yards away from each other this whole time. Why? Is it a big deal if your sister and your ex-girlfriend are in the same building at the same time?" Hannah couldn't imagine why it would be.

"My what? There has never been anything between Mena and myself. Where would you get such a peculiar idea?"

"From Gabe, in the bar after I got shot. You wanted to call Mena and he told me you guys used to be a thing, and you spent a whole lot of lifetimes together. Why is that such a peculiar idea?"

Maybe Asher didn't recall the event as well as she did, but Hannah remembered eavesdropping on the conversation between him and Gabe, who turned out not to be the friend Asher thought, but in league with Amara. Payback for his dishonesty turned out to be a very permanent death for Gabe not too much later.

"Oh," Hannah added, "and Mena has a creepy piece of your hair on her desk in a block of glass."

Asher ran his hand up through his hair in frustration, standing it up. That wasn't good.

"Hannah," Asher said, "Mena and I did spend a great deal of time together—a very long time ago—but only because we had a common goal. We both hoped Amara could be made to reform her ways. Knowing my sister as I do, I was less convinced it was possible, but Mena, she was certain there was hope for her."

"Obviously that was a lost cause."

Asher shook his head. "You understand that, and I understand that, but Mena, she would never give up hope for Amara. She loves her. She would do anything for her." He pulled open the door and yanked the hood down over his eyes, pulling Hannah after him.

"Given enough time, Amara might be able to convince Mena to let her out. I am shocked she has not done so already. And even as a human, I daresay Amara would still be formidable. Our need to escape from here has become more urgent, before Mena does something foolish."

Hannah pulled out Noble's card and waved it in front of the elevator sensor, jiggling impatiently at the wait. "Mena's too smart for that, isn't she? She wouldn't do anything too dangerous or stupid for Amara."

Asher shook his head as the door finally slid too slowly open.

"Mena is a brilliant mind, and I believe a truly good creature at heart. But it has been my experience that when it comes to my sister, Mena's heart overcomes her reason," he said. "I fear she could be convinced to set aside any of her normally sane thoughts and moral actions for Amara's sake. Especially because Amara is endlessly and creatively manipulative. And love makes people do irrational things. If Mena let Amara escape, it would not even come close to being the worst thing Mena has done for Amara's sake." That was hard to believe.

"How much worse?" Hannah said.

"Amara once convinced Mena to attempt to create a poison so deadly it would kill even an immortal, so they could truly die and be together forever in the beyond. Then she got Mena to take it first. It obviously did not kill her permanently, just sent her to her death and far away. Amara of course did not take it, but while Mena was away, eighty-two children and a dozen nuns at an orphanage found Amara's dose stirred into their morning porridge."

"Oh my god, Asher. Why?"

"Why? Why does Amara do anything? Mena founded the orphanage and patronized it; maybe Amara thought she was giving too much of her time to them, rather than her. Or maybe because she could. It was not the first such instance, and it certainly was not the last—or the worst."

What could be worse than that? Hannah wasn't sure she wanted to hear.

"I imagine you have heard of Chernobyl."

"She didn't?" Hannah said, growing anxious as the elevator moved downward. "Funny how none of this made the book."

"Made what book?"

"I'll tell you later." Hannah's hand clapped across her mouth in horror. "I guess this isn't a great time to mention that Mena has some of my blood," she said through her fingers. "I handed it right over to her. Mena said she was going to stabilize it so I didn't have to draw blood as often. You don't think Mena would give my blood to Amara, do you?"

The line of light crept its way down the side of the door as they dropped toward the lower levels.

"Why would it matter, if Amara does end up with more of your blood? She might wish to use it on me, but we can be gone before then. Do you think she might want to turn Joel or one of the others here?"

"No," Hannah said, "because maybe Amara thinks the same thing Michael did. The whole reason my father wanted to find me was because he was sure my blood could put him back the way he was. What if that's true?"

His answer was interrupted by the chime of the elevator reaching its destination. It was going to take more than a little luck for them to walk out without anyone seeing them looking suspicious. Any time Hannah tried to look subtle it screamed guilty. She didn't remember seeing any of the standard fire alarm pulls in the building, but there had to be some. Maybe it would be better to create some disorder and attempt to slip out with the rush of people trying to get out of the building.

Someone must have beaten them to it. Before the doors could open, the klaxon sound of an alarm made them both jump. A thin red band began to chase itself around the top of the elevator, and a digital script appeared on the door in front of them, spelling out an alert. Hannah felt her pocket buzz. Pulling out the tablet, she saw the same message flashing on the screen.

Gold alert Level 5. Gold alert Level 5. Nonessential personnel, confine to quarters. Gold personnel will be directed to assist in containment. Key cards will revert to emergency pass procedures.

"How did they discover me so quickly?" Asher pushed himself in front of her, waiting for the door to open.

"I don't know," Hannah said. "I don't know if this is even about you. What I do know is level five is the prison."

Hannah swiped Noble's card futilely in front of the door, trying to convince the door to open. Instead, the red band stopped circling the top of the elevator and turned a solid bright yellow. The digital message on the door changed.

It now read, *Gold personnel key card recognized. Proceeding to Level 5.* The elevator began to move, dropping toward the last level they wanted to find themselves on.

18

The corridors were silent, cast in a weird pulsing redness from lights hidden somewhere in the molding. They walked as fast as they could without making it look overly suspicious.

"Maybe it will be easier to get out now. A lot of people are going to be locked down until this is figured out," Hannah said. "Less chance of us getting noticed." Provided they could actually get out of the building. She flashed Noble's card in front of the next elevator they came to; thankfully the door immediately slid open.

"Take the card and get out the quickest way. Leave me here and tell me which way to find them. I cannot let Mena free Amara, or worse, attempt what you think she might be attempting," Asher said. "God forbid it is successful."

"Who's the one using all the *me* and *I* crap now. I'm not going to just leave you at the prison. Let's get out of here." Hannah waved the card again and the door slid shut, and she closed her eyes with relief, opening them again when it slid back open immediately. She tried it again to the same effect; the door closed temporarily, then slid open again at the same floor.

"It must be Noble's card," she said. "Whatever's going on, it must be programmed to funnel only the immortals to the prison. Probably since they're the ones most likely to be able to take care of the problem without getting hurt."

They stepped out of the unmoving elevator and looked down the hallway. "Maybe there's stairs around here or an emergency exit.

There has to be a way off this floor, and we need to find it quickly, because if we get caught down here, you're probably going to end up right back in one of those cells," Hannah said. "Mena wouldn't really do something as stupid as trying to put Amara back the way she was, would she?"

"Good people make very bad decisions for people they love," Asher said. He pulled her behind him but she shoved herself back in front.

"I'm pretty sure they're on strict orders not to shoot me," she said. "You—not so much."

As they crept down the hallway, Hannah felt like a fool for not even trying to arm herself before they'd left the residence. Even a butter knife would have made her feel better than this, skulking along empty-handed. And maybe they could have used it to jimmy open the solidly sealed door that closed off the corridor. Asher's fist, even with all his substantial weight behind it, didn't even make a dent in the metal, the impact swallowed up in a dead thud.

Suddenly a garbled scream reached them from the other end of the hallway.

"Mena," Asher said, head swiveling in the direction of the sound. One last look at the impenetrable door, and without a word, they turned toward the other end of the hall—toward the prison.

As they approached, something crunched under Hannah's shoe. Beneath her was a litter of scattered glass. She looked up to where a camera had been shot out. Just ahead of them, at the end of the remaining stretch of hallway, the first set of doors were propped slightly open.

"Well that isn't good," Hannah said when she saw what was keeping the doors from closing. The ever-present guards were still just inside, but crumpled to the floor, legs splayed out. There was a red-tipped dart protruding from each of their necks. Asher rolled one of them over and removed his sidearm from its holster, then stepped over him to creep down the hall.

"Stay behind me," he said.

Hannah yanked the back of his shirt. "Whatever Mena plans to do with it, she has my blood, so you stay behind *me*."

Asher pointedly ignored her, continuing cautiously down the short hall. Hannah stayed half a step behind but slipped in front of him as they approached the next set of doors. When he moved to get around her once more, Hannah stepped slowly and purposely on his foot, jerking her head back angrily. Asher shook his head and flattened himself against the wall next to her, out of the line of fire as much as was possible for him.

Hugging the wall, Hannah peeked through the wire mesh of the door. "The other two guards are down too," she said.

Through the dark glass she could see one of the figures on the ground had been subdued the same way as the first two, unconscious from the effects of the dart hanging sideways from where it had lodged in her scalp. The second guard was motionless and white, his neck canted off at an unnatural angle and a thin stream of blood running from his nose. It didn't bode well for whatever was happening beyond the doors in front of them. It didn't stop them, though, and as quietly as possible, Hannah pushed one of the doors open.

At first no one was visible in the space in front of the line of illuminated cells, eerie in the blinking blue lights. Hannah stopped just before she put her foot down on another scattering of broken glass. It was flickering in the flashes from the wires of the shot-out camera that sparked erratically over her head. Carefully avoiding the shards, Hannah moved silently toward the first cell. Asher was so close behind her she could feel the heat radiating from him. He reached out and pulled her to a halt.

The thick glass door that had been between her and Amara before was gone, slid up into the ceiling. All the doors were retracted. Every cell was open.

Hannah looked back at Asher in horror. Maybe they were too late and Mena had already released Amara, and she was gone. There was no way to know what their real intentions were, but if there was any chance Hannah's blood would turn Amara back into the monster she had been, the thought of her outside her glass prison was terrifying. It was bad enough if she was plain old human. Hannah started to back up, pushing against Asher, until she heard a faint whimper. It had come from Amara's open cell.

They saw the blood on the floor first, before they could see inside the cell. There was a splatter of it, artificially red against the whiteness of the cell. The air smelled of the electricity sparking from the wires, and something else ripe and ferric. Another step and Hannah could see the figures inside. They were both covered in blood.

"Oh great. You two are the original bad damn pennies."

Amara had a wiry arm clamped around Mena's neck. There was blood flowing from Mena's nose, down over her lips, and falling in drops onto the floor. The arm under her chin was the only thing keeping her from sliding to the floor along with it.

"I knew I could trust my sainted darling to come to my rescue. Oh, your glorious plans, my love." Amara jerked Mena's head up and gave her a bloody, smacking kiss on the cheek. "Of course, her plans were a little different than mine. They usually are. It's sad though, how easy it was to convince her to relieve you of a little bit of the red stuff."

Amara flicked a bloody finger their direction and Hannah felt the droplets against her face. "Can you believe she came down here absolutely ready to make herself a gross old human like you." Mena made a mewling sound and Amara jerked her upward. "Seriously, sweetness, you were willing to give up an eternity because you actually thought we were going to live happily ever after, just growing old and incontinent side-by-side." Amara shook her head in mock amazement. "Was changing each other's diapers for the remainder of our pathetic lives an appealing option for you?" Amara looked down at Mena and shook her head mockingly.

Hannah saw movement out of the corner of her eye, but so did Amara, jerking Mena up more fully in front of her with one arm and pulling out the syringe that had been hidden behind her back with the other. "Put the gun down, Asher. We both know you're a shit shot. And don't get too close," Amara said. "I've got a little bit of baby girl's blood left in here for you."

Feeling Asher pull closer behind her, Hannah pushed against him, trying to get him to back out of the cell. Trying to budge him was like leaning into a brick wall.

"Seriously, you're all idiots," Amara said. "Idiot, idiot, idiot." She pointed the syringe at Hannah, then Asher, and finally tapped Mena on the nose with it. "Every one of you. Hannah, you're an idiot—well, still an idiot—for giving your blood to Mena." Amara rolled her eyes. "Like the first time she asked. Come on, have you even heard of playing hard to get?" Amara gave Mena another shake, making her head flop back and forth like a rag doll's. "And Mena, she's an idiot for believing me. Duh. And for actually handing your blood over to me. She could have just dosed herself in the bathroom or something, but she always buys what I'm selling. It never gets old."

Amara reached the hand holding the syringe over and tilted Mena's head up; it flopped back down. "Wake up, dear, you don't want to miss this berating. It's going to be your last one." Amara smiled wickedly at Hannah. "I squeeze out a single damn tear about wanting to be with her when she does it—so we can be together when she makes the change to being human—and she shows up with your little blood donation. It's surprising really, she was never into having people watch."

A garbled, wet sound came from Mena's mouth. Somehow she managed to lift her head far enough up to look forward. There was no fear in her eyes, no pain. Just sadness. Tears were cutting tracks through the blood on her face, like pale pink rivers dividing and flowing down over her cheeks.

"And she just stood there and let me do it. She let me turn her into nothing," Amara said. "You'd be interested to know it doesn't even take that much. I gave her just enough to get her off my back. Or to get her on her back, because humans ... they're about as tough as toilet paper. The rest was for me, plus a little bit left over just in case, for getting out of here. But I'll give that to you, brother. God, what a feeling that's going to be."

Amara smiled her cruel smile, the only thing about her that had never changed. "I can feel it," she said. "My life, my strength. It's coming back. And then, I'm coming for you."

Without warning, before they could react, Amara reached up and grabbed Mena's head, wrenching it to the side, forcing a sickening, strangled cry from Mena's throat before letting her slide to the floor. She landed on the tile with her head awkwardly twisted, but somehow still alive, eyes rolling back in her head in anguish.

"I'm still a little weak," Amara said, "but really, guys, it's all coming back to me now."

While Hannah stared at Amara in horror, Asher made a move toward his sister. She waved her arm, glossy and red with Mena's blood, brandishing the syringe like a knife.

"There's just enough left in here for you, Ashy-boy," she said. "This is all your fault anyway. It's time you paid the piper."

"Amara, please." Asher backed up, lowering the gun, pulling Hannah behind him. He edged her out of the cell, keeping her from ducking past him to help Mena who lay there panting like a wounded animal. Her porcelain skin had somehow grown paler—a deathly, blanched white, filmed with sweat. "Amara, just leave," he said. "You can go. Just go. Let us help her. You loved her, you know you did. Let us try to save her."

Amara shook her head. "Did I not just tell you. You really are idiots, all of you. Love?" she said. "It amounts to nothing at all, when your body is just going to end up a slimy oozy mess in the ground. How could I love anyone stupid enough to want that?" She looked down at Mena. Then Amara raised her foot and brought it down on Mena's neck with a crunch. Mena gurgled.

"No!" Hannah pushed past Asher as Amara raised her foot again, to grind her heel into the windpipe of the woman who had been willing to give up an eternity to be with her. The foot never fell.

Amara's movement was interrupted by the appearance of a perfectly round hole above her right eyebrow. She stood frozen for a moment, until a tiny black ribbon began to trail its way over her wide-open silvery-blue eye. It blinked once, the blood spreading and coating the lens, turning everything to red. Amara crumpled to the ground.

Hannah saw Asher's arm drop out of the corner of her eye, the barrel of the gun in his hand still trailing a wisp of smoke. Asher backed away, but Hannah couldn't move. She couldn't quite turn her head away from the bodies on the floor.

A river of blood was flowing in a neat course across the tile, down into a drain set in the center of the room, next to which two heads were gently touching. Mena's dark locks rested against Amara's honey-colored hair. Both were terribly still, and both were clearly, and finally, dead.

It was the thud that finally made Hannah turn, to where Asher had sunk down onto the narrow bench across from the cells. He was staring at the bodies.

"Ash." Hannah didn't know what else to say. Mena was dead. Amara was dead. She might have been a killer, a monster, a broken and corrupted being, but she was his sister. Amara was his only family, the sole remaining tie to his beginning, and she knew that no matter what Amara had done, Asher had never wanted to witness this. He certainly hadn't wanted to be the one to end her life. Yet there she lay. And he had killed her.

"She is still there. She did not disappear," he said, his voice airy and disbelieving. "Amara thought it was working."

"Amara wanted to believe it was working," Hannah said. She took a step forward to sit down beside him.

Hannah didn't make it. Hands reached into her hair and jerked her painfully. She was hoisted into the air by her scalp, her feet kicking out off the ground.

"Fun, fun, fun," a reedy, childlike voice piped. "Everyone wanted to come out and play today. It was growing so dull in here."

Hannah choked, her vision starting to waver from the downward pressure on her neck from the weight of her own body.

"Roman, put her down." Asher took a wary step forward.

"Okay," Roman said. He let Hannah's feet touch the ground, and she struggled, kicking at him and stomping, but she couldn't get away. He yanked her hard again by the hair, jerked her ear toward her shoulder, and tore into her neck with his teeth.

Asher charged, ripping Hannah away from Roman and tossing him across the floor like a rag doll. Hannah clasped a hand to her throat, blood running between her fingers, fuzzy headed from the pain. When Asher reached for her she reeled away, stumbling backward.

"Hannah," he said.

"Don't. No. Don't touch it." He pulled the shirt over his head and handed it to her and she wadded it against her throat, still backing away from him. A lighthearted laugh made Asher pause in trying to help. His head whipped toward Roman, who was dragging himself up from the ground.

"It seems it didn't work for your sister, despite what she thought she felt. But I thought I'd give it another try, straight from the cow." Roman smiled, his chin streaked with Hannah's blood. "Not a good year. She tastes so disgustingly human. Like musty old grave dirt." Roman had risen to his feet and he cocked his head back and forth with a series of cracks. "Ah, much better," he smiled through red teeth. "I think I'll have another bite, it's still better than the food here."

Bending down without taking his eyes off Roman, Asher groped for the gun where he'd let it slide to the ground. His hand had just touched it when Roman laughed crazily and threw himself at Asher. The gun came up as the flying figure reached him, but the shot meant for Roman went wild, bouncing dangerously around the room, ricocheting off the hardened surfaces.

For a moment there was a pile of moving parts, arms and legs rolling, the two bodies coming in Hannah's direction. Just before they reached her there was a distinct snap, and everything went still.

Leaning against the wall, hand pressed on the blood-dampened shirt held against her neck, Hannah waited, not daring to draw a breath. A moment later, Asher rolled Roman's unmoving form off him.

Asher lay there for a moment, breathing hard and staring up at the ceiling. When Hannah made her wobbling way over to him, he sat up and looked at her. He scooted himself closer.

"Let me see it," he said, reaching toward her. She shook her head, making herself wince.

"I've had worse," she said. "It's fine." He nodded, getting to his feet. *Good*, she thought when he relented. Hannah didn't need him any nearer to her blood than he'd already been today.

When she started to stand up he grabbed her shoulders carefully and pulled her to her feet. They looked at the chaos, and blood, and death all around them. He paused when he reached the place where his sister was lying.

"I'm sorry, Ash. Not that I'm sorry Amara is gone," Hannah said, "I won't pretend I am. You can take back what you said about loving me, for my being that heartless. I'm not sorry she's dead, but I'm sorry you had to see it. I'm sorrier you had to be the one to do it."

He shook his head. "They ended up dying together in the end. Of all the things that seemed an impossibility." The momentary sadness in his eyes turned to resolve. "There will be time to consider all that has happened later. We need to get you some help." Asher once again put his hand out toward her neck, the bite bleeding through the fabric.

"Don't touch it," Hannah said, jerking away and feeling dizzy again. "Geez, she was right. You are an idiot. I'm fine. I don't need help. I need us to get out of here."

It was a minor miracle there wasn't a room full of guards on top of them already. Her brain was in better shape than her neck, clear enough to know someone was going to find them soon.

"I'm okay. Do you want to have to explain this? You're supposed to be in one of those cells."

Asher took one last look at his sister but didn't argue. He didn't have time. He heard them first, of course, just before she did. The slap of footsteps—lots of footsteps—coming down the hall. Hannah leaned against the wall for a moment, steadying her spinning head, then squared herself.

"Stop! Put your hands up."

Seeing the jiggling green dots of a dozen laser sights dancing across their chests, they froze, though neither of them bothered raising their hands; Hannah because she didn't want to take the pressure off her neck, and Asher, well, he wasn't used to threats of bodily harm carrying much weight.

Joel pushed his way through the line of guards and stopped short, his eyes widening when he saw Asher standing just behind Hannah.

"Sedate him," Joel said.

All the green dots suddenly focused into a clot of green on Asher's chest.

"Fire."

19

"**H**annah, move aside."

Joel waved the first line of guards forward toward Asher, who wove drunkenly for a moment, then slumped to the ground in a heap. He reached one limp hand toward Hannah before his eyes rolled back into his head and closed.

She stepped in front of him, throwing a hand up. "Joel, wait. What are you doing?"

"Please return the prisoner to his cell," Joel said to the guards. "Hannah, don't get in their way."

They shouldered her aside and she watched helplessly as four people struggled to drag the unconscious Asher into a cell.

Joel took a step forward and she pulled away from him. He reached past her and touched a button. A thick sheet of bulletproof glass slid smoothly down to the ground, sealing the prone Asher behind it. Another button made the glass opaque, hiding him from view.

"Get the other two in here and lock them down. Then get this mess cleaned up." Joel grabbed Hannah by the arm and started to pull her out of the room.

"Joel, what are you doing? Why are you keeping Asher in there? Let him go."

"Silence."

There was an iciness in Joel's expression that was new to the face she thought she'd known so well, and his tone made it clear nothing she could say would change anything.

"We'll discuss this later. Right now I'm taking you back to your room until I can get things straightened out. One moment I'm bringing back two dangerous psychopaths, the next I'm getting a call telling me the entire place is in a code-red lockdown," he said. "I rush back to make sure you're safe and find three dead immortals."

Hannah wobbled a little when Joel pulled on her arm, and he looked over and noticed for the first time the blood saturating the shirt wadded against her neck. She was desperately concerned about Asher, but the pain and blood loss were making her too woozy to put up much of a fight.

Joel sighed, then wrapped an arm around her shoulders and swept the other under her knees. He called back to one of the armed men who had fallen in behind them. "Radio medical and tell them to send someone up to my suite."

———•✦•———

"Now, tell me what happened," Joel said. "I gather Mena was the one who disabled the security systems, since the last visual I have is of her taking out the cameras in the prison."

Hannah had to close her eyes and open them again to get the two wavering Joels to merge into one. Whatever the quiet doctor had injected her with while he was tending to her neck made her feel boneless and sleepy. But she was still coherent enough to hold her tongue.

"Mena was one of the very few people who could pull it off and who knew the prison cameras run independently. They needed to be disabled even after the system was down," Joel said. "I don't know what she cooked up to dose them with, but the three guards that survived are still out. I'm sure they'll confirm it when they wake up. What was she trying to do?"

It seemed Joel didn't know Asher got out of his cell the hard way and came back next to Hannah. As far as he knew, Asher had just stepped out of his cell a moment before Joel showed up. She chose not to enlighten him.

The entire situation was horribly unclear, and she needed to tread carefully. Hannah had never once thought that Joel would harm her, but maybe she'd been very wrong. It wouldn't be the first time. And it wasn't only her life at stake now.

Joel looked at her sternly, his questions having gone unanswered while she thought. He watched her touch the thick bandage on her neck and his demeanor softened a little. He sat down next to her; she froze but didn't move, as much as she wanted to lean away from him.

He looked out the window in front of them into the blank, starless night. "If you keep playing with that you're going to get an infection," he said.

"I'm pretty sure most of what's flowing through my veins right now is antibiotics. I'm more concerned about sprouting wings and fangs. Roman went after my neck like he was Dracula."

Still, Hannah took her hand away and tucked it down at her side.

Joel laughed dryly. "Well, you read the book. Old habits die hard, I suppose." The laugh died off. "None of this is funny. Tell me what happened."

He reached over and took her hand. Hannah didn't brush him off, letting him turn it over and stare at the palm. She'd decided to tell him what happened—just not all of it. Hannah apologized mentally for throwing Mena under the bus.

"Did you know about Mena and Amara?" she said.

His thumb froze where he'd been running it over her palm.

"Mena and Amara? Mena and Asher, you mean?"

Clearly he hadn't known, which she'd suspected, since nothing concrete had appeared in his book. Hannah filled him in on some of the details, telling him the truth—mostly.

"It was sad actually, about the two of them," Hannah said. "Amara convinced Mena they could both be human and happy together. She talked Mena into getting some of my blood and turning herself so they could leave and live out one last life together as humans. But Amara was using her, as always. Amara really just wanted to see if my blood could bring her back to being immortal. I guess we know for sure now it doesn't work that way. There's no going back."

201

"I trusted Mena," Joel said, his voice low and concerned. "I had no idea she would do anything like that. I knew she had a history with Asher and Amara, but it wasn't what I thought, and it certainly wasn't left in the past."

He leaned back and ran his hands through his hair. "Mena was an amazing person and she did a great deal of good. But that same big heart was what made her vulnerable to someone as manipulative as Amara. And you gave her your blood?"

Joel didn't sound exactly accusatory, but Hannah thought it might be the result of some effort. Probably because she'd handed it over to Mena and hadn't instantly offered it up to him. Hannah explained to him how Mena had convinced her she could stabilize it, making it easier for Hannah to protect herself.

"I liked Mena. I believed her and I trusted her. She'd still be alive right now if I wasn't so gullible." Hannah wiped a rim of tears from her eyes. The memory of the thin, childlike figure lying still on the floor made a sob escape she didn't bother trying to hold back. "It's my fault she's dead," Hannah said.

"Is it?" Joel said. "Mena was kind and good, but she wasn't a fool. Rather the opposite; she was incredibly intelligent. If Amara convinced her to get your blood, and you said no the first time she asked, Mena would have found another way. In all the time I knew her I never saw her encounter a problem she couldn't find a solution to."

Hannah ducked her head at the memory of the sound of Mena's neck crunching under Amara's heel and the hair splayed out in dark waves on the floor. There wasn't a solution to this problem. Or maybe this was the solution, and Mena had no more problems to solve. Never would again.

She turned to Joel. "But why would she let them all out? All the cells were open. Mena couldn't have wanted Roman out." *Or known Asher was supposed to be behind door number three*, Hannah thought.

"I think she found she didn't have a choice. She overrode the entire system, but that still wouldn't have gotten her access to an individual cell without my approval. Mena had to cut the power to the whole block and reset everything so she could get to Amara. She had to; it was the only way in without me."

"And now they're dead. They're all dead," Hannah said. Funny, it just occurred to her that her two biggest fears were gone. "Amara's not a threat anymore. She's dead for real. Roman too. Why don't you just let Asher go? He was there, and if he hadn't been, Roman would have killed me. Let him leave. He's not going to hurt anyone." She'd stay here if she had to—at least until she could figure something out—if Joel would let Asher go.

Joel paused just briefly before he spoke. "I know he's put on a decent facade for you, Hannah, but Asher is a dangerous man. I did this to protect you. Think about how many people he's killed, just in the time you've known him."

It was true, she'd witnessed it, but only when he'd had no choice and was defending her.

"Multiply that by nearly a thousand years," Joel said. "The world is safer with him in there, and so are you."

He dropped her hand and stood up, the icy look returning. "Some people can't be trusted and will never do anything but endanger the people around them. I thought you would immediately realize your role here and accept what you were meant to do. Now I see you're going to take some persuading." He reached down and pulled her to her feet. "In the meantime, we need to go see about our new guests."

———•••••———

"Joel please, I don't want to do this right now." Hannah tried to say it calmly and resolutely without sounding like she was begging. She hated to beg, but she would if she'd thought for a second it would work. But Hannah knew Joel hated begging even more than she did.

"You're going to do this," Joel said. "It has to be done. I believe you'll come to see things my way when you really weigh your options, but we can't wait for that."

He nodded to the guards who peeled away from their stations in front of the door at their approach. Not only did Hannah not want to do what he was asking, she really didn't want to step through the doors that led to the cells again. That Asher was in there somewhere was the only thing keeping her from trying to make a run for it.

When they walked past the first cells, Hannah was stunned to see they had already been returned to sparkling whiteness. She wondered where they'd taken the bodies. Were they lying somewhere blanched and drained on a metal table, growing cold and stiff?

"Here we are." Joel stopped in front of a cell. "Meet our new guests. They aren't very energetic today, mind you. I'm keeping them nice and calm so we don't have any problems. Once we're done, there's no chance they'll escape. They probably won't even know what happened when they wake up human."

In front of them a woman was strapped upright, manacled to a board like Roman had been. She could have been the model for a Raphael *Madonna*—maybe she had been—with her flawless white skin, shining coppery hair, and pursed rosebud lips. Delicate blue veins showed across her closed eyelids, and there was a twitch of movement under one, like she was having a dream. The appearance of a beautiful angel gently sleeping was marred by the band strapped across her forehead, holding her head tightly in place.

"Deceptively lovely, isn't she? She and Amara were quite a pair at one time. Beauty still has a value, of course, but back then it was a powerful commodity, and my, did they exploit it. But I promise you, she's black as coal underneath that alabaster." Joel moved on to the next cell. "And this one as well."

Jeremiah. He was average in height, in size, and in appearance, with longish brown hair and regular features. He was attractive—as all their kind were—but not in an overly stunning, remarkable way. Joel looked over at Hannah, as if daring her to question him and all the evil he'd attributed to the man.

"Can't you just keep them here and see what happens? Maybe they want to be human. We'll ask them, and if they want it, I'll happily let them have it." It seemed like a long shot, but it was a nice thought.

"They're monsters, Hannah. They can't be allowed to go on and on doing the same terrible things."

"Look what happened to Mena. She did terrible things, made mistakes, but she didn't deserve to be dead."

"You don't get a choice." Joel motioned to someone through the door they had entered. Charlie walked over and handed him something. "You don't get a choice because they need to be neutralized now."

Hannah started to back away. Joel clamped a hand down on her wrist, grinding the bones together.

"If you don't willingly give me your blood, I'm going to hold you down and take it, and then I'm going to give it to them anyway. And after, because of your refusal to help, I'm going to do the same thing to Asher. Now sit."

She sat down woodenly on the bench against the wall, not staring at the people behind the glass in front of her, head turned instead down the length of the room to where a single dim light was visible. She knew he was in there, even though the cell glass was obscured. Hannah could feel it, the way she had before.

And because of that, Hannah sat without moving. She didn't flinch, only glancing up at Charlie who stood there with a triumphant smile pasted on her face as Joel carefully pushed the small needle into Hannah's arm and pulled back the plunger. They all watched the barrel turn ruby red as it filled, until carefully he drew it out. Eyeing it for a moment, Joel knelt in front of her, put his hand under her chin, and turned her head toward him.

"You are doing a great thing, even if you don't appreciate it right now."

He stood up and handed the syringe to Charlie. A great thing? Hannah wanted to scream. Then two great things? How soon would there be another? Maybe not today, but there would be more. These would only be the beginning, and the deaths would follow soon enough.

But Hannah was selfish, and didn't speak, because Asher wasn't one of them, at least today, and that mattered more to her than the rest. Her compliance was the only thing keeping him from being human, and if he was human, he'd likely soon be dead. She refused to let the tear gathering in the corner of her eye fall, because it was a selfish tear. After all this time, she knew how Asher felt—which was the same as she'd felt since she'd met him. At least Hannah had gotten five whole minutes of what she hoped for before everything went to hell.

She jumped when the two glass panels slid up in front of her. Delphine continued to slumber gently, but Jeremiah's eyes opened at the sound. They shot back and forth in confusion. Joel motioned Charlie forward.

"Do it. Inject them both. Leave them in restraints until they wake up. After that, double the guard on them. We don't want a repeat of what just happened," Joel said. "I'm not sure how long it will take. Amara looked visibly different, but nearly a year had passed in the interim. No matter, it's worked in every other instance. Odds are Delphine and Jeremiah won't be any different."

He doesn't know, Hannah thought. He didn't know that Mena had figured out how to tell if one of them had succumbed to the effects of her blood.

"You and I, Hannah, we're going to change the world. We're going to fix it, whether you understand right away or not. We're going to keep going until mankind is safe. It's the beginning of a new era. Every dangerous evil will be under control. And then, I'll let Asher walk away. And you too." Joel had raised her to spot a lie.

"Go ahead." Joel looked back at Charlie, who was standing next to Delphine. She pulled aside a lock of russet hair, slid the needle into the white neck, and depressed the plunger halfway. She smiled at Joel like a child looking to be praised.

"Good. Now him."

Charlie walked out of the cell, pushing the button to close it behind her, then slipped into the next one. The eyes fluttered open again.

"Joel," a quiet voice croaked, pale blue eyes fighting to focus. "Joel, my friend, what—"

Charlie jammed the syringe into Jeremiah's neck. His eyes sprang open, then closed again and stayed shut.

"All done," she said.

She closed the door and stepped back to look at her handiwork. Nothing looked different than it had been a moment ago. But for the people behind the glass, everything had changed. Today was the first day of what might be a very short span of remaining time.

20

"**G**et dressed." Joel opened her door without warning and stuck his head in. Hannah looked up at him but didn't move. "Get yourself put together. Put on something nice. I want you to be ready in half an hour."

"Where are we going?" she asked, thrown off by the light tone in his voice. There had been a fair amount of stony silence and general avoidance since their return from the prison the day before.

"Things have gone a bit differently than I would have chosen, but I think you and I can work this out. We've always agreed, haven't we? Come on, I want you to join me."

He ducked back out of the room as quickly as he had appeared, and Hannah pulled herself out of bed. She was leery of Joel, but she was rational enough to know it would be best to appear to oblige him, for now at least.

After she combed the tangles from her hair, she pulled up the front and speared hair picks through to keep the knot in place. On a whim she walked through the fine mist from the atomizer perfume bottle that sat on the vanity. It was vaguely familiar, though she couldn't place it, with an exotic, herbaceous scent. Nice, but not something she would have chosen for herself.

Nor was the dress. It was one of many that hung in neat ranks on either side of the giant closet. She wondered if Joel had a hand in selecting them, and as she flipped through the clothes, she tried to imagine which would be his favorite, based on what she knew of him.

Settling on something pretty, but at least marginally comfortable, she pulled it on, fiddling with the silken wisp of a belt in front of the full-length mirror.

The dark green silk turned the normally subtle red undertone in her dark hair fiery. The skillful cut of the expensive fabric made it hang perfectly, clinging to her waist then flaring out over her hips. It gave her a better figure than she possessed, and except for the white wreath of bandages around her neck, Hannah thought she looked well enough, though completely unlike herself.

Doubling up Asher's necklace to shorten the chain, she tucked it up under the bandages so it disappeared without a trace. She couldn't bring herself to take it off and hide it, but she didn't want it on display. It rested in the hollow of her neck, the pressure of it against her throat comforting, a smooth metal shield over her jugular vein.

"You look stunning, darling."

Hannah jumped as Joel's reflection appeared behind her. He reached out and grabbed her hand, twirling her around. She let him, though her first instinct was to pull away.

"Relax." He let her hand drop and smiled over her shoulder in the mirror. "I can't stand to have you angry at me. All I've ever done is love and protect you, and this really is much the same thing. You'll come to agree with me, I know it."

She couldn't look at him because she was afraid he would read the falsehood on her lips. "I'm not angry," she said. "Of course not. How could I be angry with you? It's just a bit much to process right now." The words stuck in her throat. Hannah wished she was a better liar.

Joel turned her around, holding her out at arm's length. "Don't pretend," he said. Hannah's heart skipped. "Don't pretend you weren't upset with me. I think we both know that's not the case. But I'm sure we'll be best friends again soon."

There was no threat in the tone—it came out of his mouth all care and kindness—but Hannah could feel it under the surface. She pulled her lips up into a smile and gave a tiny shrug.

"Well, you've got all the time in the world."

She tried to sound flippant and light, hoping she was pulling it off. He took her hand and twirled her again. It was fitting, since she was in an impossible dance, stepping as they both were, so lightly around the truth.

————◦•◦◦•◦————

"You said you wanted to go outside?" Joel said. "How's this for some fresh air?" He held open the door and Hannah was caught by a gust of wind that flung up her skirt and wound strands of hair around her neck. "I couldn't wait to bring you up here. You can't beat the view."

His words were picked up by the wind and thrown away over the waist-high glass wall around the perimeter of the building. Joel led her toward the edge and pointed down at something on the ground. She leaned over, looking down the side cautiously, stomach churning at the height. They were perched on top of the roof of the highest point of the tallest building, above the residence where they stayed. Hannah was closer to the tops of the mountains in front of her than to the figures of the guards milling around like ants below.

A gust of wind hit her from behind. Her hands clamped down on the edge of the glass wall in front of her, Joel's hands gripping her shoulders at the same time.

"Careful, Hannah. I wouldn't want anything to happen to you." There was a snakelike hiss in his voice, and they stood frozen for a moment, her clinging to the railing, him squeezing her painfully. Then, with a rush of blood back into her arms, he let go. "Over here," he said. "Let's get out of the wind."

Joel crossed to a clear glass box perched atop one corner of the roof. When he paused and looked back, she peeled her hands off the railing and followed. Opening the door, he waited for Hannah to enter the small room. It looked toward the only exit from the sprawling compound she could see, a single road leading to a guard box and a tall forbidding fence that ran around the edge of the facility and out of sight.

"No railing here to worry about."

Joel's voice was back to his usual smooth, bantering tone. Hannah took a step forward—away from him—but stepped back with a jerk when she looked down. Part of the floor cantilevered off the edge of the building, and it was glass, a clear view straight down to the ground so far below. The transparent floor was gridded with vents, the air moving up from them making it feel like she was walking on nothing.

She backed up into two utilitarian chairs stacked against the wall. They'd been moved to make room for an intimate, rounded loveseat and an embroidered ottoman supporting a tray with two glasses and a silver champagne bucket, dewy with condensation. It was all so ridiculously out of place in this location and in this situation.

"There's nothing I don't see." Joel didn't mince words, just stared pointedly down at the seat beside him. Hannah sank into it, wary eyes on the glass beneath them. "Nothing I don't know. So I think it'd be best if you and I had a little conversation, to clear the air."

He picked up the champagne bottle and deftly opened it with a gentle pop, filling their glasses with the light pink liquid topped with a froth of foam.

"See, I remember how much you like this," he said. "You were always surprisingly attracted to pink, despite your more beige disposition. I planned this for my triumphant return with you, to make you happy and celebrate everything we have to look forward to together."

He handed her a glass and held his up. "This might not be quite the celebratory occasion I was envisioning, but a toast nonetheless. Here's to you, dear, and how you will never, ever lie to me again." Joel clinked his flute against hers where it hung limply in her hand. "I don't blame you, love. It's the bad influences you've come under since my supposed death. Drink your champagne, it'll get warm."

Hannah didn't move. He raised an eyebrow and she quickly tossed it back.

"Where is it?" he said, reaching for her glass and refilling it.

"Where's what?" she managed to croak out.

"Don't be coy. You can't hide things from me," he said, tossing back his second glass, then nodding for her to do the same.

She stiffly obliged. Hannah didn't realize her hand had drifted to her neck until his eyes locked onto the white bandage.

Quick as a snake, a finger dug up under the bandage and the pendant fell loose, dropping on its chain. A second later it was ripped from her neck, the chain digging into her skin, tearing into the raw edge of Roman's bite mark. It came free, ends of the broken chain dangling over Joel's hand. He turned the pendant over, looking at it with surprise. Then he let out a laugh, letting it slide over his hand.

"Not at all what I was expecting."

He pulled the cloth napkin out from under the ice bucket and reached toward her neck. She leaned away.

"Hold still." Joel dabbed at her neck, then pulled the bandage back down over it. The napkin came away with a bright red dot of blood. "Can't let that drip down and ruin that lovely dress."

Joel examined her face, one eye squinting shut the way it did when he was puzzling something out.

"Where's the rest of the blood, Hannah?" he said quietly.

She had no idea what he was talking about, and it must have been evident, because the lifted eyebrow dropped and suddenly his eyes were crinkling into an amused smile.

"Well, well. What a quandary. You really don't know, do you? Maybe it *was* our dearly departed—and apparently not as bright as I thought—Mena. Sadly, no one can really be trusted, can they. Especially my kind. Drink."

He tipped over the empty bottle, then reached down behind the seat and retrieved another. "Always be prepared," he said, opening it and refilling their glasses yet again. Just the sight of more of the sickly pink liquid had Hannah's stomach in her throat.

"The blood, sweetheart. I want to know where the rest of the blood is. I've pored over the video, and one of the vials Mena drew is missing. I thought you might have taken it, for insurance. I would have."

The rest of the blood. Hannah hadn't even thought about it—her mind had been a little occupied otherwise. Mena had drawn two vials but had only one small syringe in the cell with Amara. Hannah forced the next glass down at his insistence. She realized he was plying her with alcohol to loosen her tongue, but as well as he thought he knew her, Joel had left her, and in that rough period—she wasn't proud to admit—she'd built up an impressive tolerance.

"I'm rather pleased to find out you weren't just waiting with a syringe full of blood for an opportunity to send me on my merry way. Good thing too, because the first thing I would have done if I found it on you was put it directly into Asher's neck."

Joel held his glass up toward the sun that was beginning to set in burning shades of orange, like shining red coals heaped on top of the mountains.

"Glad we've cleared that up then. I'm sure I'll locate it. It'll mean tracing everyone's whereabouts and watching footage, but it's only a matter of time before the rest of the blood you handed over to Mena like a simpleton turns up."

Joel turned to her again. He let Asher's pendant drop from his hand, catching the broken ends of the chain at the last second. The teardrop of metal swung back and forth.

"You understand I can't have your blood floating around for just anyone to get their hands on," he said. "I'll decide to whom it's administered and when."

He followed the flash of silver as it swayed back and forth like a hypnotist's pendulum, his green eyes reminding her of an exotic snake, smooth and deceptively beautiful.

That's what Joel was, she realized. A snake, a viper shedding layers of skin: rescuer, savior, doting uncle. And those were the Joels in her lifetime. There might have been hundreds through time, though she thought the cunning and power-mad creature she glimpsed now might be the true man.

Joel jerked up on the chain and caught the teardrop of metal in his hand. "Without fail," he smiled. "How corny." He pulled the mask of the man she'd once known back down over his eyes. "We'll forget this little unpleasantness. I've always told you there's no need to dwell on what can't be changed. And we'll have plenty of time to work every-thing out."

He picked up the champagne and poured the last of it into the bottom of their glasses. She was relieved there was no other bottle tucked away to use against her.

"You will remain here—permanently, of course. I'm sure you understand it can't be otherwise. Can't have you falling under the sway of any other unscrupulous immortals. I know your head was easily turned, but I blame myself for being too lenient with you growing up. Spare the rod and spoil the child, as they say.

"But it'll all work out. I'll keep your giant, lumbering Prince Charming locked in the dungeon, and you can live out an indulged, pampered life in a tower, if that's what you prefer. Until you forget him, which you will. Humans don't have the lifespan to gain real perspective. That's why they need people like me. They need to be saved from the bad ones of my kind, but also from themselves."

She'd been sitting in silence, staring through the glass, looking at the hills in the last of the pale light.

"I'll do it," she said. "If you let him go, I'll give you what you want. I'll forget he ever existed."

And she would, at least the first part, if she knew Asher wasn't confined in a glass box below here, a subterranean version of the one she was in now. Joel looked at her. It was an alarming look, because it was so clearly filled with pity.

He picked up his half-full glass. Hannah didn't bother to lift hers. She'd had enough—of the champagne and the games. He held his other hand out. And opened it.

Asher's necklace fell, not catching on the floor but dropping straight through the grate. It disappeared in a flicker of silver and was gone.

"Oblige me? Yes, you will. And forget him? I think you're going to have to. It may be hard, because he's going to be here for a while." Joel tipped his glass toward her. "A toast. To us. To this new chapter of our lives. You and me forever. Well, me forever. You, slightly less so."

He tossed back his glass with a smile while she looked woodenly downward where the necklace had disappeared, to the ground around the fortress she was confined to. A place she would not be leaving any time soon, maybe ever.

Joel saw the look on her face and rolled his eyes, setting his empty glass down with a clink.

"Really, Hannah, you have to learn to look at the big picture. As long as you do what I want, you're safe, he's safe, and the world is safe. You'll realize that. There's no great hurry. You're relatively young. And I have nothing but time."

21

Joel left her abruptly at the door of the residence. Hannah didn't notice anything different at first, but things had changed while they'd been on the roof. In the kitchen she filled the kettle with water for tea in a weak attempt to settle her jangly nerves. When Hannah pulled a lemon from the refrigerator and opened the cutlery drawer for a knife, there wasn't one. All the knives were gone. Everything was gone, replaced with an unopened box of plastic spoons. Opening the cabinet in front of her, she found the china had been replaced as well, with stacks of plates and bowls made from plastic.

She was sitting at the island, turning the empty unbreakable mug around in her hands and listening to the kettle scream itself dry when the door opened behind her.

"I see you've discovered the little safety measures I've had put in place. Can't have you taking the easy way out." Joel turned off the stove and the whistle of steam died with a hiss. "You can't imagine how surprised I was to hear you almost did once, with that stunt off the side of the bridge—though I give Asher some of the blame for that." He took the mug from her and dropped in a tea bag, pouring the water. "I'm always concerned about your safety—and mine of course."

Probably mostly his, Hannah thought. For all his claims about no one deserving more than one life, he wasn't at all in a hurry to risk shortening his.

"Are you sure it wouldn't be better to just put her somewhere more secure, for her safety, of course." Hannah hadn't heard Charlie slip into the room and come up behind her. "I'd hate to think something might happen to her."

Hannah felt something touch the back of her head and she jumped, slopping hot tea over the counter. Charlie rolled her eyes, holding the sharp picks from Hannah's hair in her hand while Joel mopped the granite and refilled Hannah's mug. He looked at the sharp lengths of metal and nodded to Charlie for her good thinking.

Joel planted a fatherly kiss on Hannah's head that made her skin crawl. "I'm sure you and Charlie are going be fast friends soon, since she's going to be spending any time with you that I can't."

Hannah glared at Charlie, who was probably about as pleased as she was with the turn of events, but unlike Hannah, was managing to keep the emotionless mask on her face.

"Just until things are more settled and I can rely on your judgment. I've told you often enough that trust has to be earned," Joel said, heading for the door. "I have a great deal to do today, what with our current guests and organizing for the pickup of our next ones. And finishing the planning for our little get-together. I'll be back before dinner, my dear." He nodded to them and disappeared.

"It's all about trust, Hannah," Charlie said, sneering at her. "Maybe you can have a fork next week, if you behave."

Hannah glared at Charlie, quickly deciding she wasn't interested in standing here and being mocked. Grabbing her sad plastic mug she stalked her way to the door, swiping her card. Nothing happened.

Charlie laughed out loud. "You're even dumber than you look. I wasn't sure that was possible. Did you really think your card was going to work anymore?" She smirked and leaned against the counter.

Hannah hadn't really, but she had to give it a try anyway. "I was going to go for a run."

She didn't think Joel was going to let her just waltz out of the place, but it was probably better for her to be as far away from Charlie as possible, since Hannah was fighting the urge to slap the snide smile off her face.

"For some reason Joel thinks you're worth all this babying. Don't tell him I said so, but I think it's because he doesn't want to believe raising you turned out to be a total waste of time. It would be sad to think he spent twenty years on someone who turned out not to be smart enough to see how important what he's doing is," Charlie said. "I think you belong in a cage with your boyfriend, but he's the boss, so maybe he can have a treadmill dragged in, if you need to burn off some of your ungrateful stupidity. But you'll step out that door next when Joel or I need you to."

Hannah whipped the card on its gold chain in Charlie's direction. It didn't even make it halfway there, and Charlie shook her head, entertained. Hannah considered doing a number of things that were absolutely stupid, like tossing the hot tea in the same direction and making a grab for the key she knew Charlie must have on her somewhere, but she knew neither would probably do her much good. She settled for walking into her bedroom and reaching out to slam the door.

It was gone. Hannah almost hit the floor when she got a handful of air instead. Cursing at the hot liquid that spilled on her feet, she threw the cheap mug at the window where it bounced off harmlessly. Charlie popped her head through the doorway.

"I have orders to make sure you don't lose your shit and hurt yourself throwing a tantrum. I'm sure I can get some restraints brought up and have you strapped to a chair for your own protection."

Hannah flopped down on the bed, staring at the woman who was leaning against the empty doorframe to taunt her.

"Why are you doing this? You're a regular human like me. You can't be okay with keeping me here as a prisoner. Even if you are swallowing the whole keeping humanity safe bull, doesn't that include me?"

Charlie smiled a snotty smile. "Oh, I'm more than okay with keeping you here, though I'd rather you were down in one of the cells. You deserve whatever you get, for not being able to appreciate what's happening here. You could be doing something that matters, but instead you're being an idiot, complaining about having to do your part for once. And you're not even special. You're a fluke." She turned and flounced off. "And you're nothing like me," Charlie shot back over her shoulder. "I'm more like them."

Hannah sat down on the bed, unable to focus. She felt like a trapped animal. Sick of staring at the unwelcome fabric of the dress Joel had chosen draped over her lap, she went to the closet and took it off, tossing it in the corner in a pile.

She went to the nightstand and opened the drawer, surprised to find the book was still there. Maybe it wasn't dangerous enough; the worst she could do with it was give someone a paper cut. Unless she could sneak up on Charlie and hit her over the head with it. Hannah didn't rule out the possibility.

Opening the embellished cover, she flipped idly through the pages. As the names passed by she thought about how many of them she might be forced to sentence to death. Hannah wondered about the altered pages and what the truth about Jeremiah was.

Joel had gone to some trouble to make her believe she was doing the world a service by helping rid it of dangerous immortals. She wondered if Joel would bother changing the pages after this. If any of it had ever been the truth, it meant nothing now if he was going make the book into a work of fiction and create villains to suit his needs.

Picking up her tablet, Hannah pulled up the camera. Turning it to video, she flipped through the pages, pausing on each one for a moment before turning it. If he altered anything, at least she'd know. When she reached the end of the entry for Zoa she turned back to the M's.

Leaving the book on the bed, Hannah went back to the kitchen where she rummaged around the drawers until she found what she was looking for. Charlie eyed her suspiciously but didn't say anything. Thankfully they hadn't been deemed weapons, and she returned to her bedroom and crawled into bed with a handful of colored markers.

Finding Roman's pages first, Hannah drew a fat red line across the bottom of the first one, taking care to make it straight and even—a match for the lines across the sections for Gabriel and Michael. She did the same to Amara's, forcing her hand steady, keeping the bloody red stripe neat, except for a small bump where a shiver made her hand jump. She recalled the final, permanent wound appearing above the perfect arch of Amara's eyebrow. It gave her stomach a sickening twist and took her back to when she'd met Asher. It was the first time she'd witnessed the bloody finality of death, when she'd thought she was watching life ebb away for good. When Amara had died, Hannah had witnessed it again, blood snaking a trail through golden hair, flowing and growing quickly cold, life permanently extinguished.

Hannah returned to Mena's page. One more time she inked the same thick red line. It sat like an incision across a pale, creamy throat. In the blank space above it she penned a notation, adding the date, the manner of her death, and how her only failing had been in believing some people can be redeemed. It was a sad eulogy in leftward slanting cursive, a pathetic ending to a glowing string of lives.

Setting the red marker aside, Hannah turned to the page for Delphine. Picking up the yellow marker she drew the mark across the bottom of the page—yellow for the time being. Eventually it would be red. She turned to Jeremiah. Picking up the book, she climbed out of bed and went back to the kitchen.

It was slightly gratifying to see Charlie look surprised for a change when Hannah plunked the book down in front of her on the table.

"What? Need me to help you sound out some of the words?" Charlie said.

"Tell me about Jeremiah. I know his section was altered. And he called Joel his friend, before you jabbed him in the neck."

Charlie sat back and crossed her arms, looking amused. "Why would I tell you?"

"Never mind. I figured you didn't know." Hannah picked up the book and started to walk away.

"Of course I know."

Pausing, Hannah turned back toward Charlie but didn't speak. She'd been right in thinking Charlie wouldn't be able to resist demonstrating just how much she knew about what went on here.

"I know more about Joel than you ever will," Charlie said, "but Jeremiah wasn't really his friend, despite whatever sad claims he might have made trying to save his own immortality. He was far too much of a nothing to ever be a friend of Joel's."

"If he was so much of a nothing, then why bother? Why pretend he was so bad and waste the time bringing him here and making him human?"

"Why do you care?"

"I knew you didn't know."

This time Hannah walked away and returned to her bed. Charlie followed her, only waiting long enough to make Hannah think she might have misjudged her.

"I know you think you're clever, that you can bait me into talking. You're not, but I guess there's no harm in telling you. It's done anyway. And maybe you need a little more information. It's unbelievable how clueless you are."

Charlie flopped down on the edge of the bed and looked around the room, turning up her nose. "Sure, Jeremiah and Joel had some history. When Jeremiah was alive for the first time—in oh sixteen something-teen—he was one of the more forward-thinking men of his time. Joel was good enough to take him under his wing and help him make some discoveries in astronomy and guide him in writing some poetry. I imagine most of the mental heavy lifting was Joel though. Jeremiah would have been nothing without Joel."

Hannah tried not to roll her eyes.

"Joel even clued Jeremiah in about what he was and enlisted him to help with his cause. He did at first." Charlie sniffed disdainfully. "Problem was, Jeremiah was also a clergyman. Apparently he took issue with what Joel was doing, said mankind didn't need his protection or governance—that was what they had god for. And it seems there'd been some human collateral damage when Joel had taken down an immortal—it might even have been your dear friend Amara—and Jeremiah was offended by that as well, since Joel was willing to lose a few lives for the greater good. What a fool.

"Jeremiah died shortly after. It was sheer chance he was an immortal like Joel."

Laughing lightly, Charlie got up and stared down at Hannah—looking annoyingly teacher-like and superior. "You'd think he would have realized Joel was right after that and helped him. I've been told Jeremiah was intelligent, but apparently not. Though I think Joel once called you bright, so he's a bit generous with the descriptions.

"Since he came back, Jeremiah's been a thorn in Joel's side," Charlie said, "unwilling to support his cause and poisoning others against him. He doesn't think it's their job to interfere, and that interferes with the plan."

Hannah stared. "So that's why? That's it? Joel turned Jeremiah human just because he doesn't agree with what he's doing?"

"Isn't that enough?" Charlie said. "If you aren't for us, you're against us and you're a danger. You should keep that in mind."

Looking down at the book, Hannah shook her head. She inked the yellow stripe across Jeremiah's page, wondering if she'd be here to mark it over in red.

She turned to Asher. Running a finger down the page, she frowned, thinking about where he was now. Hopefully in a dreamless slumber, in no pain.

"Might as well make that one red."

Hannah was surprised to see Charlie still there at the foot of the bed, a nasty smirk on her face.

"What do you mean?" Hannah scowled back, eyes narrowed.

Charlie didn't answer, just pasted on a plastic smile. "It's only a matter of time. There was plenty of come and go out of those cells before you came, but now, it's a roach motel. They check in, but they don't check out."

Hannah stood up. She might not be able to do any permanent damage to some of the people here, but if she gave Charlie a black eye, at least she was going to have to live with it for a couple weeks. Maybe Hannah could get two in.

"You act like you matter," she said to Charlie. "At least Joel needs me alive. I don't know what you get out of being such a bitch, but don't bother. It doesn't matter to anyone. Not me, and not Joel, since if he can raise me and turn on me, you're even less important."

It was the first time she'd seen Charlie show emotion. It was brief, but it was there, a flush in the skin. Hannah had struck a nerve; she just wasn't quite sure which one.

"You don't know anything. And you'd better think about what you're saying before you run your mouth anymore. Because I'm the only one you have anything to trade with, if you ever want to see your boyfriend again."

Charlie hadn't said another word after her cryptic remark about Asher. Hannah tried waiting her out, wearing a rut in the floor walking back and forth in front of the wide bank of windows. She hoped it would work again, leaving enough empty air that Charlie would cave and fill it—she clearly had something she wanted to say—but it hadn't worked so far. They stewed in the silence. Charlie sat while Hannah paced.

There was a knock on the door and Hannah jumped out of her path to answer it. Charlie stepped out in front of her.

"Ooh," she said, "maybe it's your ankle chains." She waved Hannah back and opened it. "Shoot. It's only dinner."

Charlie pulled the cart inside the door and quickly closed it. She pulled the plastic plates out from under the domes and set one on the table and one at the island. She tossed a plastic-wrapped spork at Hannah, who let it bounce off her chest and fall to the floor.

"Don't be a baby. Sit down and eat." Charlie pulled up her chair at the island and glared at the utensil Hannah was ignoring. Hannah resumed her pacing, watching out of the corner of her eye as Charlie poked at her food, before quickly giving up in irritation.

"I'm not going to ask you again. Sit the hell down before I have them send me a cattle prod with dessert. Your toddler routine is annoying the crap out of me." She continued under her breath, "I didn't graduate from MIT so I could spend my day babysitting some hillbilly idiot."

There was only a small pause in Hannah's pacing.

"Ugh," Charlie huffed in exasperation, abandoning her food and getting up. She poked through the cupboard, clearly not finding what she was looking for. Slamming the last door in irritation she crossed to the door to Joel's office. Punching in the code on the panel next to it, she disappeared inside.

Hannah raised an eyebrow when Charlie popped back out with a glass decanter. At the island she slopped a couple of fingers into a plastic cup.

"You better pour mine for me. Wouldn't want me to get my hands on any glass," Hannah said, coming around the island and reaching past Charlie to take down another cup. Charlie glared for a moment, then poured some for Hannah. Hannah sniffed it, then shot it back.

"God, you are such an unwashed miscreant. This is a forty-year-old Laphroaig, not Wild Turkey."

Charlie took an affected sniff of hers, rolled the glass around, then took a small sip. Hannah reached over to refill her glass but Charlie snatched the decanter away.

"Now, now, children mustn't touch." Charlie poured a little more into her own glass, then turned and dribbled a stingy amount into Hannah's. This time Hannah sniffed it, mostly hoping the appreciation would get her another pour. On top of the smell of disposable plastic cup it smelled like smoke, but underneath that, raisins and a sticky sweetness like molasses. It still burned like fire going down.

"It's not bad," Hannah conceded.

"It's exquisite, you Neanderthal. Don't even pretend you can begin to appreciate it. Joel has exceptional taste. He's not going to drink that toilet wine you probably like."

"If this is so amazing it's probably expensive. Do you think he's going to be happy we're drinking it? I mean, he keeps it locked in his study."

"Ugh, you're an idiot. Unless you're blind—which I guess is

possible on top of stupid—it's usually out on the side table. It's in his study to keep the glass decanter away from you. Joel is above anything as mundane as the cost of a bottle of Scotch." Charlie tossed her head superiorly.

"But not above booting you out of your bedroom for me?" Hannah took the shot at Charlie, a shot she was fairly sure would hit home, seeing how familiar Charlie was with the place, how she knew the code to the office, how she lit up for Joel and only Joel, but mostly on the single blond bobby pin she'd found in the bathroom. She knew she was right by the way Charlie's hand clenched around her glass so tightly the shatterproof plastic gave a little squeak.

"Did he give you time to pack before he brought me back," Hannah said, "or did he just change the locks and leave your stuff all garbage bagged for you somewhere?"

Charlie sniffed and tossed her head back, snatching up the decanter and turning away.

"Hopefully he booted you to somewhere better than the cell you tried to stick me in when you had the chance. So where *do* you sleep now, since your old room is taken? Hanging upside down in a closet probably." Hannah said to Charlie's back. "I'll trade you if you want. It's got to be better than here right now."

Charlie froze, turning back to Hannah, her face red, lips pursed.

"That's what you want, isn't it?" Hannah said. "Me gone so you can crawl back into Joel's bed. Wow, it must have killed you when he moved you out so he could move me in. How's it feel, knowing you're stuck with me here as long as I live—which is going to be as long as he can manage, because while he may not give a crap about me, he needs me. As long as I live? That could be about as long as you live too. You and I, we don't have their longevity, do we?"

Hannah tossed back the last of the Scotch, happily feeling the warmth sink downward into her stomach. "I want to be out of here just as bad as you want me to be," she said.

"You don't know anything, you silly little fool. I told you, I'm the only one you have anything to trade with." Charlie came over and clunked the decanter back down. She looked at it for a moment, then filled her glass, watching the level of amber liquid behind the cut glass drop, pretending she didn't care.

Charlie tossed it back. Hannah gave her credit for not even blanching—her own stomach was already rolling.

"You don't know anything about me," Charlie said, her voice rasping. "I was part of the plan. I was perfectly willing to do what needed to be done. I even helped Joel cook up this little fantasy so you would get with the program right off the bat. I put it all together; the bullshit about him wanting you here, having your room all ready and waiting in case you ever came. I picked out your damn clothes, which you don't even have the class to wear."

Hannah looked down at her sweatpants. There was an embarrassing stain on the leg, though she didn't think Charlie noticed it, since she was pink cheeked and staring daggers directly into Hannah's head.

"Even letting you see the book was my idea. It's a painstakingly compiled piece of history, and I suggested it would make things more palatable, seeing the horrifying histories of people like your hulking friend's creepy sister. Granted, I didn't expect to have Jeremiah fall into our laps and need to change the book to keep your pristine little conscience satisfied. I'm surprised you even noticed, you're so busy whining and running pointlessly around the track like a deficient."

Hannah reached over for the decanter. Charlie didn't stop her, just stared her down, a little glassy eyed. The decanter was hefty, but Hannah wasn't sure she could get enough oomph behind it to make it worth it, so she refilled her glass instead. They were doing a solid job on emptying it, so she filled Charlie's as well.

"So if you're so on top of everything and didn't mind a bit that Joel dropped you like a hot rock to clear out a bedroom for me, why are you so impatient to get me out of here?"

Charlie picked up her glass and eyed it but took only a small sip before setting it carefully back down. "I want you gone, that's for damn sure, but as long as Joel needs your blood that's not going to happen.

But that's going to change. I want something else, and you're going to give it to me."

"You're repeating yourself. You must be drunk. What could you possibly want from me and why would I do anything for you?"

"I'm not drunk. I have an incredible tolerance," Charlie said. "And you'll do it." She picked up her glass and looked at it but set it back down without taking a sip. "They're dead. Did you know that?" Charlie said.

"Who?"

"Delphine. Jeremiah. They're dead."

Hannah didn't say anything. She didn't believe it.

"I could take you down and show you, but I wouldn't risk it. Why would I do anything for you that doesn't benefit me? But they're dead. At this rate we're going to need to start stacking them two-deep in the morgue."

"How? Why would Joel do that?"

"He didn't, though saving the taxpayers from having to spend a gazillion dollars keeping Delphine on death row would have been a good reason, for starters. But he didn't even have to kill her. The minute Delphine was awake and free she took herself out—bashed her head against the wall until it looked like a squashed tomato. Joke's on her, I guess."

Hannah felt sick at how nonchalantly Charlie described it. She pushed away her Scotch. "And Jeremiah?" Maybe she didn't really want to know.

"Oops, that was my fault, I think. For some reason, he just never woke up. Maybe I gave him a poke somewhere a little too deep. Or maybe it was your blood, and you poisoned him. I guess we'll have to wait for the autopsy results."

Charlie sat back down at the table and crossed her arms. "Good riddance to bad rubbish. Joel's working on bringing in the next ones right now. Hopefully the same thing happens to them. You might want to think about taking an iron supplement, with all the blood you're going to be donating," she said. "At this rate, how long do you think your little friend—sorry, gigantic overgrown doofus friend—is going to survive? Joel will eventually get tired of having to use Asher as leverage and do him just to free up some cell space—it's going to be a hot commodity if everything goes the way it should. Going to be rough for you when he ends up dead, which he will, but at least Joel won't kill you outright, since you're necessary."

Now completely in control of herself again, Charlie paused, looking sideways at Hannah with a sly smile. "Unless you weren't necessary. No one would care about either of you then."

"Not much chance of that happening. Aren't you supposed to be super smart?" Hannah said, shaking her head.

"Just because you barely scraped by with an associate's degree in redneck survival doesn't mean everyone else is clueless. And even Joel doesn't know everything. But I'll clue him in, and then—well, I don't care what happens to you."

"What do you want, Charlie? I'm tired of this conversation."

Charlie got up and tidied everything neatly, lids back on the untouched dishes, cups emptied—with a sigh for the contents poured down the sink—then carefully washed and dried and put back in the cupboard. The decanter was returned to Joel's office and the door relocked. Finally she sat back down across from Hannah.

"I want the same thing Joel wants," Charlie said.

"World domination?"

Charlie rolled her eyes. "Your blood, dumbass."

Hannah raised an eyebrow. What good would her blood do Charlie?

"I tried to get my hands on it when you were brought in, but Mena stuck her dead little nose into things." Charlie looked at Hannah, an excited gleam in her eye. "I'm going to tell you another little secret. The blood that's missing? I took it from Mena, out of her pocket after she died."

Hannah's eyes widened. What would Charlie want with it, unless she was going to hand it over to Joel for a pat on the head. The only person it could have an effect on was …

"Oh calm down. I didn't give it to your meathead boyfriend. I wanted to get my hands on it for my own purposes. Joel's going to be surprised, and in the end, thrilled at what I've found out. But I need a little more of it. And a little more time. You're going to give it to me, and you're going to keep your mouth shut about everything I've told you until the little event Joel has planned. If you can manage that, I'll do something for you."

22

"**C**harlie was supposed to make sure this included all the appropriate accessories, so I'm sure everything you need is in here."

Hannah jumped when Joel dropped the long white box on the couch next to her. She'd been sitting, staring blankly at the swirling clouds that sat just below the level of the windows and blocked all view of the ground. It was like being stranded on a floating island in a sea of uninspiring gray. It had been that way for days, dreary and isolating. With nothing else to do, not permitted to set foot outside the residence, Hannah had spent most of her time looking blankly out the window, thinking until her head hurt, swallowing her anger and apprehension.

"What is it?" Hannah eyed the box suspiciously.

"Your attire for this evening."

"This evening?"

Joel nodded, sitting down on the opposite side of the couch.

"I believe I mentioned I was planning a little something. It popped into my head as soon as I decided to bring you here. I was just waiting for the right moment—and here it is," he said. "I intended tonight to be a celebration, a grand announcement of the new development and to introduce you officially since you're the key to all of it. This is the pinnacle of everything we've been trying to do for so long. The effect it'll have on morale is going to be incredible." He turned to look at her sternly. "Granted, I hadn't anticipated your obstinance. But despite our current difference of opinion, I see no reason why the evening shouldn't proceed."

"You want me to get dressed up and go to a party and just act like I'm not a prisoner and you aren't threatening me to make me do what you want?" Hannah shoved the box away with contempt.

"Indeed I do," Joel said. "I expect you to be ready and willing, with a smile on your face. If you're a prisoner, it's only because you choose to be. And Asher's current state will only be necessary until you come around to seeing things correctly. Think of yourself more as a treasured guest who must be protected at all costs, even from herself."

He must have thought her silence meant she was taking his words into consideration, and he slid closer until they were shoulder to shoulder. It was the strangest feeling, that something so familiar as sitting beside him that would have been a comfort in the past now gave her a little shiver of disgust. He mistook it for a chill and rubbed his hand up and down her arm.

"I expect you'll come around; you're going to have to. Tonight will be a good indication of your ability to operate as required." There was a ding from his phone and he hopped up. "Duty calls, as usual, though I think it'll settle down quickly after this. All the time and effort spent locating and trying to hold people in those cells can be refocused on a single objective. Find them once and make them human. One and done, and then we can move on, instead of chasing the same ghosts again and again." He opened the door to leave. "Yes, it's going to be quite the evening. I'll be back for you. Who knows, maybe you'll even enjoy yourself. Charlie will be by shortly with your meal and to help you dress."

He closed the door, and the clap of the lock echoed around the empty room.

⸻

She was still glaring at the unopened box when Charlie pushed a cart through the door. Hannah watched her take the covered dish from the cart and plunk it on the table. She whipped off the white cloth to reveal bottom shelves that were packed with items, pieces of small lab equipment, boxes and bins of things, all jigsaw puzzled together.

"Get over here. We don't have much time and we both have to be ready when Joel gets back." She eyed Hannah. "And some of us are going to take longer than others to not look like a train wreck." Charlie began to unpack things, pulling a blood draw set out of one of the bins. "Give me your arm."

Charlie clamped a hand around her wrist. Hannah pulled back, and they stood there for a moment in an arm-wrestling match.

"How do I know you're going to do what you promised?" Hannah said.

"You don't. But you don't have any other options. And every minute you wait makes Asher's chances of ever walking out of here that much slimmer." Charlie jerked Hannah's wrist. Her thin arms were deceptively strong. But so were Hannah's. "Stop. You're just wasting time."

"All of this, just to get back with Joel." Hannah relented, letting her arm be pulled straight. "Turns out he's kind of a dick. But I guess there's no accounting for taste."

"You think this is all about Joel and me? Granted, we were happy enough before you came along. But I'm not a fool. I know what would have happened. I'm not going to look like this forever, and he would have lost interest eventually. This, though, this is going to make and keep me a top priority. I get what I want, he gets what he wants, and we get to fulfill our life's ambitions, without having to risk you screwing it all up."

"There's no way this is going to work," Hannah said, "but fine, as long as you keep up your end." Hannah stared down at the needle and didn't flinch when it slid into her arm. "That's enough." Hannah reached up and pulled out the needle before Charlie could clip a second vial in. "I don't want any extra sitting around in case you get any bright ideas."

"Bright ideas are the only kind I have, dim bulb. I have enough anyway, and it won't be such a hot commodity soon," Charlie said. "Joel and Mena were surprisingly dense about the possibilities. Just goes to show that age doesn't necessarily come with any added wisdom."

Charlie held the vial up to the light, looking at the red inside. "All they wanted to know was what your blood could do to *them*. They never even considered what it might do to another human. It took me about two minutes of basic tests to see the possibilities. Disappointingly short-sighted on their part."

She suddenly looked like she'd forgotten Hannah existed and returned to busily setting up whatever she'd brought on the cart. Hannah stepped back and watched her as she bent over the table, focused on the equipment in front of her.

Hannah wondered if there really was any chance it would work. Charlie seemed convinced, and Hannah had to concede that while the woman might be a snake, she was no idiot.

From the outset, Charlie had a plan it seemed even Joel hadn't considered. From the moment it was known what Hannah's blood did, Charlie had wanted to recreate the effects in the lab. It would have meant the success of Joel's master plan wasn't dependent on the length of Hannah's life, and it would have meant an unlimited supply of what he needed to make anyone he wished human. It was why she'd tried to get her hands on Hannah's blood when she arrived, and why she took the missing vial from Mena.

But she'd failed miserably—that much Charlie had admitted when she presented Hannah with her little deal. What made Hannah's blood do what it did was still a mystery, and all Charlie's attempts to reproduce the effects had come to nothing.

What Charlie did discover, however, was that Mena had been close to the mark about one thing. Hannah was like a virus. When her blood was introduced into immortals it took over, and they changed. But it changed humans too, in a different way.

"Go start getting ready. And use conditioner, for god's sake, so I don't have to break a comb making you look presentable. Be quick. I'll be in as soon as I'm done here."

Hannah turned and made her way to the bedroom, leaving Charlie bent industriously over the table, a small, confident smile on her face.

Soon, Charlie was going to make herself like Hannah. If it worked the way she was confident it would—the way it had when Charlie had introduced the blood to a sample of regular human blood—Hannah would be unnecessary. Hannah wasn't sure what that meant for her own future, but what Charlie had promised to do—her end of the bargain—was to let Asher leave before the night was over.

⊶⊷

The elevator ride down was silent at first, Joel only removing his hand from Hannah's waist to brush an invisible speck of dust from the sleeve of his tuxedo. Someone who didn't know anything about the situation might think them a well-heeled couple on their way to a fancy event.

The dress in the box hadn't been another shade of the blues and greens Joel favored but was a deep dark red, in a softly shining fabric that flowed like spilled wine. *Or like blood,* Hannah thought, which might have been behind the color choice. The fabric slithered around her feet when Hannah turned around. It felt like a snake weaving its way around her ankles.

Hannah reached a finger up and pulled at the uncomfortably tight high neck that covered the bandage on her throat. It was snug and stiff and felt like a choke collar. Joel pulled her hand back down to her waist, and she stifled a shudder at the feeling of his hand against her skin.

She watched the light bar whisk downward, so intent on it she jumped when Joel spoke.

"I can see by the scowl on your face that you haven't come around to my way of thinking yet. I daresay I don't need to remind you, but it would behoove you to behave. Remember, while your survival is assured at present, Asher's is not."

Joel took her arm, squeezing until she winced. Hannah twisted to get out from his grip, but he jerked her roughly into place beside him.

"Surviving, of course, does not guarantee freedom of movement, or even consciousness. Don't force my hand." He dropped his arm and straightened his sleeve. "And try to act like it's just a party, dear, one you're delighted to attend. Remember, you are the guest of honor. Behave as if life depends on it. Someone's does."

The elevator suddenly dropped into open air, clear glass replacing the dark of the elevator shaft. Joel stood straighter, a bright, relaxed smile appearing on his face, suddenly a different person as they descended toward a vast outdoor space filled with people milling around tables swathed in white cloths and a large stage where a band was set up.

"Smile. I insist," this charming Joel said as the car stopped and the door slid open. Hannah dragged the corners of her mouth up into a ghost of a smile. The mellow, bright music and sounds of laughing voices invaded the silence through the open door and jarred with the tension of a moment ago.

A neatly pressed waiter in black holding a tray of champagne waited for them just outside, and Joel took two glasses and handed her one. Hannah took it unenthusiastically, in no mood for champagne after their last toast.

"Charlie, there you are. Is everything going smoothly?"

Charlie gave Joel a radiant smile. Of course she looked undeniably stunning. Her usually precisely restrained hair hung in long, silvery waves down her back. The green silk of her dress was fitted so closely it was like paint against her skin, the neckline a puzzle of straps and mesh that managed to look enticing without revealing an inch of actual skin.

Looking at them side by side as Joel gave Charlie his other arm, Hannah didn't wonder the two of them were a pair. Besides both being terribly attractive and intelligent and sharing a single-minded and absolute belief in their misguided cause, they were both more than a little crazy.

Charlie nodded stiffly at Hannah behind Joel's back as he led them across the room, nodding and smiling as he went. The room was a swirl of well-dressed, excited people. Everyone present seemed happy, thrilled at the prospect of a night of unaccustomed looseness and celebration.

Craning her neck to look over the faces, Hannah realized all of them were obviously human. Anyone who might have reason to disagree with Joel's plans, who might be concerned with who he chose to take down and why, was missing. She didn't know if they had all drifted away like Nobel had insinuated—she wasn't surprised he hadn't returned himself—or if Joel encouraged them to leave. Not that she blamed them for leaving, whatever the motivation. Proximity to

Hannah hadn't worked out well for people like them in the past, and she doubted anyone wanted to be next. It was safer for them, but it left Joel with no one who might oppose him, and a legion of employees convinced of the rightness of his self-imposed mission.

Joel pulled out a seat for her at a table set with gold-rimmed china and silverware set in soldierly ranks. He left her there with Charlie standing stiffly behind her. She'd probably been ordered to be on guard so Hannah didn't decide to slip a butter knife down her dress. Just the thought made her finger twitch toward the flatware. The band abruptly stopped, and there was a tap on the microphone.

"Thank you all for coming." Joel's voice brought a swift end to conversation, and all eyes turned to him. "We're here tonight to celebrate. I know how hard you've all been working, and that we've had some hard losses, but I'm about to give you some news I guarantee will make every one of you leave here a changed person."

He looked around at the faces turned up at him with almost worshipful attention. From the benign, satisfied look on his face, she could see he enjoyed it, was soaking it in, taking in the moment.

"But first"—his expression changed into a look of sadness— "as is sometimes the case, good news is preceded by a less happy note. I know all of you loved Paige and mourn her loss. Few of you know, however, that she was recently joined by another, who also made the ultimate sacrifice. This person, too, knew the importance of our mission and shared it with me for a very long time. The safety of humanity was her driving force and her primary concern. Please raise your glasses."

There were hushed movements and the clink of glassware.

"To Mena, who will be greatly missed."

There was a buzz of conversation, even a few laughs at what probably seemed like a joke about the death of someone who'd died so many times.

"Please, I know some of you may be puzzled. Let me clarify. By death, I mean a true and final death, not the temporary kind that was hers until now."

There was confused silence, glasses held in midair.

"Mena died bravely in the service of her mission," Joel said, "but I take comfort in the knowledge that when she passed, she knew our mission had been accomplished in a real way. She knew we had finally reached the day we've dreamed of, where the same people we've continued to fight against can now be made permanently human. They will be a threat to the world no more."

A few soft gasps were heard, a rise in conversation. Joel raised his free hand and again there was dead silence.

"Don't be sad. Be joyful. Both Mena and Paige would have wished you to. Eat, drink, dance, knowing they would be overjoyed, their hearts swelling as mine is, with the knowledge that we are no longer fighting an endless battle that cannot be won. Let me share with you how."

Joel was the consummate actor, eyes ablaze, glass still held high, the room in his thrall.

"Hannah, please join me."

She didn't move at first, until she felt Charlie jerk her chair backward. Hannah didn't wait for the woman to dig her nails into her shoulder and make her get up, but stood, straight and rigid. Somehow she made her way up the stairs without tripping on the fabric that slithered bloody and red around her legs, grabbing at her shoe heels.

"Very few of you are aware of what we've discovered," Joel said, "though I know all of you have sensed the undercurrent of change and excitement. You've heard rumors about immortals who've dropped off the map, virtually disappeared. We recently discovered why. The source stands here next to me."

Joel looked at Hannah, his expression telling her clearly that she needed to smile. She did a half convincing job and gave a small, embarrassing wave.

"Everyone, this is Hannah. She was just an infant when I rescued her, near death at the hands of her father Michael, the evil murderer of so many. I raised her, not knowing the blood in her veins—a result of her being a human descendant of an immortal, the only one of her kind—would be the key to relieving the world of the threat we've been fighting against."

Joel grabbed Hannah's limp hand and pulled her closer to him. She looked out over the faces below them, every one of them intently staring excitedly, none of them fearful. Not like she was.

"Look happy, darling," he whispered into her ear. "You're going to be spending the remainder of your life with these people. Best to make a good first impression."

Joel squeezed her hand until the bones protested. She forced her smile a little wider until he loosened his grip and continued speaking to the crowd.

"Here she is, and here she'll stay. We'll keep her protected and safe, so together we can complete our mission, finally bringing to an end the scourge of evil immortals who terrorize the human race."

He yanked Hannah's arm up and smiled broadly at the thunderous wave of triumphant applause.

23

When the applause finally died down and Joel waved the band into an annoyingly peppy, triumphant tune, he escorted Hannah back to their table and pulled out her chair. Joel moved to pull out a seat for Charlie next, but she ducked away instead of sitting.

"You'll have to excuse me for a moment," she said. She smiled and disappeared as the first course was placed in front of them.

"I know you'll love the meal. I had you in mind when I was choosing it, while I was arranging everything really," Joel said, raising his glass and draining it quickly, holding it up for the hovering waiter to refill.

The meal may have been chosen for her, but it was glue and sawdust in her mouth. The courses blurred together, everything pushed in circles around the gold rims of the plates. It seemed like an age passed before the chargers were whisked away and the table was finally set for dessert, the soft conversation and clink of glassware around them slowly rising to laughter and louder voices, happy and relaxed faces all around. All but hers.

Hannah saw Joel nod his head from the corner of her eye, and the band—who'd been playing softly throughout the meal—suddenly grew louder, moving into a more upbeat song.

"Come, let's dance," Joel said, standing and reaching his hand out to her.

"Joel, I really don't feel—"

His hand dug into her elbow and she stood, knocking over her glass, spilling a stain of pink over the stark white cloth. A waiter immediately retrieved the upended glass and replaced it with another that he filled. Hannah hated the sight of it, hated all this precisely planned fake enjoyment. "Fine," she said, relenting to the hand clamped on her arm and forcing her to stand, "let's dance. Could I at least use the ladies room first?"

Joel looked over toward Charlie, who'd spent dinner sitting rather silently on the other side of Hannah, looking ecstatic though pale, her face blanched to nearly the color of her hair.

"Of course," he said. "Charlie?"

Charlie didn't look as put out as usual and stood up, motioning Hannah ahead of her. She didn't seem worried Hannah might jump her and make a run for it. Unless maybe she wanted her to. Hannah kept an eye on the figure beside her as they skirted the edge of the veranda, in case Charlie had the order—or the urge—to push Hannah off the building. It would be an even more expedient way of getting rid of her.

"Did you do it?" Hannah paused outside the bathroom door. Charlie didn't say anything, but the smile at the corner of her mouth was her answer.

"How do you know it worked?"

Rolling her eyes, Charlie twirled a lock of her hair around her finger in the most human gesture Hannah had ever seen her make. Maybe she'd been a robot this whole time, and Hannah's blood had turned her into a real girl.

"I know because I'm smarter than you. Which is why I won't bother explaining the science, because it would be like explaining physics to my goldfish," Charlie said.

Hannah didn't believe for a minute she had a goldfish. Charlie opened the bathroom door and looked inside, and when she confirmed it was empty, held it open for Hannah.

Before she stepped in, Hannah asked the question she really wanted the answer to but was afraid of hearing, if Charlie had decided not to honor her end of the bargain.

"Where is he?"

Charlie jerked her head toward the bathroom, for Hannah to get on with it. "His sedative drip is off and so are his restraints. If he can't figure out how to kill himself and get out of that cell while he has the chance, then he's too stupid to be running around in the general population."

"Kill himself? You were supposed to let him go."

"He's immortal. That's why we keep them knocked out, dummy, so they can't pull a Delphine and bash their heads against the wall to escape all the time. What did you think was going to happen? That I was going to have him walked to the front door? Even I couldn't have managed that without Joel finding out. It was hard enough to do what I did without being caught."

Hannah stumbled into the bathroom. If Asher died, he was going to end up right here where she was, and they were both going to be in serious trouble.

●◆●●◆●

Hannah felt eyes following her as she and Charlie made their way back from the bathroom. She looked down to make sure there wasn't toilet paper hanging from her shoe. The staring continued, picked up even, with more eyes—all eyes—on her when Joel led her out onto the dance floor and twirled her around.

Pulling her in, Joel placed his arm around her waist, against her bare back, making her feel naked and exposed. He leaned his head near her ear. "Good job, darling. I'd almost believe you're enjoying yourself. With behavior like you've shown so far, this might not be the last fresh air you breathe for the foreseeable future." He spun her away again with the change in the music.

Other couples began to fill the space around them on the dance floor. A waiter came by and Joel retrieved yet another glass for both of them. She reached for hers but wobbled, snagging her heel in the hem of her dress.

"Shoot."

She tried to tug it away, but it was caught and she nearly lost her balance.

"Stop, dear, you'll end up on the floor." Joel handed her the glasses and reached down, pulling the heel free. "You look marvelous, but you never did have a great deal of luck navigating in anything less than functional."

Hannah handed him his glass, looking past him to where the moon was a full yellow disk that looked as if it were resting on the edge of the railing.

"Come on, might as well have a look." Joel led her to the edge of the wide veranda, in the dim shadows beyond the party lights. They watched in silence as thin clouds drifted over the moon in lacy patterns, until Joel set his empty glass on the ledge and turned to her. "It really is a beautiful night."

"I've seen better," she said. Joel froze. "Feel that? You're a genius, so I'm sure you can guess what it is."

Hannah jabbed the syringe she was holding just a little farther into his side, so she was sure he could feel the tip of the needle breaking the skin. Joel turned his head to her very slowly, until he could look at her face where she stood next to him, glued to his side.

"Clever girl. Wherever did you get that?" He shifted slightly, and Hannah gave him a poke to make him freeze again.

"Out of my underwear. When I pretended to trip. I know how to walk in a pair of heels, Joel." She wiggled the needle a little bit to remind him it was there. "Or did you mean where did I get it before that? I'll give you a hint," Hannah said. "She's wearing green, which is about the color of her face right now."

Joel's eyes flicked to Charlie, who stood a few feet away. Where she'd been pale when she'd taken Hannah to the bathroom, now she was obviously and seriously ill. Her hand was clamped down on the back of a chair and she was clearly struggling to stay upright.

"What did you do to her?" Joel said, starting to move toward Charlie. There might have been some real concern in his words, or maybe he was trying to throw Hannah off, but she stopped his movement with a jab.

"I didn't do anything to her. She did it to herself. She was trying to use my blood to make herself like me," Hannah said. "Why she decided to do it in the bathroom and put the needle in the trash can, I can't imagine, since she's supposed to be the smart one. Probably wanted to do it at the most conspicuous time, for effect. Or maybe it was getting uncomfortable stuck down the front of her dress."

Charlie suddenly jerked upright. Then she heaved forward and vomited a stream of red down her dress. She stood there for a moment, swaying gently back and forth, a dark, wet slick down the front of her. Charlie collapsed to the ground.

Joel twitched, and Hannah drove the needle deeper, finger on the plunger.

"What do you want, Hannah?" he said.

His voice sounded choked. She wondered if it was because he really cared about the woman who loved him and was probably dying in front of him right now, or because of the possibility he was a thumb's pressure away from being human himself.

"You can have someone call for help for her," Hannah said. "Tell them they better hurry, because on their way here they're going to need to stop by the prison. Tell them to bring me Asher."

Joel nodded slightly to a nearby guard, one of the many Hannah had picked out among the guests, sidearms tucked discreetly into their tailored jackets. The guard slipped out of sight, past the small ring of people around where Charlie lay on the ground. She convulsed—one last disjointed quake, gobbets and strings of red pouring from her mouth—then lay still.

The sight turned Hannah's stomach, but if it bothered Joel, he gave no indication. He'd recovered from the emotion he'd let slip a moment ago and now stood perfectly in place, preternaturally calm.

Hannah, on the other hand, was struggling to remain still. Her hand was growing sweaty, cramping from clutching the needle. It was a deadly waiting game now; for her, for Joel, and for Charlie. Charlie looked like she was losing.

Little by little, all the attention had been drawn their way. Conversations had slowed until every head was turned toward their corner, the band dying out with the blat of a trumpet, cut off by the conductor at the sight of an alley parting in the silent crowd.

At the front of the group pushing its way toward them were two medics laden with emergency duffle bags. To their credit, they took one look at Hannah with a needle stuck in their boss's side and gave their attention to Charlie instead. Hannah didn't see what they were doing to her, because she was quickly drawn to the group that appeared behind them.

"Asher," she whispered, shocked and sickened. What had they done to him? How had he managed to deteriorate so quickly in such a short period of time?

He could barely stand on his own. The burly guards on either side of him were struggling to move Asher along, with his bare, deformed feet stumbling and dragging against the ground. His face was battered, purple and red and green, and his lips were cracked and split. Trickles of blood had dribbled and dried down his chin. Hannah felt herself choking at the expression of pain in his single remaining eye.

When they let him slide to the ground in front of them, he looked up, but his remaining eye only focused for a moment before closing.

Hannah poked Joel so angrily she felt the needle strike bone, though he didn't react. "What have you done to him, Joel?"

Joel didn't answer. He struck, as quickly as a snake, in the distracted second when Hannah looked at Asher crumpled on the floor. Joel wrenched her arm back and shoved her away from him, sending her crashing into the nearest table in a clatter of dishes and glass.

He had the needle. Before she could untangle herself from the pile, he bent over Asher. When Joel stood up again, Hannah could see the depressed syringe standing like a flag from Asher's back.

Shooting his cuffs, tossing his hair back into place, Joel smiled a wicked smile.

"You wanted him, and here he is. Now you've really done it. You are quite the poison apple today, aren't you?" He looked to where the medics stood by Charlie—no longer working—then to Asher, who had rallied enough to pull himself to his knees.

"Clearly you're too much of a danger to the population here to be allowed to roam free, Hannah," Joel said, shaking his head at her. "And I see now that you won't let yourself see reason, and your ungratefulness won't be easily mended. So a vegetable in a cell you will be." Joel waved his guards forward. "Maybe I'll be generous and put you two next to each other. He'll be even easier to manage now that he's human, for as long as he lasts anyway."

Joel didn't make a move to stop her when Hannah threw herself at Asher, trying to pick up his head and see his face. A slit of silvery blue eye showed for an instant, then slid shut.

"He'll be beneficial to study of course, though that kind of research has a habit of shortening the lifespan. But I'm really interested in finding out how much a person can take after they've lost the ability to come back. Real fear, and real pain. Knowing that after all this time your true death is coming at any second. I think it'll be very important scientifically."

"Just let him go, Joel. I'll do whatever you want."

Joel laughed and shook his head. "Hannah, Hannah. You'll do that anyway. You had a perfectly good chance and you wasted it. I'm sad you had to make it so hard on yourself. I thought I raised you better, really, but you never could see the big picture."

Hannah ran a hand through Asher's hair, tears leaking from her eyes. She couldn't believe she'd ever wanted him to be human. "Ash. I love you." The only movement was his breath against her arm. "Ash. Do you trust me?" He didn't move. She brushed aside the golden hair and placed a gentle kiss on his forehead. "Can you stand up?"

Joel took a step forward, eyes narrowing. He'd heard her. He cocked his head at the guards. "Pick him up. Put him back where you got him."

Hannah felt Asher's body shift. His head moved. He nodded almost imperceptibly.

"Trust me," she said.

Hannah stood up and looked at Joel.

"Asher. Jump."

She didn't know where he found it—the strength to move—but he did, despite the injuries, the clearly shattered bones showing through his feet. There was no pause, no hesitation. Joel's head swiveled as Asher gathered the last of the energy that remained in his abused body and pushed himself to his feet.

Then, in a burst, he was moving. He took a giant step forward and, planting his hand on the wide railing, heaved himself up onto it. For a split second he looked back, and his mouth moved in words she couldn't make out.

Asher disappeared over the edge.

Joel and everyone else stared in disbelief. Hannah used the moment to try to move away. She almost made it, but Joel caught her by the wrist just before she slipped past his reach.

"Not so fast." He yanked her over to the railing, grabbed her hair, and bent her over it.

"It's too dark." He leaned over. "Someone get the lights on down there," Joel yelled. "I want to see the body."

Hannah pushed herself away from the edge with both hands, but Joel pressed himself against her to keep her from escaping.

"Where's your white knight, Hannah? I'm going to get a spotlight so we can see him splattered all over the concrete."

"I am right here." The voice came from behind them.

Hannah felt the weight lift from her back. She spun in time to see a perfectly restored—and of course entirely naked—Asher, easily holding Joel off the ground.

When the guards who were now assembled around them in a tense ring drew their weapons, Asher lowered Joel to the ground and wrapped an arm around his neck.

"Be careful, Ash. If you squeeze too hard he's gone for good. And he's not going to come back this time." Hannah walked boldly in front of Joel, who was silent for a change. It might have been because of the arm closing off his windpipe. Asher released it, just a little bit.

"You lie. You didn't get me. I put the needle in him," Joel rasped angrily, struggling against Asher's grasp. Asher snaked his other arm around Joel's chest and squeezed till there was a crack, quieting him.

"You did. Good for you, Joel. You put the needle in Asher. Too bad it was empty then, like it was the whole time. I mean, at least by the time I got it into you. I wasn't sure I was going to even get that chance, and since you taught me to err on the side of caution, I emptied it into your glass while you were untangling my dress from my shoe, just in case. That stupid pink champagne actually hid the color perfectly."

Joel's face blanched. He looked over at the empty glasses sitting on the ledge, at the color of the dregs in the bottom.

"And now," Hannah went on, "you're going to tell your men to move aside, and we're going to take a walk."

Hannah didn't wait for an answer. Joel had no choice, with Asher holding him just shy of a death grip. She wondered what was going through Joel's mind. Maybe for the first time in a very long time he was considering how very fragile—and potentially very short—a single human life was.

The crowd separated for them. When they passed Charlie, Hannah looked down, saddened. Despite her cruelty and misguided worship of Joel, she hadn't needed to die.

When they reached the door, Hannah fished Joel's card out of his pocket and swiped them through, off the falsely cheerful veranda and through one set of doors after another. Midway through their route Asher paused, hearing something she couldn't.

"Call them off," Hannah said.

By then she too could hear the whisper of the footsteps of the guards trying to quietly close in on them. Asher lessened the pressure on Joel's neck.

"Stop. Let us go through," Joel said, voice a hoarse croak.

"Louder," Hannah said.

"Stop. Get back."

There was a shuffle. The sound retreated. Finally, finally, they came to a door. A single door with a square window, the smallest bit of moon showing through. Hannah swiped the card and heard the door unlock with a click. Asher let go of Joel's neck, letting him slump to the ground.

"We're going to walk out of here," Hannah said, "and you're going to let us."

"You know I can't just let you go. You're too valuable." Joel rubbed his neck. Asher leaned toward him, and Joel leaned away warily.

"You can, and you will," Hannah said, "because I'm going to give you what you want." Asher growled under his breath, but Hannah silenced him with a nod and continued. "If you keep me here, one of us is going to wind up dead sooner rather than later. The moment you let your guard slide, I'm going to figure out how to kill you and watch you take your last breath, your real, permanent last breath. You're going to be spending the last short years of your life looking over your shoulder for me. Or for him." She pushed open the door. "And even if you somehow managed to keep me here, and keep him away, *and* keep your life, you still wouldn't get what you want. If you keep me here and I can't figure out how to take your life, then I'll take mine. Try me. You won't get what you want either way. That's what is going to happen if you don't let us walk away."

Hannah took a step toward the door, Asher close behind. Joel didn't move to stop them, but he didn't need to. He could call down a hundred people to stop them the moment they left the building. But he wasn't going to.

"But what's going to happen is that I'm going to give you my blood. It's not what I would choose if the situation was different, but I'm going to have to learn how to live with that. You can keep on fulfilling your misguided master plan for as long as you live after this—if that still interests you, of course. Maybe you'll find your priorities have changed."

They stepped out, and the door started to close behind them. "I think you should take my offer," Hannah said. "I'll give you what you want, and you can right every immortal wrong, settle every old score you want—while you have the time. You keep me here, and well, we'll see what happens."

Joel didn't say anything, just looked at her through the crack of open door. She could see him running the scenarios, weighing his options. She knew the expression, the look when he rolled the facts through his head and ran all the possible outcomes. She got the same look on her face when she was weighing all her options. Everything she knew, she'd learned from him.

Finally he nodded. Hannah walked out the door.

24

They moved down the stretch of paved road until they came to the squat concrete sentry box. The guard inside stared, but he didn't step out or move to stop them. For a moment they stood in front of the tall gate, but just as Asher began to take a step toward the guard there was a crackle of a radio, and the gate began to move. It swung open only far enough to permit them to pass, then shut swiftly behind them with a quiet electronic whir.

A few minutes later the pavement petered out to uneven gravel.

"We should keep going," Asher said when she paused to lean her back against a tree. Hannah was trying to work a hole into the fabric of her dress with her fingers.When she couldn't get the fabric to separate with her hands, she used her teeth.

"He knows where we are. If Joel was going to stop us from going, we'd know. He isn't."

When she finally managed to make a hole big enough to get her fingers in, Hannah wrenched the fabric apart, trying to tear the bottom of her dress off. It looked so easy in movies.

"Here." Asher reached over and pulled, the fabric separating like tissue, around and around, finally freeing an uneven foot of fabric. He handed it to her.

She handed it back. "That was for you."

It seemed she was the only one conscious of the fact that he was still naked. He wound it around his hips and tucked the edge in. It looked like he was wearing a red stretch miniskirt. Unconventional, but not the least attractive thing she'd ever seen by a long shot.

Hannah pulled at her shoes, struggling to undo the tiny buckles at the ankles. When they were off, she tugged at one of the spiky heels, trying to pop it off. Also something that looked easier in the movies.

Asher took it from her and yanked. Instead of the heel coming cleanly off, the shoe broke at the instep. He looked at it, in two small pieces in his big hand. Hannah took them from him and tossed them over her shoulder. The other shoe swiftly followed. She smiled and took his hand.

"We're going to get some looks when we hit the main drag."

They continued picking their way barefoot down the road, slowed by the darkness and sharp stones.

"Maybe Joel will be wise enough to let you go entirely, his priorities having changed, as you said. Now that he is human he might think differently, with a care for his shortened life," Asher said. "I hope there is no need for you to buy your freedom with your blood."

"I wish that too," Hannah said. She was free of her prison, but she wasn't happy about how she could still be forced to participate in Joel's war against his own kind. "But I don't think that's going to happen. Joel's going to figure out he got played pretty quickly. He may be a huge ass, but he's still smart. Where do you think I learned it all?" she said. "But I think at the end of the day, the risk of trying to hold on to me far outweighs the reward for him. He's seen the risk. He knows I won't live like a prisoner."

The gravel path started to run left in a gentle curve and the cover of trees thinned out. The clouds had cleared and the bright orange moon was visible overhead, a perfect circle like a child would draw. She stopped and turned toward Asher, who was standing still in the middle of the road behind her.

"What does that mean, 'got played'?" he said.

"It means Joel's not any more mortal than you are."

Hannah started walking again, hearing him come up beside her.

"How? You said you gave your blood to Joel, in his drink?"

Hannah shook her head. "There was never a chance. When I found out Charlie hadn't actually let you go, I had to act fast. It was pure luck I was able to get my hands on the needle. I didn't have time to put anything in it. And even if I could have, there was never a moment when I could have slipped it to him. Which is how I knew if you jumped, you'd come back in one piece."

She was the one who stopped this time.

"You jumped anyway. You didn't even hesitate."

"Because I trust you, and because I was willing to face the outcome either way," Asher said. "And because you said you love me. If that was going to be one of the last things I heard, it was not a terrible option."

This time it was her turn to hurry and catch up with him. She wondered if he could see her smiling in the dark. She guessed that he could.

He shook his head. "But you did not give Joel your blood? He is not human. I wish you had."

"I couldn't, there wasn't a chance. And even with everything he's done, I'm not sure I could have done it." Asher didn't say anything.

"There are a lot of people dead because of me, Ash," she said. "Even Charlie's death, that's on me—apparently my blood is killing humans now too. But not once have I done it if there was any other choice. I never want to be the one to decide who lives and dies."

"So escaping from here, from Joel, it will not be the end."

"No. It won't. But we'll cross that bridge when we come to it."

She was hobbling now, the stones in the road cutting into her already sore feet. Suddenly her legs flew out from under her when Asher picked her up. They'd rounded the full curve of the road before he spoke again, and in the silence, Hannah thought she could hear traffic far off in the distance. There were vehicles somewhere up ahead, and people.

They continued slowly onward, following the path the moon made on the road. She was deep in thought, until she felt him kiss the top of her head.

"What did you say?" she asked. "When you were about to go over the edge?"

"I made a promise I was not sure I would be able to keep in this world but hoped to in the next."

"What."

"That I would find you. Without fail."

He walked on in silence, carrying her in her destroyed gown and bare feet, him wearing a scrap of hem like a loin cloth. When they finally reached people, they were going to have some explaining to do.

EPILOGUE

The knock on the door made Hannah jump. She looked out the peephole and saw the back of a retreating delivery man. Hannah started to turn the lock, but Asher stopped her.

"Wait, I will get it," he said. "I am going to go around. You stay here."

She nodded and watched him step out onto their small balcony and push off the wrought iron railing with one arm. He disappeared neatly over the edge into the blinding sunshine. A moment later she heard another tap at the door. Checking to make sure it was him, Hannah let him in.

"A package," he said, "for you."

He didn't hand it over; they shouldn't be getting any packages here. Asher turned it toward Hannah and she saw her name written on the front. She knew who it was from without needing to look for a return address. She recognized the hurried, crabbed handwriting.

"It's from Joel," she said.

It had only been a matter of time. Not that he would find out where they were; he'd probably done that weeks ago. They'd been tensely waiting for him to want payment on his end of their shaky truce.

"Let me open it," Asher said. "Just to be safe."

She nodded.

Asher set the box on the table and began to carefully remove the layer of tape and then the neat white paper. He stepped in front of her before he lifted the lid of the cardboard carton.

Underneath it was a rectangular velvet box. The type that jewelry came in.

"This isn't exactly what I was expecting. Why would he send me this?" Hannah asked. She reached out, and Asher pulled it away.

"I will do it. Stand back."

Hannah rolled her eyes. "He's not going to send me a bomb. Give it here." She reached over and took it, opening the hinge.

Her eyes widened. It was the necklace. Asher's necklace. She'd never imagined she would see it again.

The chain was expertly mended, and it was snapped down to the blue velvet in a circle, on display. It wasn't all the box contained.

She set it back down on the table. In the space inside the circle the chain made, a rectangle had been carved out. It was perfectly sized to hold the two plastic stoppered vials. A fold of paper was wedged between them.

Hannah pulled it out and opened it up. Inside was an address, neatly typed. Underneath, Joel's handwriting appeared again. It simply said, "once a month." She looked up at Asher grimly.

"You were right. It wasn't the end."

ACKNOWLEDGEMENT

Thank you, first and foremost, to my husband, Nathan, who never once agreed with me when I considered that writing another book very few people might ever read was a waste of time. In the end, it's okay if the only life an author's work changes is their own.

To Meredith Tennant and Beth Dorward, thank you once again for your mystical, magical editing abilities and endless patience. Natasha MacKenzie, your covers are works of art, and Catherine Williams, your attention to detail and design is perfection.

Note to the Reader

Asher will live forever, but what does the future hold for Hannah?

Dear Reader,

Thank you for reading *Reverberation*. If you're here, there's a good chance you followed Hannah from the beginning, through the first book in the trilogy, *Echoes*.

That was the beginning. What comes next, is the end. See what the future has in store for Hannah when the journey comes to a close in *Dead Quiet*.

Most of us don't have as much time at our disposal as Asher, but if you have just a few extra moments on your hands, I would be grateful if you would kindly leave a review for *Reverberation* on amazon.com

P.S. Sign up for my email list at amcaplan.com for a personal heads-up about future releases.

Turn the page for more on *Dead Quiet*, available October 2020.

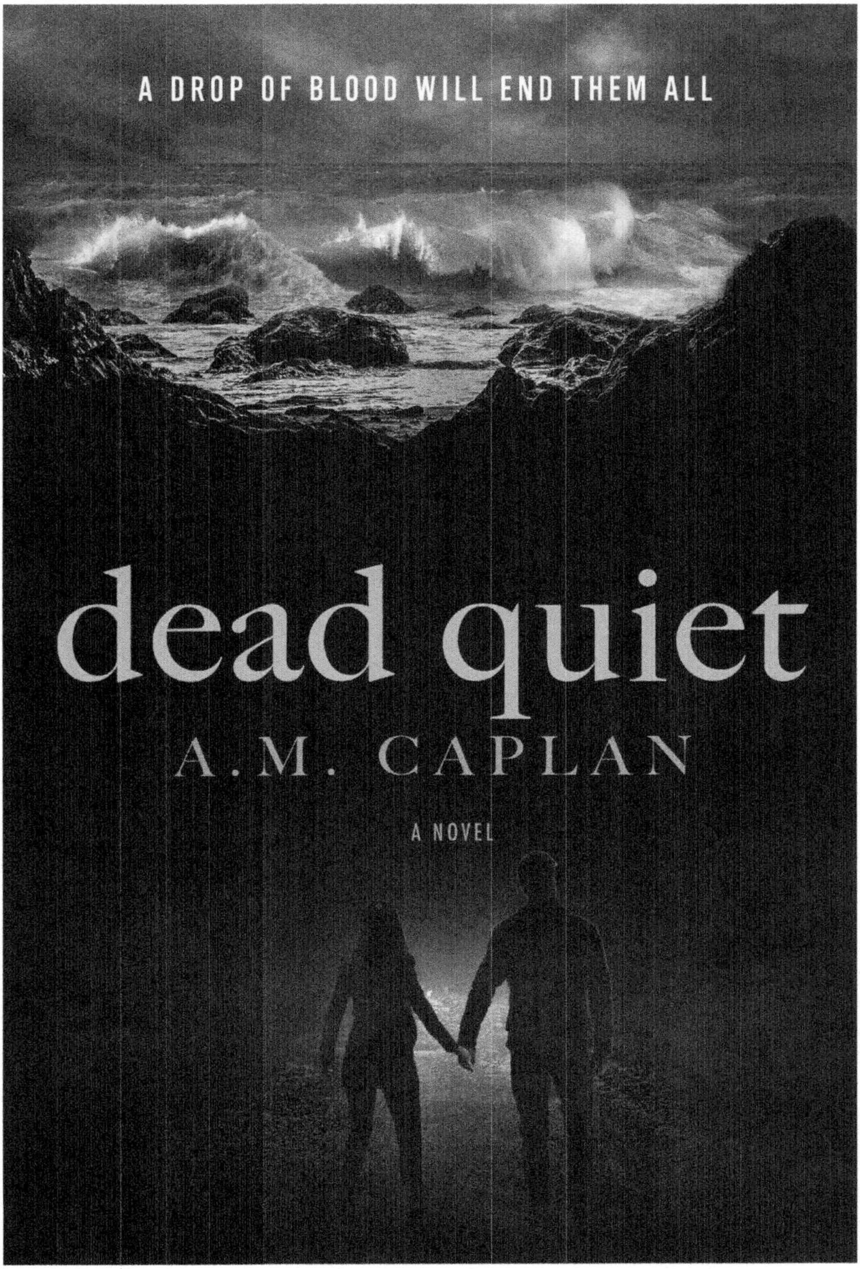
A DROP OF BLOOD WILL END THEM ALL
dead quiet
A.M. CAPLAN
A NOVEL

Hannah is so tired of running. With her uncle using her unique blood to turn dangerous immortals into humans, she's desperate to find a safe place for the life growing inside her. But the pregnancy has unexpectedly changed her into a lethal toxin, and now, eternals want her dead.

With nowhere to hide, Hannah is terrified her unborn child will never see the light of day. And when an old enemy resurfaces to lead the mob determined to end her, the last place she'd ever want to return could be her only refuge.

Can Hannah finally escape this undying nightmare before her little one pays the ultimate price?

Dead Quiet is the explosive conclusion to the Echoes supernatural thriller trilogy. If you like big-twist endings, unlikely love, and bloody combat, then you'll adore A.M. Caplan's high-octane finale.

Available October 2020

About the Author

A.M. Caplan is the author of *Echoes, Reverberation* and *Dead Quiet*, the *Echoes Trilogy*. She resides in scenic Sayre, Pennsylvania, watching the river roll by with her husband and writing about people that only exist in her mind.

You can connect with me on:
https://www.amcaplan.com
https://www.facebook.com/annmarie.caplan.7

Subscribe to my newsletter:
https://www.amcaplan.com/page-2

Printed in Great Britain
by Amazon

43533567R00152